# Finding Balance

# Finding Balance

## KATI GARDNER

flux
®

Mendota Heights, Minnesota

First Edition
First Printing, 2020

Book design by Sarah Taplin
Cover design by Sarah Taplin
Cover images by ractapopulous/Pixabay, Sarah Taplin

Flux, an imprint of North Star Editions, Inc.

This is a work of fiction. Names, characters, places, and incidents are either the product of the author's imagination or are used fictitiously, and any resemblance to actual persons living or dead, business establishments, events, or locales is entirely coincidental. Cover models used for illustrative purposes only and may not endorse or represent the book's subject.

**Library of Congress Cataloging-in-Publication Data (pending)**
978-1-63583-052-1

Flux
North Star Editions, Inc.
2297 Waters Drive
Mendota Heights, MN 55120
www.fluxnow.com

Printed in the United States of America

*Jason Gardner, who holds my heart.*

*To those who found their loves at camp. Thanks for showing us how it's done. Sunshine Forever, baby.*

*For all the cancer survivors who have felt the weight of that word. I see you, and I hear your stories.*

# Prologue

The pavement around the swimming pool at Camp Chemo was problematic. Tile and grout blended together when wet. The sun hit the ground in such a way that Mari couldn't tell if it was a puddle or just the sun reflecting off the tile. Even after going to camp this many years, she was still cautious.

"Hey! Princess!"

The voice, God, she knew it everywhere. She knew it in her five toes and ten fingers. That voice was the one that filtered through her dreams and into her stomach, leaving behind a trail of warmth that wriggled into her heart—and had been doing so since she was twelve years old. Now, at sixteen, Mari Manos still tingled when Jase Ellison and his distinctive gravelly voice were in her space.

Mari rocked the one-legged look and was an expert at moving her crutches like legs. She got comments all the time about how graceful she was and how her crutches were an extension of her body.

"Jase." They'd spent this entire week together, and she wasn't ready for it to be over. With the end of camp giving her a bit of urgency, she stopped watching her step, watching the boy in front of her instead.

A rookie mistake.

There was a slide, the rubber of her crutch tip hitting one

of the slick spots. The crutch continued to slide, and Mari went down with it. She saw Jase running toward her, and she threw out her arms to catch as much of herself as she could before crashing into the ground.

"Mari, are you okay?" Jase was kneeling down, dark-blue eyes staring at her, a worry crease between his brows.

"Well, Jase." She moved so that she sat on her butt instead of splayed out on the wet concrete, her one leg in front of her, an angry red scrape on her knee. "It appears I'm falling for you."

"Seriously." He rolled his eyes at her. "Do I need to get Tiny or Heather?" He mentioned her counselors.

Mari stood up on her one leg, pushing her arms through the cuff on her crutches, and offered Jase her best smile. Hiding her bottom teeth like she always did. Orthodontics were expensive.

"I'm good. No worries." Mari did a mental check of her remaining appendages, and all of them seemed to be intact, maybe a little bruised, but that's it. She tightened the towel around her waist, a little bit of covering so she wouldn't feel quite so vulnerable in front of him.

"Well, I'm taking you to the infirmary to get a Band-Aid anyway."

Jase pulled at her arm and then helped her slip her one flip-flop back on. She hadn't even realized it'd come off in her spectacular fall.

"Do I get any say in this?" Mari felt the way his hand cuffed around the top of her arm, the heat moving through his hand into her body and, subsequently, into her heart.

"I'll make it worth your while." He smiled at her, his hair

more brown than blond, water clinging to the ends and dripping down onto his T-shirt.

She had to fight not to touch him.

"We'll see," she flirted back. They'd spent most of the week this way. Jase constantly working his way into her space, filling it up, working his way into her brain when she really did not want him there. Because when Jase Ellison was in her space, in her brain, he was almost all she thought about. It wasn't a relationship, because it would be over as soon as they went home tomorrow. It was a camp thing.

A flirtationship.

Jase did stop by the infirmary for some ointment and a Band-Aid, but instead of sitting in the air-conditioned area under the eyes of their nurses, he guided her along toward the rocking chairs on the porch just outside.

"Sit."

She did, mostly because she wanted to see where this was going.

There was a little scrape on her knee, something that at home she probably would have ignored altogether. She wasn't really bleeding, and it would eventually scab over.

But Jase dabbed it gently with a cleaning swab. She could feel his breath against the top of her knee. He was close, maybe looking to make sure it was just a scrape.

Mari's breath was shallow.

She was going to need a nurse for real.

Jase blew a little over the scrape, maybe afraid that it would sting, before applying the ointment and covering it with the bandage.

"All better," Mari said, her voice much thicker than she wanted.

Jase looked up at her, his eyes seemingly darker, and something was swimming around in them. "Almost."

He moved closer, a soft smile on his full lips, and with a smoothness Mari didn't think really existed, he reached out and pushed at one of her curls, tucking it behind her ear.

"Just missing one thing."

And the sounds of camp faded around Mari. There were no other campers. There were no counselors. There was nothing but Jase Ellison and his beautiful face in front of her. Her breath was stuck somewhere around her sternum, and she didn't spend any effort to get it to move again. His hand was warm against her cheek, his eyes moving from her eyes to her lips.

And Mari knew it was going to happen.

He was going to kiss her.

"Mari?"

And that was another voice Mari would know anywhere.

Her breath started moving, and her heart pounded for a completely different reason. She was frozen, a breath away from Jase and a kiss that she had spent too much time dreaming about.

She didn't know whether to laugh or cry.

Standing just behind Jase was the director of Camp Chemo.

"Hi, Margaret." Mari's voice strangled in her throat. "Nice day."

# Chapter One

A grape ended Mari Manos's student career at South Side High School.

She worked her way through the hallway. As always, it was crowded, and even with teachers yelling for students to "Walk, please," students pushed and ran. Mari breathed deeply through her nose and fought her way to her locker. She was one of the few students allowed to carry a backpack. One of the advantages of having one leg, she guessed. She flipped her bag off of her shoulder, hanging it on a makeshift hook inside the locker before changing out her books. Her crutches were propped against the row of lockers, and she balanced without them.

She should have paid more attention to what was happening around her as she went through the motions to get to her next class. She wasn't thinking at all about being in school or plans for the rest of junior year. School was school, not something she loved or loathed. It was just something she had to get through before she could go back to camp in the summer.

Mari was zipping her backpack, hanging on its hook, when she heard someone shout "FIGHT!" But this was a common enough occurrence that Mari first finished putting her bag on before looking up. Her crutches were still leaning against the lockers at her side.

"Mari!" Leo, her older brother, yelled from farther down the hall, motioning for her. "MOVE!" But it was too late.

Two hulking bodies barreled into her, fists and knees flying, and Mari was caught in the middle. No one connected. They mostly just bounced off of her and continued down the hall, pummeling one another. But the back of her head slammed into her now-closed locker, the force of the impact caused Mari to see stars and sink down onto the hallway's gross carpet.

"Well, shit," she said, stars swimming in her vision.

"You okay?" Ellie, her best school friend, ran to Mari from her locker down the hall.

A teacher—Mari thought it was the Spanish teacher—and Leo were also at her side. Other teachers were breaking up the fight while a large section of the student body continued on with their lives, ignoring the hallway drama.

"Yep." Mari blinked hard, and the stars moved out of her field of vision. "No big deal." She let Leo help her up, and he handed over her pink forearm clip crutches.

"You sure?" Ellie asked, taking her bag for her. "They slammed right into you."

"Never better," she lied. "We gotta go. Delufuente will not give me a break for being tardy."

"I'll write you a pass." The Spanish teacher shook her head, smiling.

Mari was sure the teacher was thinking about how precocious and inspirational she was. Teachers did that. This one in particular had stopped Mari more than a few times last year to tell her how "brave" she was and how much "harder" things must be for Mari. That had to be what caused the nausea now, not a possible head injury.

"Thanks," Ellie said to the teacher, taking the slip of paper as they moved toward the elevator. "You coming, Leo?"

"Mari?"

Leo was a great big brother, because he didn't try to impose any sort of big brother antics on Mari. Nick, her oldest brother did that. Mari never worried about Leo threatening another guy if he wanted to date her. (Not that that had happened anyway.) Leo was Mari's closest ally, helping her navigate this world that wasn't built for her. He had taken her cancer diagnosis when she was only ten the hardest, but now didn't worry the way the rest of their family did. It was probably because they were a mere fifty-one weeks apart, more like twins in many ways than regular siblings.

"Go to class," Mari said. "I'll see you out front later."

"Okay."

He might have been a little hesitant to leave her, but Mari thought that was probably more about his lingering crush on Ellie than Mari's well-being.

"I fall all the time," she reminded her sweet and probably concerned brother. "I'm made of steel—I don't break." She didn't bring up the fact that she had indeed broken her leg before the cancer was found. Mari did fall occasionally. Not *all* the time, like she had said to Leo, but enough that she knew how to get up and keep moving. Heck, last year she'd nearly broken her arm in a wrestling match with a vacuum. But getting caught in a hallway fight was unusual, even for her.

Mari's headache only got worse through AP Chemistry, but she was pretty certain it was from the formulas and not from the fall. By the time lunch came around, she was feeling better. Ellie had fourth lunch, so Mari was alone, heading to the table where she sat with her friends from debate class. She brought her lunch from home most days, preferring her mom's PB&Js over the school's food any day.

That, and carrying a tray was a problem.

And Mari hated asking for help.

But today was one of those days she really should have asked for some help. Even if it was just to have someone walking beside her.

Because a stupid squished grape was going to be her downfall.

Literally.

Her one foot stepped on it, the miniscule fruit giving enough slide that her foot slipped out from under her, causing her to land on her ass with a resounding thud. She was just thankful she didn't hit her head again.

Everyone was staring at her.

"Only an 8.5," she announced to the silent cafeteria. "I didn't quite stick the landing."

Brooke and Hannah, friends from Mari's lunch table, came to her rescue, grabbing her crutches and bag before helping her up. Murmurs filled the space around her and slowly morphed into more talking, and Mari hoped people had moved on and were already discussing something else. This would be a great story by the end of the day, no doubt. Gossip traveled fast in any school, and gossip about the disabled girl falling was always going to be a hot commodity. Especially because she'd fallen *twice* now in the space of a few hours. That had to be a record, even for her.

"That was pretty awesome," Megan, a freshman, commented as Mari took her seat at the table. "Like, you landed so gracefully."

"Thanks." Mari was used to these types of comments. People always wanted to make her feel better, but she knew that they were really putting themselves at ease. And Megan was naïve, young in the way that she just hadn't lived a lot. But then again, compared to Mari, her entire lunch table was years behind.

"Are you okay? Anything hurt?" Brooke slid a fry into a mound of ranch dressing.

"Oh, just my pride." Mari smiled, but her head still hurt. "I'm fine, promise."

Thankfully, her friends moved on quickly from her feats of clumsiness to more pressing matters like the auditions for the fall play and who had been cast. Mari was one of the few debate team members who wasn't involved in the drama club.

Listening to her friends' chatter, Mari scrolled through her phone, even though it was just torture. She needed to leave it alone. To move on. But she wanted to see what he'd posted today.

And there Jase was. In his school-required blazer, the fancy logo of Atlanta West Prep on the breast. In the selfie was Jase and a girl who Mari assumed was Lindsay, kissing his cheek, and Jase was looking both annoyed and not at all annoyed. He hadn't posted the picture, but @ActuallyLindsAy2001 had tagged him.

"Jase?" Hannah asked from Mari's side.

Hannah and Ellie were the only two who knew the whole story. The week of incredible flirting at camp. When he had literally lifted Mari off the ground to keep her team from winning at Capture the Flag. The almost-kiss outside the infirmary. Being caught by Margaret. Not even Mary Faith and Paige, her two best friends from camp, knew about that.

"Yeah, I need to stop doing this to myself." Mari scrolled some more, finding another picture of him and Lindsay. She tried not to compare herself to this girl, someone she hated based totally on the fact that she was with Jase. But how could Mari ever compete with perfection? @ActuallyLindsAy2001 had strawberry-blonde hair that could only be achieved through the best salon in the city, and her bright-blue eyes never looked tired or sunken. And she was thin in the athletic way that Mari could never be. Mari, with her hips, curves, thick thighs, curly brown hair, and dark eyes . . . She was the exact opposite of Lindsay.

"Or text him and get it out of your system," said Hannah.

Mari didn't want to admit that she didn't have Jase's number. That on the last day of camp, she had nervously put her number in his phone, and her heart had cracked a little when he hadn't made a move to do the same.

"Sure," she said instead, because it wasn't like there weren't other ways to get in touch with him. "I could do that and then face the humiliation of him ignoring it."

"And then you could move on." Hannah scrunched her long, wispy blonde hair into a careless ponytail and then took a bite of her sandwich. "There are lots of guys here."

"Sure. And all of them want to ask out the one-legged girl." Mari said it as a joke, but there was a lot of truth to her words.

"Mari?" It was the Spanish teacher from earlier, putting

a gentle hand on her shoulder. "Mrs. Fulston wants you in her office."

"The assistant principal?" Mari's brows drew together. "Did I do something wrong?"

"I'm sure it's just about this morning."

~

It was not about this morning.

Mari walked into the office and was surprised to see both of her parents and Mrs. Moore, the school's counselor, there. Karen and Nicholas Manos did not just take off of work and show up at the high school in the middle of the day. Mari immediately noticed the line between her mother's eyes and the deep-set frown lines around her father's mouth.

This was not good.

Even Mrs. Fulston, the AP, looked irritated.

Mrs. Moore looked embarrassed.

"Hello, Mari," Mrs. Fulston began, motioning for her to sit in the chair between her parents. "Sorry to interrupt your lunch, but the administration thinks this is an important matter, and it would be best to resolve it quickly."

"What?" Mari asked, fear and worry in her voice, looking back and forth from the principal to her parents.

"I have spoken with your parents about the incident this morning." Mrs. Fulston's hair was a frosted-blonde football helmet, and there were creases around her eyes and lips. "The administration has come up with some new accommodations we would like to add to your 504 plan."

Mari had a legal document set up by the school that listed the accommodations she needed to be successful at school. It was because of that document that she got to keep her bookbag and use the elevator.

"I think my 504 is fine." Mari's brows drew closer together as she looked at Mrs. Moore, who was in charge of her 504. Mrs. Moore looked down at her shoes. "I haven't had any issues."

"The administration thinks that it would be best for everyone, to make school as successful as possible for you, that you either use a wheelchair during school hours or pursue using a prosthetic limb." Mrs. Fulston spoke with an eerie calmness, the same as you might do with a wild animal.

Mari had heard the words, but that couldn't possibly be what this woman had said.

"Mom." Mari turned to her mother. "Is she serious?"

Karen took her hand. It was shaking the tiniest bit, telling Mari that a rage was building.

"You realize you are asking our family to spend money on very expensive medical equipment?" her dad said, an edge to his deep baritone—the same tone Mari heard before one of her brothers got grounded for life.

"And it is not like we can snap our fingers and Mari will have a new prosthesis. They typically take months to fabricate correctly." Her mom spoke in clipped tones.

"It's about the safety of Mari and the entire student body," Mrs. Fulston said. "We ask that you make a decision, or we will have to consider moving Mari to a self-contained classroom."

"This morning wasn't even my fault." Mari's voice was rising.

"But you did fall in the cafeteria as well." Mrs. Fulston's

look of concern, her flattened smile and sympathetic eyes, only pushed Mari's ire. "That could have been prevented."

"Yeah, well, if people cleaned up after themselves . . ." She had officially raised her voice at this point. "I slid on a grape. A *grape*. And I would have slid on it with a prosthesis."

"That's an idea," Karen started. "Why don't you offer a course on how to dispose of trash correctly, and *we* don't have to spend potentially thousands of dollars on a prosthesis that Mari has no desire to use."

"But, Mari, you could look like everyone else," Mrs. Fulston stated, like it was some goal for her. "You could walk without your crutches."

"This is ridiculous." Mari's brain blurred with anger. "And maybe illegal? Like, can they really do this?" She knuckled tears of frustration. "I will never look like everyone else. I had cancer, and my amputation saved my life."

"Well, there is always the option of a self-contained class-room. You wouldn't have to change classes."

This woman was delusional. This wasn't a real suggestion. Mari might as well stay home and go to school virtually.

"Mrs. Fulston, this is obviously about the school being scared that we might sue because of the incident this morning," her dad said. Nicholas Manos did not suffer fools. His hands were big and warm on Mari's arm, a little dirt under his nails, as he tried to comfort her. "We saw the video, and it is clear that who you should really be discussing self-contained classrooms with are the two boys who were fighting this morning."

"What video?" Mrs. Fulston's voice rose half an octave. "We have taken care of the boys."

"Please, if you don't think students film these fights and

put them on YouTube, you're out of touch," Mari's mom said through gritted teeth.

"A couple of days of ISS is not taking care of it," Nicholas added. "We have had two other boys come through this school and have two children here now. I know what goes on."

"If you have a problem with the way that we handle discipline here, you are welcome to speak with Mrs. Carter, the principal." Mrs. Fulston's face was red and splotchy, her voice now tight and tinny sounding.

"You know what?" Karen Manos was officially over it. "Why don't you just draw up the paperwork to unenroll Mari from this *lovely* institution of learning."

Mari sat there, mouth hanging open, mad, hurt, and a million other feelings.

Stupid grape.

# Chapter Two

Jase threw his car in park and ran into his house, cutting through the four-car garage. He'd left his USB with the visuals for his speech at home. Of course, if he'd saved it to the school's cloud like he was supposed to, this wouldn't have happened. Today was not working out the way he'd planned.

"Jason?" Olivia Ellison was in the kitchen, pitting an avocado for her lunch. "What did you forget?" She smiled at him.

"Speech presentation." He ran past her, up the steps and into his room where the gray thumb drive sat on his desk, right where he'd left it last night as he'd hurriedly finished the stupid assignment. He snatched the thumb drive and raced back down the stairs.

"Maybe we should think about doing some of the testing Dr. Miller has talked about."

"Mom, I'm fine."

Olivia thought a cough was a sign of his leukemia coming back, even though he'd been off therapy for almost eleven years.

"She said at your last cancer survivor program appointment that children treated for leukemia sometimes have short-term memory problems." Olivia was staring at him, her eyes narrowed as though she was looking for signs of visible defects and disability.

"Mom, it's not a short-term memory problem. I was in a

hurry this morning and wasn't thinking." Because he had gotten up late, because sleeping was hard when you couldn't breathe because of a stupid cold, and because he was really thinking more about breakfast than his presentation.

"Maybe we should still—"

"No. I'm fine. But I will be in trouble with Harker if I'm late to class." He pressed a kiss to her cheek, grabbed an apple from the bowl that was always full, and ran back out to his car. His mom always thought whatever was wrong with him could somehow be traced back to his leukemia, and that was just, well, stupid.

Jase didn't even remember having leukemia. In fact, if he didn't go to Camp Chemo or that pointless doctor's visit every year, he would never even think of it at all. None of it was a part of his life. What he knew about his leukemia could be summed up in one sentence: I had leukemia when I was three. After that, it was all irrelevant. Hell, none of his friends even knew that he'd had it.

Thank God.

~

"God, I hate these speeches." Lindsay slid onto the couch next to Jase.

Only at AWP did your English class have couches, as well as desks. An "open learning plan," they called it. Jase took it for granted that he'd be able to recline while listening to the ridiculous speeches. He hated the public-speaking element of his AP lit class, but since the speech and debate classes were not mandatory, AWP worked it into this class as well.

"Do any of us really care what each other did for volunteer

hours this summer? And why do we have to have these stupid hours? I hated working at our church's clothing ministry."

"It could be worse." Jase smiled at her. She was cute, but she was starting to get to him. When they'd first started hanging out—he wouldn't even call it dating—her shallowness had been something he could overlook, but lately it had become glaringly apparent that Lindsay had no life experience outside of their private school bubble. "You could have had to get a job."

"Jason, you're up." Mr. Harker motioned for him to come up to the podium.

Jase stood in front of the Smart Board, pulling up a picture of himself with a young, bald patient taken a few weeks ago.

"This summer, I helped Heather McNeil, the Child Life Specialist at the children's hospital. I worked with her to put together 'busy bags' that keep patients and their siblings entertained while waiting at the clinic. I also collected gift cards for the families of the patients being treated at the hematology and oncology clinic." He talked about spending days in the tiny Child Life office, working with Heather and coming up with different busy bags.

Jase did not talk about how he knew Heather from the hospital and camp.

He did not mention that the picture of him with a little boy who was receiving chemo for leukemia had been snapped while the boy's mother had wept at meeting a survivor.

Meeting *him*.

"That sounds amazing." Lindsay smiled as Jase joined her back on the couch, her strawberry-blonde hair curling just around her shoulders. "What you must do for those poor kids."

"I mean, it was okay." He didn't want to talk about it.

"Maybe I could come."

"Maybe." *Never.*

"But aren't you afraid of catching it?" She asked the question like an afterthought. "I'd be nervous the whole time."

"You can't catch cancer." He would have been angry if she wasn't being so honest. "It's not contagious."

The bell saved Jase from thinking too much about what she'd said. It was easier to ignore it than to try and educate her. And even if she was a little obtuse, answering her might lead to more questions. Like, how did he know so much about cancer? So instead he moved through the halls, easily opening his locker—none of them had locks anyway, perks of a private school education—grabbing his notebook for his last class of the day.

AP Chemistry wasn't his favorite, mostly because he had to work a little for a good grade, but he did like the teacher. Mrs. Yother was smart and made sure that everyone understood the material, which was saying something, given how hard the class could be. Since it was an advanced class, it was dominated by seniors, with only a couple of juniors (and one random sophomore who was smoking all of them).

"How was the speech?" Lucas asked, sitting down at their lab table. Even at the high-top desks, Lucas seemed to fold himself to fit on the stool.

"Fine." Jase shrugged, beginning to feel a little guilty for what he'd presented in class. "Volunteering" was a stretch, since he'd mostly shown up at the hospital and given Heather some gift cards he'd bought on the way there and then spent thirty minutes straightening the busy bags. In the simplest of terms, he'd lied on the form that said he'd done ten hours of community service.

"Hey, did you hear there's a new girl?"

"Yeah, haven't seen her yet." AWP was small enough that a new student was big news. It was especially unusual for a student to transfer in once the school year had started. "Is she cute?"

Lucas was still talking, but Jase couldn't really hear him.

Because crutching into his AP Chem class was Mari Manos.

Jase watched her eyes light up, their brown color turning nearly gold with happiness. She smiled, and it was big enough that he could see her two bottom teeth. They were slightly crooked, and he knew she was self-conscious about it. Relief seemed to slide over her, and she released a pent-up breath. But his heart was racing so loud in his ears that it dominated everything.

"Hey." She smiled over the word and walked toward him.

"You know her?" Lucas asked, disbelief in his words.

"I—" Mari started.

"No," Jase said, stopping Mari in her tracks. "I just have one of those faces." Smugness dripped from his voice. He turned to the front of the classroom, unable to look at her, because what if everyone saw the lies that had spilled from his mouth? What if Mari saw them?

Jase didn't want to watch as Mari was assigned a lab table. But his eyes drifted toward her as she sat just out of his line of vision. He didn't want to hear Mari as she asked if she could speak with the teacher after class, but her voice permeated all of the class chatter around him. Jase did not want to acknowledge

Mari. But his brain seemed unable to do anything else. He could practically hear her breathing throughout the class.

And class was long.

He didn't want to look Mari in the eyes, because he knew he'd been cruel.

He had been an ass to Mari.

He had been an ass on *purpose*.

The bell rang, signaling the end of class and the end of the day, and Jase was out the door before Mari even left her desk.

Jase hooked an arm around Lindsay's waist, doing his best to ignore Mari as she crutched carefully through the halls behind him. He stood with Lindsay near a bank of lockers, but his brain was watching how the student body seemed to part for Mari, like the Red Sea, and hearing all the whispers. It was such a bad movie moment. They were all acting like total clichés.

But he didn't do anything to stop it.

"Does she have one leg?" Lindsay asked in horror. "God, that's horrible."

This was not the Mari he knew. Jase didn't look at Lindsay as she slid into him, unable to look away from Mari. This Mari was not at all like the girl from Camp Chemo. There was no joy in her eyes, and he'd done that. This was not the girl who he had picked up, crutches and all, to keep her from winning the most competitive game of Capture the Flag ever. This girl, the Mari who was moving through the halls, was lost and alone. He felt a sliver of guilt in his belly. And the guilt sloshing around with the fear was enough to make him sick.

Addison walked over to Mari. "I'm Addison. We have

Chem and Debate together." Addison Miller was better than anyone else at the school. "Are you a junior or senior?"

Jase looked back to Lindsay, trying not to listen to Mari's conversation, but unable to stop himself. Why did he home in on every word Mari said? It was as if his body was tuned in to what she was saying, doing, maybe even feeling. And Jase needed that to stop.

"Junior." Mari's voice wasn't quiet or quivery. In fact, she sounded pissed.

Jase watched as Mari walked past him with Addison. And there she was. The girl he'd known since he was eleven. She glared at him for a split second and crutched down the hall and out of view.

"God, why doesn't she wear a robot leg?" Disgust dripped from Lindsay's voice. "It's just gross to be out there like that."

"She doesn't like them," he answered without thinking. "I guess, or something."

"God. Her life must be awful." Lindsay shook her head, like she might actually feel sorry for Mari.

"I gotta go." Jase's brain burned with the need to get away from Lindsay. From everyone. It was as if his classmates could see into his skin, could see his once-diseased cells. And he had to get away from them. Not even stopping at his locker, he ran from the building and to the pool.

~

Swimming was a second language for Jase Ellison. He could forget the world existed while the water surrounded him. His feet pounded on the brick pavers that connected the main school building to the natatorium. Once inside, he ran to the locker room, unable to change fast enough, shoving his clothes in his gym locker. He'd have his mom deal with the wrinkles later. He had to get in the water, to escape his own mind.

He didn't have swim practice this afternoon, but he needed to hide, and the pool was the best place for that. He didn't bother with a swim cap, dropping it on the side of the pool, his goggles barely pushed on before he dove into the water. He pushed through the water, his strokes even, but his rhythm was off. His was heart pounding a lot harder than it should have been as his right arm came over his head and glided back into the water. Mari could unravel everything.

And there she was, even here at the pool, in his quiet place, in the place he didn't have to think about anyone or anything.

Mari. She was in his head.

The way she'd looked at him when he'd said he didn't know her.

It was nothing like the way she'd looked at him when he'd nearly kissed her. And that was something he regretted: that he hadn't *actually* kissed her. That Margaret had appeared. Her apparent camp director magic meant she knew exactly when they were going to kiss. But he could still feel Mari's skin under his palm.

Mari could ruin everything. Fear trickled inside, reminding him of the same fear that had lived in his stomach all through middle school—his old school, where his classmates knew about his past. Afraid of the students, the school building, what had been waiting for him inside. The comments about his mutating cells. The constant questions about his leukemia. The prying and the relentless teasing from some of his classmates. Any absences led to rumors that he was dying. Jase could still taste the hate in his mouth, the absolute hatred for leukemia and all that it brought.

He pushed through the water. Typically, he just moved, letting the water be his friend and push him forward. But today, with the thoughts of Mari and the endless teasing he'd endured back in middle school rambling through his brain, he was fighting it. Pushing and pulling like a bull might. The water was his enemy, just like his own traitorous mind.

Stopping at the end of the lane, he held on to the wall.

"Shit." He said it aloud, slamming his open palm on the water, splashing himself and the concrete outside the pool.

"Shit!" Frustration began to pour from him. His skin began to feel too tight for his body; irritation prickled over his scalp and down his neck. And it wasn't Mari's fault, but damn it, if it didn't feel like it was.

Climbing out of the pool, he ran toward the locker room to change. There was no chance she was still around, but he could text her or something. Maybe try to explain where he was coming from.

He dried only enough that his clothes still sort of stuck to him. He shoved his blazer into his bag and didn't bother to tuck in the white dress shirt. Wrinkles creased his pants, and he shoved his feet into the school-mandated loafers.

Taking off in a sprint out the door toward the parking lot, Jase could still see the way Mari had all but crumbled in front of him in Chemistry.

He had to talk to her.

Yes, he needed to apologize, but he had to explain.

Because she could make his sandcastle of a life dissolve.

God must have been on his side. Mari stood at the corner,

the muted orange, blue, and white of the MARTA sign not too far above her head. She was waiting for the MARTA bus. Jase hadn't even noticed that there was a MARTA stop near school.

School had been out for an hour or more, but there she was, still waiting. Her dark curls were down, and she wore one of the school-required polos and the kilt most girls wore in the warmer months. She wasn't staring at her phone. Instead, she seemed to be taking in her surroundings.

"Hey." He stopped in front of her, breathing heavily, wiping the sweat off of his forehead.

"I'm sorry, do I know you?" Her dark eyes narrowed back at him. "I must have one of those faces."

# Chapter Three

Heat filled Mari's stomach, and a hard knot was in her throat. She swallowed and turned away, refusing to look at Jase again. She wouldn't give him the satisfaction.

"Mari, let me explain."

She didn't want to hear it. She knew everything she needed to know from Chemistry. She untangled her earbuds, not caring how rude she was being. In this instance, her mother would forgive her. With all of the disinterest she could muster, she put them in her ears and continued waiting for the bus.

"Come on, Mari."

Instead of answering, she scrolled through her friends' updates on her phone. Ellie had a bright-purple star sticker just beside her eyes, because she was a star, standing outside the theater, waiting for rehearsals to begin. Then there was a pic of Davis standing outside of the Daily Grind, where he had obviously spilled an entire iced coffee. Despite Jase's unwelcome presence, relief moved through her, happy to see Davis sober and at work. Something that, before this summer, would have been unthinkable.

And she could have been with either of her friends, hanging out after a day at her old school. Instead, she was wearing an itchy secondhand Atlanta West Prep polo and a nearly too-big kilt. Her shoe had no support, and she missed her black Vans.

And Jase—no, *Jason*—Ellison had been a total asshole.

She wouldn't think about it with him standing right there. She wouldn't let him see the tears that had been dying to release for a week now. Since the day she had been told she had to get a wheelchair or a prosthesis to attend her own damn high school. Because they were "afraid for her safety." It was such ableist bullshit, and Mari was paying the price for it.

"Please, Mari." Jase reached out, taking her hand.

She pulled it back, pushing back the memory of how warm his hands were, how they felt when they touched her. How easily his hand had cupped her cheek—she had been replaying the moment nightly since camp.

"No." That was all she was going to give him. Thankfully, she was saved by the MARTA accessibility bus that decided to finally show up. She walked to the bus, not looking back at Jase Ellison. Not looking at him as the bus pulled away from the school.

She would not let him hurt her again.

~

The ride back toward the southeast side of Atlanta was long.

Mari had to ride the MARTA accessibility bus to the North/South line stop. Then she'd ride to the Five Points station and then transfer. It was only a little ironic that she could easily navigate the large city of Atlanta and its notoriously frustrating public transit, but her own high school had been "unsafe."

Mari had been carefully connecting dots in a game on her phone when the blue message screen popped up at the top.

Davis: I'm at work, but tell me about how the first day went.

Mari: Oh, totally fine. It's going to take some adjustment. Did you know rich kid schools don't have locks on lockers? They just trust people and stuff.

She was deflecting. Davis was being thoughtful, checking in on her, but she didn't have it in her to give him the real deal. To tell him just how awful the whole place had been.

Because it wasn't exactly true. It was Jase who had been bad. Addison had been nice, and Zeke, who sat behind Mari in English, but most everyone else had reacted exactly like she had thought they would. Staring, pretending not to stare, that one jerk who thought it was totally okay to pry into her life because she lived while disabled.

Davis: Meet me at the Grind? I'm here until about 7:30. Coffee's on me.

Mari: Thanks ☺ But I'm beat. And I'm sure the cavalry will be at my house waiting on me. 😳

Davis: You sure? You can try to find out what my plans are for Capture the Flag this summer.

Mari: That's cheating, Davis Channing! You know full and well I'll make it my job to find out what your plans are.

Davis: 😖

One look at her house—cars in the driveway and on the street—told Mari that *everyone* was at home. And they were all waiting to hear how her first day at AWP had been. The mail was sticking out of their little mailbox next to the door. She wasn't going to grab it, but there was something addressed to her.

Examining the envelope, she groaned. She couldn't deal with this right now. The envelope felt like lead in her hands, and she momentarily thought about putting it in the garbage bin on the corner before anyone saw it.

Because Mari knew that what she was holding in her hand was an interest mailer from Wilson Prosthetics. And after the crap from her high school and then today at AWP, the feelings of inadequacy because she chose not to use a prosthesis seemed to be bubbling inside her.

Was the universe out to pummel her?

She didn't throw it away; she ripped it open. A cursory glance at the words talked about a clinic for hard-to-fit amputees. Shaking her head, unable to really process what it meant, she stuck it in her bag's outside pocket. She'd decide later what to do with it.

Mari closed her eyes, pulling every single reserve she had left up within her, and took a deep breath.

Then she smiled and walked into her home.

Mama and Daddy were in the kitchen, pretending to be fussing over the way the dishwasher was loaded, but even Mari knew that was just a ruse. Kris and Nick sat at the table. Both had their computers out and were likely coding something for fun.

They needed better hobbies.

Leo was drying his hair with a towel. Mari knew he usually swam for a couple of hours on Mondays after school. Everyone was there to hear her report.

"Hello, family. I have returned from the north side of the city, and I have lived to tell the tale." She put on her most affected voice, praying that it covered the exhaustion.

"How was it?" Mama demanded. Her dark hair was streaked with gray, making her look a little witchy.

"Let her get in the door, Karen."

Dad laughed, but Mari could see it in his face: the deepening in the lines around his mouth, the nervous laugh—they all said *worry*.

"It was fine." Mari dropped her bag and sank down onto the couch that faced the kitchen. The kitchen and living room combined into a large, single room. "I only saw Giselle for class."

"She had a staff meeting, so I haven't heard anything from her." Nick, her oldest brother, came over to sit with her. He had the Manos curls, but his need for order meant he kept his hair close cropped, the complete opposite of Leo. "She did say that the faculty and staff are excited for you to be joining the school."

*At least someone is.* "I think her class is going to be fun. I met a girl from it, and she seems cool."

"I'm picking Giselle up for dinner later." Nick hugged Mari. "She was happy to help you get the scholarship and to go to bat for you."

The underlying message—*Don't let her down*—was loud and clear.

"Well, you should think about proposing at some point," Mari teased.

"She is absolutely right." Mama came into the family area, wiping her hands with a worn dish towel. "Gisele isn't going to wait forever . . ."

And the conversation turned just the way Mari wanted it to. The focus was no longer on her, thankfully. Nick was irritated with Mari in the way older brothers are often irritated with sisters, but instead of whining, he got up, explaining again that he *would* propose . . . later.

Kris joined Mari on the couch. His way was all ease and quiet. He didn't push for details, but let Mari rest her head on his shoulder. Kris was the nurturer, and he was in full effect for his exhausted baby sister. He was all recessive genes from some other part of their nationality. No dark curls or brown eyes, just blond and a dark hazel that Mari had found sweetness and comfort in for as long as she could remember. Kris didn't need to say the words. Instead, he just wrapped her in a warm hug and let her rest.

Her phone sat on her thigh, the buzzing pulling her focus from her brother.

**Jase: I need to talk to you. Please.**

# Chapter Four

Mari stared at the phone, thinking before responding—not something she was known for. But her heart was still pierced in the right ventricle where Jase had looked through her. The ego filling his voice—"I just have one of those faces"—pulsed in the recesses of her brain. A week ago, Mari would have gotten down on her knee to thank God that Jase was texting her. Now she wanted to sulk or, really, hurt him the way he'd hurt her.

And also still be kissed senseless by him.

And she despised those feelings.

She got up, signaling to Kris in their unspoken language that she needed a minute, quickly grabbing her bag while most of her family was distracted, several conversations happening at once around her.

**Mari:** Sorry. New phone. Who's this?

It was a terrible lie, and while it might have been funny to someone else, it just sat in Mari's chest like wet concrete, hardening and sinking into her. Now in her room, Mari climbed onto her bed, and with little thought, she grabbed the offending letter from Wilson Prosthetics and slid it under her pillow. A faded hunter-green-and-burgundy comforter was pulled up enough that her mom would think of it as made.

**Jase:** Really? It's Jase. We need to talk.

**Mari:** No, we don't. You made yourself clear.

Would this be where he apologized? And when he did, what was she going to say? She hated that she was angry with him. She didn't want to be angry with Jase. He was the one who had listened to her vent and cry at camp when they had found out about Davis being arrested and going to rehab for his addiction. Jase had been the one to assure her over and over that she had done everything to help Davis. That it wasn't her fault.

**Jase: I need your word, Mari.**

This was not the same guy who had gone to Camp Chemo with her for years. Where was the apology? What in the ever-loving world was he going on about? Need her word about what? That she wouldn't tell his precious Lindsay that she knew him? That he'd almost kissed her this past summer? Jase had probably been dating Lindsay then and didn't want his almost-transgression to come to light.

**Mari: Don't worry, Jase. I won't tell her about camp.**

She'd almost written "kiss," but it wasn't a kiss, it was an almost-kiss. And that was the worst part.

It was only an almost.

**Jase: Not just camp. No one knows I had cancer.**

She had to reread the text at least twice before the words sunk in.

How in the hell was this possible? How could no one know that he'd had cancer?

That was a thing?

**Mari: Fine.**

And she nearly flung her phone across the room, but it might break, and she couldn't afford a new one right now. Throwing things had always made Mari feel better, so instead, she grabbed her well-loved and well-beaten pink bunny, Lovee. It didn't make the satisfying thwack her phone would have, but it also didn't bust into a million pieces and involve her explaining her broken phone to her parents . . . again.

"Hey, what did Lovee do to you?" Mama moved into her room like a dancer.

Mari envied the easiness with which she walked, the way that her body seemed to flow and follow, unlike Mari's, which was a clack and a step, all noise and no grace.

"He had the audacity to try and convince me that I was too old to have a security blanket." Mari smiled from her place on her bed. She wasn't upset that her mama just came into her room. That was the way things were. Mama was a welcome presence in Mari's chaotic life right now.

"As your mama, I just want you to know you can have Lovee as long as you want. I'll sew it into your graduation robes and pack it up and send it to college with you." She sat next to Mari, her scent and the feel of her arm as she wrapped it around Mari's shoulders were comforting.

"Thanks." She leaned her head on her mama's shoulder, letting her mother hold her to ease some of the burden of the day. "Hey, Mama . . ."

"Hmm?" Karen twirled a lock of Mari's curls around one of her fingers.

Mari could still remember her mama doing that as the strands started to fall out, the look of sadness in her mama's eyes. But Mari had laughed, not wanting her mama to be sad about it.

"I found this in the mail." Sitting up, Mari reached under her pillow, pulling out the letter addressed to her from Wilson

Prosthetics. She shook a little as she handed her mom the letter detailing events about an upcoming clinic for people with hard-to-fit amputations.

"What do you think?"

Mama looked over the letter, keeping her face blank, probably not wanting Mari to know her true feelings.

"I mean, they are really good at what they do." Mari chewed on her lip. "And a couple of people from camp go there."

"Are they amputated like you?"

This was the hard thing; no one was really amputated like Mari. She had one of the highest levels of amputation, and even at camp, where there were other amputees, most had at least *some* residual limb.

"No." She shook her head. "But this clinic is for hard-to-fit people."

"Do you want to go?"

Because her mom would make it work.

"I don't know," Mari admitted, shrugging her shoulders and still staring at the logo on the paper. "Like, it seems like the world wants me to have a prosthesis."

But she hadn't liked her last prosthesis.

Maybe she would if she went somewhere else.

"That's your choice, baby. Forget what the world says." Karen pushed one of Mari's curls off of her face. "But if you want to go for it, we can."

Mari stopped herself from chewing on her cuticles as she thought through the words. Did she want to go? Did she want to hear them tell her that with a lot of work she could walk "just like everyone else"? Did she actually want that? "I don't want another bucket seat." She motioned to her last prosthesis, the world's most expensive doorstop, which was propped in her closet.

"Okay." Mama nodded. "Why?"

"Mom . . ." She drew out the word. Her mother knew exactly why Mari didn't want a bucket seat, but she apparently wanted Mari to be prepared to defend her decision. "I don't want a bucket seat because it's uncomfortable, I have to take it off to pee, and it adds a couple of inches to my hips. And I am vain enough that it matters."

"Okay, then." Mama said. "What do you want? How do you want it to be different from that one?"

"I don't know . . . I guess something . . ." She trailed off as she thought about the different types of prosthetic limbs available. "A suction socket and the microprocessor knee. It's pretty amazing."

"So if they can find a way to give you a suction socket, even though you don't have any residual limb left, you might be interested?"

"Yeah. And I want good function and a lower profile on my body."

"So we'll tell them this at the clinic and see what they say." Mama smiled. "And the worst that happens is we drive out there and get a no."

"But at least we'll know," Mari agreed, feeling the smallest inklings of . . . something that felt a lot like hope.

# Chapter Five

The end of September bared down on Jase. Mari seemed to be at every turn. Every space he was in, she was there too. Even when he wasn't supposed to be watching Mari, Jase was watching her. Which meant that he was almost always watching her. It was weird. His internal radar seemed to be trained on her. She was only in his AP Chem class, but he'd find her in the hall, walking through with her bright-pink crutches, a sly smile, but with hesitancy in her movement. He could see the differences so clearly between "regular Mari" and "camp Mari."

And he missed camp Mari.

And he needed to stop thinking that way, damn it.

But there Mari was again. Every day in Chem class, leaning over the lab table, her curls hanging over her face, her bottom lip between her teeth, pencil tap-tap-tapping on her paper as she worked on the equation. His hand wanted to touch one of the curls, to feel it between his fingers and see if it had the same softness that it did at camp.

He had to stop.

Jase jerked his head as if trying to dislodge the thought and went back to his paper, staring down at it, focusing. Pencil to the paper, he listened to the murmurs through the class, pencils moving over the papers, the shuffling sounds of Mrs. Yother moving around the room.

Lucas nudged Jase while they worked. "She's kinda cool."

"Who?" His heartbeat tripled, afraid that Lucas had caught him looking at Mari. "Yother?"

"No." Lucas shook his head, light-auburn hair moving in a wave before settling right back over his eyes. "Mari, the new girl."

"Really? I didn't know you'd talked to her." His back straightened, and there was a thicker thud to his heartbeat. "She's only been here, what, two weeks?"

"She's in Debate with me and Advisement." Lucas leaned in, whispering, "I mean, she's kind of cute."

Hair stood up on the back of Jase's neck, and his brain couldn't seem to understand the words his friend was saying . . . or not saying. "Huh?"

"I'd ask her out if she . . . you know."

"No." Jase pushed his pencil against the paper, and the tip broke. "Enlighten me." But he did know. And everything about this conversation bothered him. Because his own behavior was so much worse than Lucas's. But it was Lucas's that pissed him off.

"If she didn't have one leg."

"Oh sure." He didn't want to hear more, so he tried to look busy while rummaging through his bag, looking for another pencil.

"Did you hear she had *cancer*?" Lucas said "cancer" like it was the plague. "I bet she knows that lady you did your summer hours with."

He didn't answer. His tongue was sawdust in his mouth. What could he say? Because yeah, of course Mari knew

Heather. Heather was Mari's camp counselor. Hell, they probably talked outside of camp and the hospital too.

"I hear her brother is a swimmer at South Side." Lucas just couldn't seem to shut up about Mari.

"Huh."

"We'll probably swim against him. They're coming to the invitational."

"Probably." God, it would have been so much easier to just run into Mari at a swim meet than it was to see her every day in his class. "But you seem to know a lot about her. Sure you don't want to ask her out?" Jasc deflected, but it didn't sit right, and Jase knew he should just let the whole damn thing go.

"I mean . . ." Lucas turned around on his lab stool, openly staring at Mari. "Maybe I will."

The bell rang, and the students ran from the room. It was the last class of the day. Jase had swim practice in forty-five minutes, so he didn't bother to rush from the room. That, and he had picked up on Mari's cues. She never rushed from this class. Instead, she took her time, putting her stuff into her bag and crutching out the door.

"Hey." He spoke to her a moment after the last student had left the room. It was the first time since she had started at AWP that he had spoken to her.

"Excuse me." Mari moved around him, ducked in front of him, and moved out the classroom door. Mari headed to the bank of lockers; hers was on the end. She propped her crutches upright next to it.

He moved to follow her, wanting to say more, but all of the words seemed wrong.

"How does she stand there like that?" Lindsay came out of nowhere and pulled Jase's arms around her.

"Lots of practice." God, he had to stop. "I have practice," he corrected quickly.

"Can you still give me a lift home?" Her fingers curled around the belt loops on his khaki pants. "I'd hate to take the bus."

"Sure." He pulled himself away, grabbing his Chromebook and the rest of his stuff before heading out. But as he trotted down the hall toward the pool, he could hear Mari laugh. He stopped in the middle of an archway that led from the main building to the outside corridor and turned to see her giggling with Addison and Zeke. Her eyes were lit up, and her smile was big enough that he could see her teeth, and her curls shook.

And she never looked up to see him.

She was playing by his rules. She'd kept his secret.

Why did it bother him so much?

# Chapter Six

The question on the Smart Board in her AP Chem class was mocking her. There were letters and numbers and all of the correct punctuation, but it was all written in gibberish. How could it be this hard? And why did the teacher have to move so fast? Mari's head ached as she attempted, very poorly, to follow along in the class. Mrs. Yother moved through another problem, something to do with a chemical or something that might have something to do with the periodic chart, but she couldn't be completely sure.

She was good at school. She didn't have to really work at it, and she could swing decent enough grades that no one complained. But now, suddenly, it was all too much and all too fast, and in her head, she was screaming and crying.

And she hated it.

Mari watched the other students. They all seemed to intrinsically understand what was going on, and the sounds of their pencils scraping over their loose-leaf paper were grating on her exhausted nerves.

"Mari?" Lindsay whispered her name across their shared lab space. "Do you have a pencil?"

It took a solid minute for Mari to decode all of the words that Lindsay said. Her brain was still stuck, trying to understand the problem in front of her. "What?"

"Pencil? You know? The thing you write with?"

"Sorry." Heat crept up Mari's chest and cheeks. "No, I'm down to my last one."

"Ugh." Lindsay stood, sweeping her long curtain of hair off of her shoulder and taking her broken pencil to the electric sharpener. "I'm just so lazy."

She laughed to one of her friends, a girl Mari still struggled to remember the name of. It was something with a Y in a place that it shouldn't be. Patyn or Madalyn or something.

"God, wouldn't it be nice if we could all use wheelchairs or something?" Y said.

"Uh, no." Lindsay couldn't seem to answer a question without putting a filler in front of it. "God, to be deformed or something." There was a full-body shiver as she sat back on her stool. "I would want to die."

"Right?" Y laughed, but then they both seemed to remember that Mari was there at the same time. Eyes looked at her, and she just stared at both of them.

"I don't know." Mari sighed, when what she really wanted to do was hurl things. Preferably obscenities. "I get really great parking out of the deal."

"Sorry," Lindsay mumbled. "That was insensitive. I just forget you're handicapped. It's like you're normal."

But Mari didn't believe for a minute that either of them ever forgot she was disabled.

"Yeah, I hear that a lot." Now the headache pulsing at the base of her head was from this conversation, not from trying to figure out what the "temperature to the reaction mixture" was.

But both made her sick to her stomach.

The bell chimed a low dulcet tone. Because the clanging

of a normal bell ringing would be too pedestrian for the children of Atlanta West Prep. But it still cued the same thing, and students began the ritual of packing up and heading out the door. Mrs. Yother reminded the class about the optional tutorials after school and that they had a test next week.

"Mari?" Mrs. Yother, in her ethereal long skirts and with her long, curly hair that looked effortless and suitably hippy, stood at Mari's lab spot. "Do you think we could chat for a minute?"

Mari's heart did that thing where it stopped for a half second before picking back up in a pace that was too fast to be healthy. "Sure." She smiled her I'm-Talking-to-a-Teacher smile, bright enough to be pleasing but not so big that her teeth showed.

"How are you adjusting to AWP?" Mrs. Yother pulled up a stool and sat down across from her.

"Oh, you know, it's a little different." Mari stopped putting her things away, realizing pretty quickly that this wasn't going to be a short conversation. "Not just the uniforms and no locks on the lockers; it's a different atmosphere."

"But you've found some friends?"

Was this a welfare check? Did friends come with the tuition check?

"Yeah, uh, Addison and Zeke." She wanted to chew on her lip or twist her hair or do something with her hands. Instead, she scraped at the lab table with the side of her thumbnail. "But it's always hard to find your place." She didn't mention Jase as friend. She didn't know him. Not at all.

"And classes?"

"Ah." And here it was—the real reason they were talking.

"You guys move a little faster than South Side." She was doing okay in her other classes, but her first few quizzes in Chemistry had been way south of an A. So far south that they weren't even in the same hemisphere.

"There are the after-school tutorials," Mrs. Yother said sympathetically. "I was looking over your homework, and I think you're close, just a little lost in some of the elements."

"I'm tied to the MARTA schedule." She hated the quivery feeling of "not enough" that filled her belly. "The accessibility bus will leave me if I'm not outside when it arrives."

"Right." The teacher seemed to study Mari. "I don't even understand the MARTA schedule, and I have an advanced degree."

"Yeah." Mari forced a laugh. Why was this turning so awkward? "Well, the access bus is a little easier than the regular bus line, but I've used both. My brother and I share a car, and since he has swim team and a job, he gets the car for school."

"Maybe he could pick you up after the tutorial?" Mrs. Yother went back to her desk and pulled out one of the quizzes from last week. "We both know your grades are not up to AWP standard. We could talk about moving you to Honors Chemistry instead of AP."

Heat covered Mari's belly at the thought. It was almost worse than the failing grade, the idea of dropping the AP class. She could handle this. She had to. "No, I'm sure it's just from the adjustment. I promise."

"I know that part of your scholarship is dependent on your grades. I wouldn't want lack of transportation to jeopardize your being here. If the class just moves too fast we can think of a less strenuous alternative."

A sucker punch would have been less painful, the lack of transportation informing her once again that she wasn't supposed to be an AWP student. "I'll be fine." Fear and anger clipped her tone. "Is this all you needed? I'm going to be late to catch the bus."

"That's it." There was the sympathetic smile, a touch of compassion. "Please let me know if you think you could make the tutorials."

"Sure." Mari hefted her bag onto both shoulders, taking her crutches and moving out of the classroom at what might be considered a run.

AWP was supposed to be better. It was supposed to offer her things that South Side couldn't. But all it had done was point out her inadequacies.

# Chapter Seven

Water still clung to Jase's hair as he stood outside his SUV, waiting on Lindsay. He'd seen her running off of the track, but he knew it'd be awhile before she was done with her shower and stuff. He should pull out his notebook and work on his paper for AP History, but he was tired, and his brain was on overdrive. His fingers fidgeted, his heart thudded, and he replayed his last lap in the pool.

"Hey there." Lindsay ran up, popping a kiss on his cheek. "Practice ran long."

"Let's get out of here." Jase opened his car door and climbed in, not waiting for Lindsay and definitely not opening her door.

"God, can you imagine waiting on MARTA every day?" She pulled her seatbelt across as Jase put the car in reverse and pulled out of his spot.

"What?" He followed Lindsay's line of sight, and there was Mari. She was sitting on the ground at the bus stop, across the parking lot from them. No bench or anything because no one used MARTA. "Is everyone obsessed with her?"

"I heard her family doesn't have the money to get her a fake leg." Lindsay pulled out her phone and snapped a selfie. "I guess they've never heard of insurance." She laughed.

But he didn't say anything. He didn't say anything because he knew that insurances didn't cover everything on some medical equipment or medical procedures. He didn't elaborate on the fact that Mari had no residual limb, making a comfortable prosthesis difficult to achieve. He didn't tell Lindsay to shut up, because it would give everything away. And his heart beat faster at the very idea of anyone finding out his secret. He couldn't go through that again.

Instead, he pushed the pedal to the floor and literally burned rubber out of the school's parking lot.

Jase listened to Lindsay talk the entire way to her house in Vinings, a community just north of Atlanta city proper. Atlanta West Prep was just a couple of miles from her house, making it easy for him to drop her off before he made his way across town. But it meant he was going to be sitting in traffic once he left her house. The homes in this area were newer than the ones in his own neighborhood, but still said money—just newer money.

"Are you going to the thing at Chessie's on Friday?" Lindsay asked, her hand dropping ever so casually onto his thigh.

He didn't think twice about removing it from his body.

"She mentioned something." Jase parked his car in her absurdly long driveway. "Is your car fixed?"

"It's supposed to be back today." She sighed, flipped her long hair over her shoulder, and went to grab the door handle. "But I really like you driving."

"I really like not sitting in traffic on West Paces," he said, but didn't add that maybe their thing was winding down. It had never been serious, and he didn't want it to turn into a potential mess or, more likely, added drama. "If your car's not ready, I can take you home the rest of the week. But next week is when practices really get going, and I'll need to stay at school longer."

"It's fine." She opened the door and climbed out. "I wouldn't want anyone to think we're exclusive anyway." Her smile slid into place, lifting her left eye just a little. "Later." And she walked into her house. Her school uniform was shoved in her bag, and instead she wore the athletic shorts and a non-sweaty T-shirt.

He knew without looking at labels or price tags that her "crappy" clothes probably cost more than a lot of people's nice ones.

And he began to wonder just what that said about him. He'd never given a single thought to the price tag on any of the clothes he owned. And he wondered if he should.

Jase turned the car around—the driveway was too long to successfully back out of, even with the back-up camera—and started his journey across town. Okay, it was all of five miles from her place to his, but in traffic it was going to take at least thirty minutes. And that was if the lights were in his favor.

Jase didn't think about Mari. At least, that's what he told himself as he turned back onto the main road and began the stop-and-go crawl toward his house. His phone buzzed from its mount on the dash, and his mother's picture popped up.

"Mom, I'm not supposed to use my phone." It was a family rule, but one that Olivia Ellison broke on the regular to tell him something.

"But I have something I want to tell you." She was giddy, and that made Jase smile. "It's super exciting."

"Did I get a letter to compete for the Olympics?" It was a family joke because there had been a time when swimming had consumed him to the point that he might have been able to do that. But he'd backed off. Enjoying his life as a teenager more than his life as a swim rat.

"No, but you can still try if you want." It was something his mom hadn't quite let go of yet. "But! I talked to Margaret Smallwood from Camp Chemo today."

"You did?" Why would his mom be talking to Margaret? Did Margaret tell his mom about Mari and the near-kiss she'd caught them in? "Why?"

"We'd chatted last year about a benefit, and I decided that this year's New Year's Eve Gala would be a great opportunity for that!" Her voice bubbled with excitement. "I know it's September, but it takes a lot of planning."

"I know. You've done it every year that I can remember." It was his mom's favorite event she did for charity. It was put on by the city's service league, where she was a member. The gala always benefitted some charity . . . just usually not one he was associated with.

"Isn't this great?"

Jase thought he could hear her typing, probably making notes and plans already.

"Maybe you can invite all your friends from camp."

"Uh—" He stopped short, almost nailing the car in front of him. "Let's talk about this when I get home."

"I cannot wait! You can help me come up with the theme and auction items."

"Bye."

He couldn't close his eyes because he was driving, but he wanted to. His stomach rolled and pitched.

This was a particularly terrible idea.

If his mom did a benefit for camp, people would ask questions—and everyone might find out. About him. Because Camp Chemo was for kids with cancer. And what if someone asked how his mom had found out about camp? What if she told all of them that *he* was how she knew about it? Because *he* was a camper. Jase was beginning to wonder if this was even a secret he could keep anymore. But at the thought of what that meant, Jase couldn't breathe.

# Chapter Eight

Mari had officially completed a month at Atlanta West Preparatory School. Thankfully, she was no longer much of a novelty, but she could still see the questions in her new classmates' faces—wondering what they could ask her and what was off limits. October had arrived, but the only thing it meant for Mari was that Halloween (her favorite holiday) was a little closer.

"Hey, Mari." Lucas perched next to her, sitting on the table in debate class.

A big difference between AWP and South was the fact that the classrooms had long tables instead of the single-person desks. She didn't have a little wire basket under her chair to cram all of her crap into. Instead, everyone hung up their things on the wall, keeping just what they needed for each class.

"Hey, Lucas." Mari smiled at him, feeling the early teases of a possible crush. In the month she had been at the school, Lucas had become someone she might have considered a friend. Despite the fact that he still hung out with Jase—Jason—and his friends. But he always smiled at her and, lately, had been helping her get her things from her bag to her desk.

"Plans for the weekend?"

"Just family stuff." She smiled but made sure her bottom teeth were covered. "I have to work on Saturday."

"Oh yeah? Where do you work?"

"A bookstore in the East Atlanta Village."

"Do you live on that side of town?"

"In Grant Park." She smiled because she truly loved her neighborhood. "Usually, one of my brothers can drop me off, or sometimes, the bookstore's owners pick me up."

"You don't have a car?" He asked this like she didn't have shoes or clean underwear.

"I have to share it with Leo, my brother, and most of the time he has to drive farther for work." She shrugged her shoulders. "I can drive. It's not a big deal." It was a habit for her to offer this information. So many people—including those at the DMV—made assumptions about her disability.

"Oh, do you have, like, hand controls or something?"

"Nah." She appreciated the way he was asking all of this, like it wasn't a big deal and he was just curious. "We have an automatic, which you only need one foot to drive with, and since I don't wear a prosthesis, it's not like that gets in the way of me using the pedals. I could get a pedal extender, since I have my right leg, and it would make it a little less awkward, but really it's no big deal."

"So, you wouldn't drive with your prosthesis, even if you had it?"

"Nope, it'd just get in the way, I think."

The warning sound chimed, and Giselle (or Ms. Austin, as she was called in class) came in. Lucas moved his way back toward his table, getting his things out. Mari was nearly jubilant, like for the first time she wasn't a sideshow for her classmates. She was just another student.

"God, these douchenozzles are beyond." Zeke Williamson sat next to her, his afro brushing her arm as he lay his head down on their shared table in debate class.

"What's going on?" Mari doodled in her notebook, a list of potential debate topics in front of her.

"If one more person asks if my dad can get them tickets to the next Atlanta United game, I'm going to tell them to go to hell."

"Why do they ask you for tickets? Your dad play?"

Zeke looked up at her, a little side-eye and whole lot of sarcasm.

"Uh, no." Zeke rolled his eyes. "My dad is one of the team physicians."

"Oh." Mari should have stopped being surprised by her new classmates' backgrounds, but it seemed like everyone's mom or dad was a CEO of a major corporation. Or they had a last name that was as recognizable as Vanderbilt or Forbes.

"They can totally afford them." Zeke kept his head on the desk, and his words sounded muffled against his hands.

"So, um, can you get me tickets to the next United game?" Mari deadpanned, waiting to see if he would catch her joke. Had they been friends long enough to make these?

He rolled his eyes, but he was smiling, so she was pretty sure she hadn't crossed some new friend line.

"Hello, scholars." Addison slammed her books next to Zeke's head, but he didn't flinch. Mari had already learned that Zeke could sleep anywhere and fall asleep in a matter of seconds. She wasn't positive he was asleep right then or just ignoring Addison. "Are we ready to take on the world of debate and the rules in which we live in society?"

"Are you feeling okay?" Mari laughed. "It's only Wednesday, too early for us to be delirious."

"Is he sleeping?" Addison sat at her table, bringing out her day planner and highlighters. Her life was color coded and all in that pretty little book.

"I would be if you could just reel it in a little," Zeke muttered from his place on the table.

"Sorry, just, you know, functioning in society," Addison teased.

"She's just excited to start the prep for your next debates." Ms. Austin sat down at the table with them.

Giselle Austin had been dating Mari's brother Nick for nearly three years. Giselle was a year older, having graduated from Georgia State, and was now working on her master's in education there while Nick finished up his electrical engineering degree at Georgia Tech. And she was a very big reason that Mari had been able to leave her public high school and attend this way-too-expensive-for-her prep school.

"Oh yeah, that's definitely it." Mari smiled, grateful that she was at a table with two friends, even if they were still very new. They weren't at the random text stage or anything.

Giselle smiled, patting Mari affectionately on the arm. "Don't sound too excited."

Class moved forward quickly after that, as the rest of the students found their way in and sat down. They discussed ways to counter arguments, to defend their positions, and to hold their own thoughts. Mari always wanted to make sure she could believe in either side of her debate; that way, she could find a footing in it.

"Hey, I've got to meet Harker during lunch today," Addison said as they scanned through recent newspaper articles on their topic. "Sorry. He wants to talk about something in my English paper."

"Ugh, fine. I guess I have to sit in the lounge alone." Mari tried to say it like it was no big deal, but it was. She hated the student lounge. She hated not having a larger group of friends to be with and missed her friend group from South Side. And she missed Leo. Her staunch protector and pest all in one package.

"Mari? Earth to Mari?" Zeke poked at her shoulder. "Bell rang."

"Right." She laughed.

# Chapter Nine

Most schools had proper cafeterias with lunch ladies and serving lines. Jase imagined they were loud and cavernous and packed with students. The student lounge was Atlanta West Preparatory School's idea of a cafeteria. There was no line or lunch lady. Instead, if you didn't bring a lunch from home, there was the option of ordering from nearby restaurants that the school had a deal with. Today, he had udon noodles from his favorite noodle house. The room had large floor-to-ceiling windows, and instead of tables, there were couches and plush chairs scattered in various conversation nooks. There were also several study carrels and private study pods where students could work.

"Uh, we have to talk about your epic fail in front of Mari yesterday." Madalyn Smith sat on the floor, her back up against the couch that Jase and Lindsay were eating on. "I cannot believe you said 'deformed' in front of her." She twirled a lock of dark hair around her finger, working it into a simple knot before releasing it.

"God, I couldn't either!" Lindsay laughed. "I guess I forgot she's handicapped. You know Yother had her stay after class?"

"She's tanking," Madalyn whispered. "I saw her quiz from last week."

"Maybe they amputated part of her brain when they did that to her leg." Lindsay said it like it was funny.

"That's a lobotomy." Lucas dropped down on the other side of Lindsay, filling the couch. "And I don't know. She seems pretty smart."

"I saw what I saw." Madalyn slurped her own noodles. "The girl is flunking."

"It's got to be tough." Jase tried to ease into the conversation. "She's not from here and stuff."

"I thought you had to pass an entrance test to get into this school." Lindsay picked at her salad. "Maybe they needed some diversity check-off or something."

"She's here on scholarship." Madalyn's face was lit with the excitement of gossip. "And I saw her waiting for the bus. Like, the MARTA bus."

"I wonder how long it takes her to get home. Like, where does she even live?" Lindsay didn't think of herself as classist, but to Jase it was clear.

"Across town." He had to stop answering these questions. People would figure out that he *knew* her. "I heard her talking."

"Grant Park," Lucas filled in. "Off South Ave. I asked," he said, shrugging. "That's got to take forever on MARTA."

"Probably quicker than driving, though," Jase said.

"Do you have swim today?" Lindsay changed the conversation, touching him on the knee. "I don't have cross-country and wanted to see if you wanted to go grab a coffee or something." The "something" was said with the barest hint of a suggestion.

"Maybe." He didn't outright commit. This was getting dangerously close to something some might call exclusive, and he didn't want that with her. At this moment, he wasn't even sure he liked her.

The conversation moved to the football game that weekend and the party after. Jase listened, but he could still hear the earlier conversation in his head. The one where the girls had talked about Mari. And he hated that it was even in his brain. Like, why did he care about Mari Manos at all?

"Hey, so I'm going to ask Mari to the game this Friday," Lucas said, leaning across Lindsay to talk to him. "Do you think the stairs at the stadium will be an issue?"

"How would I know?" But he did know. He knew that Mari was fine on steps. That she could handle steps—or even a high ropes course.

"You just seem to know." Lucas shrugged. "That's all."

"I have no idea," Jase lied succinctly.

"Well, I heard that the reason she's here is because South Side wanted her to wear a fake leg, and her family couldn't afford it," Lindsay gossiped.

"Old news." Jase was so tired of this.

"You would think she'd have already done that." Madalyn kept the conversation going despite Jase's best effort to end it. "I mean, then she'd at least look normal."

"It's a prosthesis," Lucas corrected. "My uncle has one because of something with his diabetes."

"God, I cannot imagine how she does life." Madalyn chewed thoughtfully. "Like, how does she even shower? Does she have to take a bath?"

"Do you think she's missing anything else?" Lindsay whispered to her friend, but they could all hear her. "Like, her vagina?"

"Oh my God," Madalyn breathed. "Could they even do that? Like, I know she said she doesn't wear a prosthesis because her amputation is high or something. Like, she doesn't have a stump."

"God, do you think?" There was shock, but maybe also a little intrigue.

There was the sharp sound of a bag hitting the floor in just the wrong way, and the entire lounge turned to see Mari. She stood there, outrage and sadness all over her face. But she couldn't speak. Her mouth opened a few times, but nothing came out. Instead, she turned, a little spin on her one foot and left the lounge at a pace that could have been considered a run.

Jase leaned back, fighting the urge to stand up.

No one said anything for a minute, just looked at the door Mari had exited. Her bag was still on the floor.

"Oh God." Lindsay laughed, but it was a laugh that was full of shock. "Do you think she heard?"

"I'm going to say yes, based on the fact that she looked like she was about to cry," Madalyn said. "Should we go after her?"

"And say what?" Lindsay asked. "It's fine. I'm sure. She's got to be used to people being curious."

"I'm gonna go find her." Jase heard the words coming out of his mouth, unable to stop them.

"Jason, stop!" he heard Lindsay call, but he didn't. He didn't wait to see what she was going to say or do. Instead, he moved through the lounge, grabbing Mari's bag, and out into the hall.

Turning quickly, he saw her in front of her locker, her face pressed against it.

"Mari." He sat the bag down next to her, but then didn't know what to do with his hands. Because Mari had been his friend for so many years, he wanted to reach out to her, to touch her, but the wall between them was currently thick and high. And he had built it brick by brick.

"Oh, please just go the fuck away." Tears thickened her voice. "I don't know this place well enough to know where I can cry in peace."

"I'm sorry." He touched her arm just above her elbow, Mari's skin cool against his warm hand. "Don't let them get to you."

"Hard not to when people are literally questioning what your body is like." She bit hard on her lip, stopping the little quiver he'd seen. "Now go away."

"Mari."

"Jase—Jason—just go away." She stomped her foot, picking it straight up off of the ground and bringing it down hard. Anger replacing her sadness. "I don't want you here."

"I—" He started to say something, but nothing that entered his brain felt right. "Okay." He backed away, watching the tension sort of slide down Mari's body, her shoulders hunching over again, the slight shake of her shoulders.

She was crying.

And he was walking away.

Adding another layer to the wall he was putting between them.

# Chapter Ten

Jase didn't go get coffee with Lindsay. In fact, he hadn't spoken to her again after the incident with Mari at lunch. He couldn't shake the way Mari had glared at him. The hurt in her face had been bad, but what bothered him the most was the fact that she hadn't seemed surprised by it. Like she had just been waiting for someone to say things like that about her. She had looked at him like he couldn't get any lower in her opinion of him.

He wasn't normally a jerk, but it was as if since Mari's arrival at AWP he couldn't be anything but. And he didn't know what to do about it. With it only being the beginning of October, fall colors were still weeks away, but at least the days were no longer in the nineties. Jase itched for change, but he didn't think it had anything to do with the stagnant heat and everything to do with him.

Driving down the interstate, he found himself moving through the neighborhood where Mari lived. The student directory had come in handy for once. The houses were all nice, with well-kept lawns, but nothing too flashy. Old bungalows and a smattering of Victorian era homes decorated the streets around the park that housed the zoo.

And there was Mari's house. The yard was nice, with some landscaping that needed to be weeded—nothing like the professionally manicured lawns in his neighborhood. He didn't see a car in the driveway but hoped Mari might be there anyway. He didn't know what time the bus would get her home.

Parking his car on the street, he slowly walked up the path to her house, noticing the large front porch with a swing, some flowerpots that needed water, and some furniture covered in a light layer of dust. But it was nice, like somewhere people might actually sit and invite the neighbors over, not just keep nice for appearances.

He knocked, not really sure what he was going to say to her. Just that he needed to see her, needed to make sure she knew he . . . he wasn't sure what. But he'd already knocked, so it was too late to turn back now.

"Ellison." Leo Manos opened the door to him. "What's up?"

The two boys didn't know each other, not really, but they'd swam against each other, and Jase remembered seeing Leo when his family dropped Mari off at camp functions. Based on the fact that Leo didn't seem to want to beat him up right now, he guessed Mari hadn't told him about their arrangement.

"I was looking for Mari." Jase shoved his hands in his khaki uniform pants. "Is she home?"

"She's over at the Daily Grind." Leo smiled, and it was pretty identical to his sister's, except there were no crooked teeth on the bottom. "Want me to tell her you dropped by?"

"I'll just see her around." He didn't say he'd see her at school. "You don't have to tell her I stopped by." His heart did a thud and then tripled its pace. Why was he even here?

"Okay," Leo said, but then his face changed, concern marring his forehead. "Is she okay? Is it something at school?"

"No." Jase probably said it too quickly. "It's nothing." He backed down the steps. "I'll see you at the invitational?"

"I'll be the one kicking your ass." Leo laughed.

"We'll see." Jase smiled, but it faded as soon as he turned. What in the hell had he been thinking when he drove all the way out here?

# Chapter Eleven

**Leo: So, random, but Ellison just stopped by.**

Mari had to read the text three times before she could comprehend the words. Jase had been to her house.

"Mari?"

She didn't really hear Davis say her name, only sort of.

"Mari?" He laughed this time as he spoke. She looked up, and Davis stopped laughing. The crooked smile faltered, his eyes filled with concern. "What is it?" He pushed at his brown hair, but it wasn't long enough to go behind his ear or anything. Not at all like the long hair he'd had a year ago.

"Nothing." She turned her phone facedown and smiled her winningest smile for him. "It's nothing." Jase—Jason—had been to her house. He probably just wanted to find out exactly how her body was shaped so he could ease Lindsay's mind. Heat filled her cheeks just thinking about it. The way those two girls had laughed. It all hurt, but the embarrassment was worse.

"Right." Davis wiped the counter she sat at. "Lying has never helped me out of anything."

His words were earnest; he was not the same guy he'd been just four months earlier. Sobriety suited him, and dear God, it was so nice to have her best friend back.

"It really is nothing." She didn't want to lay her drama out for him. Davis had missed Camp Chemo this past summer, so he hadn't been there to see how Jase had been the one she had leaned on, how he so often held her up. "How's work?"

"It keeps me busy." He wiped at the counter again. "And my probation officer is happy, and that means my lawyer is happy, and that makes my parents happy."

"But are *you* happy?" Mari stopped his hand. Davis, with his smile-with-a-wink, a side effect from surgery to treat his lymphoma. She worried about him. "Are you okay?"

"I'm sober." He smiled over the word, but there was an exhaustion just under it. "And I take it minute by minute most days."

"I like having you back." She squeezed his hand before letting him go. "How's school? Your volunteer hours?" Dr. Henderson, their mutual oncologist, had arranged for Davis to do his community service at the hospital where they'd been treated for their cancers. Mari knew it was hard on Davis to be there. To see his nurses and doctors, people who had helped him survive cancer when he was now there for an arrest associated with his addiction.

"Fine." He topped off her coffee and sat the creamer down for her. "Having my NA sponsor, who doubles as my school counselor, keeps me on the straight and narrow. My community service at the hospital is okay, still finding my way." He bit his lip. "I want to be helpful and all of that. Sometimes, I just feel like I'm in the way. But it'll be okay." Sliding her the sugar, he drilled her with a look. "Now that we've talked about my sobriety and how I'm okay, tell me what's going on. How's AWP? Do you ever see Jase?"

And that was a minefield Mari did not want to get into. "Oh, it's totally great." Lying, liar, who lies.

"I'm sure Jase has helped you find friends."

Davis said it like it was a fact, and Mari had to fight off the sarcastic laugh that burned in her belly.

"Hey, are you in AP Chem?" She flipped open her school-issued Chromebook and pulled up her homework. "AWP is ahead of where I was, and I can't seem to catch up."

"Nope, sorry. I didn't want to put too much on my plate."

Which made sense—recovery, job, community service hours.

"But if you hang around here long enough, you'll find someone who can help."

She arched a brow at him, waiting for Davis to elaborate.

"This place is lousy with college students. Surely someone will know chemistry."

"Great." She didn't want to talk anymore. It wouldn't be fair to unload on Davis that way, to tell him everything that was going on with Jase and AWP and how it would just be easier to go back to South Side. At least at South Side she would probably pass her classes, and maybe this time a prosthesis would work for her and she would be *just like everyone else.* Her brain was one long run-on sentence lately.

Instead, Mari found YouTube videos on how to do the chemistry problems. She made notes and texted Kris when she didn't quite understand what was going on. But sometimes, there were those ads that websites had, the ones that made Mari think her phone was listening to her, because on the side of her YouTube screen wasn't an ad for a chemistry tutor, but instead an ad for one of the leading prosthetics and orthotics companies in the United States.

She almost felt like she was looking at something illicit.

She put her earbuds in and quickly clicked on the video. It was a glossy and slick ad. Amputees doing "normal" things like walking step over step and going downhill. An upper-extremity amputee was cutting strawberries, and another was putting on makeup—all with their technologically advanced prosthetic limbs. Mari watched with bored fascination as a "super crip" like her friend Noah ice skated with a below-knee prosthesis, and then a bilateral-below-knee amputee broke records on her bladed prosthetics.

She could still hear the recent conversations in her head. They seemed to always be there, to be lurking in the back of her brain, about why she should *want* to wear a prosthesis. The assistant principal at South Side, Lindsay and her friend at AWP . . . Heck, even at camp, her safe place, there would be an offhanded comment. The clinic at Wilson Prosthetics was coming up, and as much as she tried not to think about it . . . she thought about it.

None of it mattered anyway. She wasn't going to get a prosthesis. She wasn't going to be Jase Ellison's girlfriend, or even his friend, outside the walls of camp. She was probably going to fail AP Chemistry and would be kicked out of AWP anyway.

Done.

Mari was done. Her head dropped onto the keyboard of her computer, her pencil flying out of her hand and across the room.

She did not care.

# Chapter Twelve

The Daily Grind was your typical coffeehouse and only a few blocks from Mari's house. It had a bar where patrons could order drinks and sit, or there were tables and other seating arrangements throughout the café. It was exactly what Jase had expected.

The pencil that thwapted him on the knee before rolling next to his foot, on the other hand, was a surprise. He picked it up and followed the direction that he thought it had come from.

Mari sat with her head down on her laptop, a notebook out beside her with a cup of coffee and her requisite cream and sugar. Davis wasn't behind the bar, but Jase did catch him wiping down a table and clearing the dirty dishes.

"Hey, man," he greeted, a real smile for Davis. "How's it going?"

"Today is good." Davis bumped his elbow in hello before moving back behind the counter. "Know anything about AP Chem? I think Mari could use some help."

She sat up when she heard her name. There were a lot of emotions on her face. Jase realized that he could name each and every one of them. Confusion. Embarrassment. A little excitement. And shame. She slammed her laptop shut, and the ire from earlier returned.

"I'm good." She said the words quickly, shoving things into her bag.

"Come on, Mari." Davis stopped her hand. "You've been here for hours, and I don't think you've moved past the first problem."

Jase walked over to her. She should ignore him completely. If it had been him, he would have.

"Can I help?"

He could see the words in her eyes. There were a bunch, and he got the feeling that most of them were not kind. But she didn't say them. She didn't say anything.

He moved to her other side, where the worksheet was still out on the bar, and sat her pencil back down. "Where do you get lost?"

"I don't need your help." Her voice was low, doing her best not to draw attention to them.

"Davis, can I get some coffee?" he said instead of answering. He sat on the barstool next to her and tried to see what exactly she was working on.

"Just black coffee, or something with foam?"

"Nothing fancy." Davis handed him the cup of coffee and Jase poured a little sugar from the canister next to Mari. "Where are you getting confused?" he tried again.

"I would like you to leave." Each word was said as its own sentence. She finally looked at him, and the look on her face was one of irritation and a smattering of just plain anger.

"I heard you were here." He didn't want to press too much; he didn't want to piss her off to the point that she stormed out. If she did, Davis would ask questions.

"Oh, so we can be friends outside of the walls of AWP?" She hissed the words quietly.

"Mari, do you want help?" Davis asked from across the room. There had been no way he'd heard Mari. "Stop being stubborn and let him help."

"Being stubborn is my brand," she said, refusing to look at Jase.

"Let me help," he tried again, wanting to get back in her good graces, but unsure as to how.

"No." She didn't look at him as she shoved the rest of her things into her bag, taking her bright crutches and starting to walk out. "I'll see you later, Davis." She smiled and stopped to give Davis a hug before going on out the door.

And she left. Jase itched to follow her, to walk her the few blocks back to her house, but he didn't.

# Chapter Thirteen

Jase was still there. Mari knew that he was just inside the Daily Grind and watching her. Her whole body tingled with the urge to stop and turn to him. To motion for him to walk with her and for them to fall into their old and easy patterns. Not this new painful tension and irritation that wrapped around her spine and pushed her forward, farther away from him.

Mari hated the way Jase had to talked to her—and Davis—like it was no big deal. Like Jase hadn't asked her to pretend not to know him.

That sentence played over and over again in her brain.

Jason Ellison had asked her to pretend not to know him.

A person she had known for years had said he didn't know her.

Someone who had spent a week virtually tied to her just a couple of months ago had ignored her.

She would not let him back in.

Mari stopped walking, not too far from the church where Davis had his NA meetings, and slowly thumped her head against the brick wall. She was making terrible life decisions right now, and she didn't know why. Was it some weird lingering crush on Jase, despite the fact that he'd been a total and complete douchenozzle?

"Hey, hey, hey! You're going to get a ticket for property damage." Leo appeared, and Mari groaned.

"I know I shouldn't hit it with my massive head," she joked, but her heart still hurt. "Are you checking up on me?"

"Maybe." He was honest. "You're being really unfair to the wall." He instinctually reached over and took her bag off of her shoulders. "How's Davis?"

"Seems to be doing okay." She was hesitant in her answer. "I'm almost afraid of how great he's doing."

"Why?"

The sun had set, and the twilight of fall brought just enough cool air that Mari wished she'd remembered a sweater. But it wasn't too far of a walk back to their house.

"He tried to get clean a couple of times," she remembered. "But always on his own."

"He went to rehab." Leo made it sound like it was a cure.

"But relapse is always a possibility." Mari listened to the sounds around her: people out walking their dogs, kids being called in, college students debating the new transportation options. Her neighborhood was alive and vibrant.

"Like cancer."

"A lot like it," Mari said, but hated the rocks it left in her stomach.

"You going to tell me what Jase wanted?"

"No." But she knew it was a lie as it left her lips.

"Mari, remember, we're almost twins." A family joke, since they were so close in age. "Tell me. And not the bullshit you tell everyone else about AWP being amazing."

"AWP is . . ." She thought through a lot of adjectives. "Privilege dressed in woke clothes," she finally said. "Like, they're all progressive and have all the right clubs and do the right fundraisers, but they all order lunch from the places around town, and they don't think twice about filling up their SUVs with the credit card Mom and Dad pay for."

"What's it like for you?" Leo stopped her from walking. The two inches in height he had gotten from their dad made him seem more imposing.

"It's . . ." A coil unraveled in her belly, filling her body with uncertainty and unease. "Hard," she finally finished, being truthful for the first time in two weeks. "They're ahead of me in a lot of my classes. The week I missed between unenrolling at South and getting the scholarship meant I missed stuff. And I feel like I'm always explaining my life to them."

"But Jase is there. This isn't the first time they've heard of cancer."

They climbed the wide steps to their home, sat on the top step, and stared out across the neighborhood. Mari had always loved where they lived, being so close to downtown, but Grant Park was a community, with neighbors who helped and businesses all around. She felt like it was the other side of the planet from the other students at AWP, not just the other side of the city.

She didn't say anything to Leo about Jase and his cancer. She knew what he would say.

"I'm failing Chemistry," she said instead.

"It's only your first month," Leo reasoned. "You'll be fine."

"Yeah, maybe." She shrugged. "I've never failed anything. Not even fourth grade, when I was only there for weeks at a time."

"You still haven't told me why Jase was looking for you."

He brought the conversation back to what Mari knew he thought was a safe topic. Ha.

"He wanted to help me with Chemistry." It was sort of the truth. "But I don't know."

"Take the help!" Leo laughed at her. "Stop being so stubborn and let people help occasionally."

It was the second time in one evening that she'd been called stubborn, and while it made her smile, it also rankled her a little. She didn't want to need help from anyone, especially Jase Ellison.

~

After dinner, the house so much quieter now that Nick and Kris had both moved out, Mari sat with her phone, scrolling through her friends' Snaps and pics. She messaged her camp friends Mary Faith and Paige, but didn't expect to hear back from either of them. With her homework done for once, she felt like she could relax for just a moment.

Mari moved through various quizzes and mindless articles about your Hogwarts house and what kind of book heroine you would be.

But then she stopped scrolling.

An autoplay video began, and she watched, dread and interest competing for her feelings. It was a series of videos, kids and adults with different disabilities doing extraordinary-for-anyone things. A bilateral amputee powerlifting more than Mari weighed. A wheelchair user climbing ropes to the top of a gym, and she was still strapped to her wheelchair. There was a below-knee amputee moving across the balance beam, one foot in front of the other, and then successfully completing a pirouette on the four inches of space that the beam offered.

Conflicting feelings buzzed through Mari. She saw these videos through very different lenses than someone who was able-bodied would. She watched and saw people doing what they wanted, doing what they loved, and giving the proverbial middle finger to what society thought. But she knew someone who wasn't disabled would see something very different. They would see *inspiration* and *strength.* And then there was the punch in the gut of "There's no disability but a bad attitude" written in bold letters at the end of the video.

"Fuck that." She dropped her phone with frustration.

She had both—a bad attitude and a disability—at the moment. She was so tired of educating, discussing, and being a ridiculous inspiration for others. She grabbed her crutches and knocked on Leo's door.

"What's up?" His massive earphones hung around his neck, and he was holding some well-worn copy of a fantasy novel. One that she was sure he'd read at least thirty times.

"I'm irritated, and I need to talk to someone."

"The doctor is in."

He opened the door, and Mari climbed to the top bunk, hopping up each rung of the ladder, where she had come to hide and think and hang out with Leo for as long as she could remember. Until her older brothers had moved out, this had been Leo's bed, but now he had the room to himself, and he slept on the full-size bottom bunk.

Leo lay down on his bottom bunk, letting her have space and privacy. She was grateful.

"I hate inspiration porn," she groused.

"I know," he said. "And that's totally valid."

"And I hate explaining to people what happened." She danced her fingers up the wall, moving them in an itsy-bitsy motion. "I wonder if it'd be easier to just tell people it was a car accident."

"Why?"

"Because then I wouldn't have the added bonus of being a cancer survivor on top of being disabled." She thought of Jase. How no one knew, and he *could* keep it a secret. "I hate that people feel like they deserve to know."

"But you still tell them."

"Yeah, but, like, no one knows that Jase had cancer." She bit at her lip, fingers still moving up and down the wall. "How is that even possible?"

"Because he looks like everyone else," Leo said. Then he was silent for a moment. "Are you still going to go to the prosthetics place?"

"Yeah."

"But it isn't for a few weeks, so you could cancel." He climbed up the ladder to the top bunk, sitting crisscross-applesauce on the end of the bed, staring at her. "Do you want to cancel it?"

Did she? Did she want to cancel this appointment with a new prosthetics place, this company who was supposed to be "the best"? Now she was quiet while she chewed her own words, thinking over them. "I don't know."

"What happens if you go?"

"Probably just a discussion. Maybe they'll show me some new low-profile sockets." She didn't mention the ones she'd seen pop up in the ads on social media or the YouTube commercials for different prosthetic components.

"So, no big if you decide it's not for you."

Mari didn't think it was that easy. Because it was a "big," regardless of what she decided.

Because there was the option of her appearing not-disabled.

And suddenly, that mattered a whole lot to her.

Because Jase could keep his secret. Because he looked just like everyone else. And Mari never would.

And right then, she kind of hated Jase because he could keep his secret.

But she would keep it for him.

Because she wished that she could have the same secret.

# Chapter Fourteen

Parking his car in the three-car garage in the back of his house, Jase grabbed his bag and went through the mudroom toward the kitchen. He loved the kitchen. Not just because food was there, something he also liked, but it was the room that he associated with the best memories. Birthdays, family holiday parties, or just a family meal—all happened in the kitchen. Tonight, it smelled like dinner: a soup or maybe pot roast.

With his dad being gone most weeks, traveling for work, his mom didn't cook a big dinner for them often. But today, the weather had turned blustery, which he knew equaled soup in his mother's mind. She was dependable that way.

"I'm home!" he called. If Olivia was home, she would come and find him. Dropping his bag on the table, he fished out his old gym clothes and dropped them in the basket that was in the hall for just this reason.

"You're a little late." Olivia came into the kitchen, smiling at him in a way that only meant love. "Long practice?"

"No." He moved around the kitchen to the fruit bowl, grabbing an apple. "I was trying to help a friend with homework."

"Oh?" His mom's smile morphed into a tease. "Is that what you guys are calling it now? How is Lindsay?"

"I'm sure you called it studying too." He laughed. "But no. I was helping her with homework." He didn't bother to correct who his mom thought he had been with. She still didn't know that Mari was at AWP, and he wanted to keep it that way.

"Sit, and I'll make dinner, and you can tell me about your day." This was their old routine from before he was busy at school, from before he was out of the house more often than in.

"It was fine." He shrugged, wondering for just a half second if Mari was doing something like this at her home right now.

"How's AP Calc?" his mom asked, but before he could answer, her phone rang. She answered and still moved around the kitchen with the same proficiency of a waitress. "Hi. Thanks for returning my call."

Jase could tell by her tone that it wasn't one of her friends.

He ate. The soup was warm and slid into his body in a comforting way. He didn't let himself think too often about how, lately, his world had been balancing on a pinhead. One wrong motion could send him into oblivion.

"Margaret, we are so excited about helping Camp Chemo with the annual New Year's Eve Gala."

The words froze his heart. He had hoped that it was only an idea, that she would get outvoted or something when it came to the charity this year.

"You don't have to do anything, of course." She was smiling at him now, like it was a thrill for both of them. "In fact, how about an older camper can come to accept the check? In the past, we've had people from the organizations speak, and I would love to open up this platform to camp."

*Dear God, please don't let her ask me.*

"I mean, I could ask my own camper, but I'm not sure he's up to it." She thought she was being so clever, but Jase felt like he needed to vomit the soup he'd just carefully consumed. "Maybe one of his friends?"

There was a pause in the conversation, but he couldn't listen anymore. His skin had that crawly feeling again, and he had to get out of the room. He mouthed "homework" at his mom before sprinting up the stairs and into his room. He shut the door—too hard but also not nearly hard enough.

The world was spiraling, and he wasn't sure what to do. How to stop it. How to find the perfectly cultured rhythm he had created again. He had spent the past four years keeping this secret because he was not going to relive those miserable years from middle school. The years when everyone had known.

*"Whatever. You're still diseased, freak."* The words from those days still hung in his brain like spiderwebs that were always being built, never being swept away.

~

Jase was drowning, he was sure of it. His body was caught in a current, and try as he might, he couldn't pull himself up or out of the water. Jase could grab a breath, but it was like sipping it through a straw. Why couldn't he fill his lungs? Why was it impossible to see the top or the bottom? He didn't have enough air to blow bubbles to find out which way was up. Everything felt off.

And if he didn't breathe soon, he knew he was going to die.

Finally, with a start, Jase jerked up in his bed.

Clammy and unnerved by his dream, he waited for his eyes to focus.

But he still couldn't breathe.

Jase emptied his lungs, pushing out all of the air, then with intention pulled in as much new oxygen as he could. But it still felt like he was trying to breathe through a straw. He repeated it two more times before he finally relaxed enough to feel like he might be able to get back to sleep.

He lay back on the mound of pillows, and his breath stuck once more. Not really thinking much about what was going on around him, he reached to the other side of the bed and grabbed another pillow, shoving it under his head. Four pillows. This cold was so weird and didn't seem to be getting any better.

Those were his last thoughts as he finally drifted back off to sleep. Finally.

~

Jase woke up with a knot in his stomach. He moved through his morning routine, heading down to the kitchen where his parents sat chatting over steaming cups of coffee. Normally, coffee was his biggest incentive to get out of bed in the morning, but today, the idea of the dark liquid burned his stomach with acid. He could feel the butterfly wings of his heartbeat in his chest.

"Morning, sweetheart." His mom smiled, bright, shining face and her tennis outfit ready for that morning's game. "I'm going to come by the school and get your car. Needs the oil changed."

"He should be taking it himself." John Ellison studied Jase over his cup of coffee. "It is your car."

"I can take it this weekend." His head started to ache.

"I've already got the appointment," his mom said. "You can do it next time. I'll have it back before last bell."

"Thanks, Mom." The headache lessened a centimeter,

but still lingered with the knot in his belly. His heart still beat faster than he wanted.

"Coffee?" Olivia was refilling her own cup, still smiling, unable to see all of the struggle that was rioting through him with each move.

"No." The word stuck in his throat. "I'm good." He grabbed an apple he wouldn't eat and went to leave for school. The knot, the tension, the slow growing irritation seemed to be building in his spine.

"It's early," Olivia said over the rim of her cup. "I can make you something."

He needed to swim.

"I'm going to get in a quick workout." The need to feel the water, the push of his muscles—his brain could only focus on that.

"Good for you," his dad said. "You have the invitational coming up, and then your real season starts."

"I know, Dad." Did he sound petulant? "Gotta go." He left through the garage door. As he climbed into his car, the cold morning seeped into his skin, his bones.

He needed to swim.

Not caring about anything else, he backed out of the driveway and pressed the gas, the gnawing in his gut pushing him faster than he thought possible.

~

The swim had only added to Jase's frustration and anger. With each stroke, instead of the water supporting him, pushing him along, he'd fought and clawed against it. His back had been tight, his strokes choppy, his breath all out of pace. He'd only done half of his normal workout before he just couldn't do anymore. And he still had a full day of school and dinner with his family at the Atlanta Country Club that night. Shaking his hair once more before leaving the locker room, he nearly ran right into Coach.

"Ellison!" Coach Bartlett had been his swim coach since he'd come to AWP in the ninth grade. "Early swim?"

"Yeah, wanted to get in some extra time before the invitational."

"I've been meaning to talk to you."

"About?" But Jase knew exactly what it was about.

"Your times have been slipping." The coach crossed his arms, studying him in the way that only a coach can. "What's going on?"

"Nothing," Jase immediately deflected, but the lie sat so wrong in his stomach that acid flipped over, making him feel sicker. "I've got a cold. It's nothing."

"Then stop swimming so much and take it easy." Coach studied him.

Jase knew what he saw: tall guy, blond hair that was long enough to be pulled back, and exhaustion.

"Okay, Coach."

"I don't want to see you in the pool after the invitational."

"Fine."

"You can do dry-land training, but stay out of the water until your cold is gone."

"Okay." Jase just wanted to go. Because this cold wasn't like a normal cold. He didn't have congestion and achy joints. He just almost always felt like he couldn't breathe. Like his breath was stuck somewhere between working and not.

Coach Bartlett sent him off with a firm pat on the back, but Jase was in another world. His brain focused on his breathing, he nearly ran into Lucas.

"Trying to impress Coach?" Lucas reached out, shaking his hand.

"My times do that." Jase pushed his hair back off of his face, then just gave up and tied it back with one of the hair elastics he'd stolen from Lindsay at some point. "Just wanted to burn off some steam." He slung the large gym bag he carried everywhere over his shoulder as they walked.

"Before school? Your dad must be home." Lucas was almost a head taller than Jase, his body automatically making a path in the crowded hallway with ease.

"Yeah." Jase's muscles were tight. He rolled his shoulders, cleared his breath from his lungs, and attempted to act normal. "Just felt the need to swim. That's all." He didn't want to get into the feelings that were sitting inside his brain.

Students filled the halls, not uncomfortably crowded or anything, just enough that you might bump into someone. Everyone sort of looked the same, Jase noticed. Same uniforms, similar hair, mostly white skinned. He'd never really paid attention to the homogeneity of the school until now, but it was definitely there.

Jase turned down the hallway where the seniors' lockers were, his bag knocking right into the corner locker.

"Watch it!" Mari said the words before she saw who had hit her, then she blushed. If it had been another morning, not one that immediately followed his mother talking about the stupid gala or Camp Chemo, Jase might have had a different reaction.

But he didn't.

Instead of apologizing or being the slightest bit kind, he just stared at Mari for a minute before jerking his bag in front of him. And because he was in a shit mood, because he'd had a pissy night and a pissy morning, she was all the catalyst that his brain needed.

"Maybe you should learn to take up less space." It wasn't a snarl or said with derision. He said it in the same tone as when he'd offered to help her with her homework.

Mari didn't speak. Her mouth hung open, and her face paled around her bright cheeks. Obviously completely taken aback by his words. She turned back into her locker, sliding her computer into her bag. Her entire posture had changed. She curled in on herself again, like the day she had cried into that locker. Trying to make herself smaller.

Maybe he should have said he was sorry, but he didn't.

"Need to hit the pool again?" Lucas asked, concern lacing his words. "That was kind of crappy."

Jase didn't respond. Instead, he found his own locker and shoved his bag into it, getting his own laptop and stuff out. That frustration from home slid into his belly. Closing his eyes, he rested his forehead against the hard wood of his locker, the coolness on his warm skin. Was he mad at Mari? Was he mad at his mom? Or was he mad at himself?

# Chapter Fifteen

"Hey, gang!" Giselle called for the class's attention. "We're going to start the next debate topics. You'll draw the topic out of my magic hat." She had an actual top hat in her hands.

Mari watched the hat go around the room until it came to her. Reaching her hand in, she swooshed the papers around until her fingers finally grasped one.

Health care as a right.

Mari pursed her lips and let her eyes close. She would have rather had almost any other divisive topic. Give her abortion or prayer in school. This one could potentially out her as having used Medicaid for years among a group of people who had never worried about their health care being paid for.

"We're going to spend the period doing research on your topics, but know that most of this is expected to be done at home," Giselle said to the class.

Mari had her computer open and a notebook with her pencil beside her. She held her pencil between her teeth and clenched just a little as she thought about her topic for class. It was all random, but she also felt like maybe God hated her for some reason. "Health care as a right." Oof. The world of insurance, premiums, deductibles, PPO versus HMO—these things didn't mean much to the average teenager.

She understood all too well what a lot of this meant. She

had watched her family work double and triple time to pay bills when she was sick. No amount of savings could prepare a person to pay for cancer. She knew her parents had done their best to make sure she didn't worry about this part, but they also didn't know how often she'd overheard their conversations.

She knew when the bill collectors began to call her mom's cell phone.

She knew that there was no way that Nick and Kris could attend Georgia Tech without student loans and HOPE scholarships.

And she knew that no one in this classroom would know what any of that was like. Based on the fact that most of them drove nicer cars than either of her parents, she had yet to hear someone say they didn't have money to get lunch that day or ask to borrow some money until the next payday.

So, Mari looked up statistics. How most people filed for bankruptcy because of medical debt. How people lost jobs after becoming disabled or sick and then losing their health insurance.

And she tried to separate herself from the topic.

But her one foot tapped. Her crutches were propped up beside her. The ache of phantom pains still stung in a foot that wasn't there.

"Lunch?" Addison whispered from next to her where she worked on her own project.

"Sure. Do you need to pick up from the lunch spot?" That was where the majority of students picked up their takeout deliveries.

"I brought mine today." Addison smiled. "I remembered for once."

"I'm so proud of you." Mari laughed. "But can we eat outside? It's gorgeous."

This was partly honest. It was a lovely fall day, just crisp enough to need a jacket, but not frigid. But, mostly, Mari didn't want to go into the lounge right now. Not after the weird showdown with Jase that morning. And to be honest, she didn't want to see Lindsay or Madalyn (whose name she'd finally learned) either. She didn't want to have to see their looks of pity or disbelief.

"Absolutely," Addison said. "I'm vitamin D deficient."

"You are such a liar." Mari laughed. Addison still carried a lovely summer tan, even in October.

"Can a person be deficient in vitamin D?"

"Are we discussing debate topics? Styles?" Giselle stopped next to their table, a dark brow arched in their direction, but the small smile said they weren't in too much trouble.

"Absolutely." Mari nodded. "I'm talking about health care, and Addison is assuring me that sitting outside during lunch will help her vitamin D deficiency."

"That's a stretch there, Manos." Giselle tapped the screen of Mari's laptop, telling her with no words to get back to work.

For a second, Mari breathed, feeling like she actually fit in at this weird school. Teachers here still treated her a little bit like she might fall apart, questioning whether she needed help or looking at her like she was something other than just another student. And it annoyed Mari. She missed the way that she melded into South Side, like she didn't matter.

She smiled and went back to work. And for once, she felt like maybe it would all work out. She would pass Chem. She would make more friends. And she would stop worrying about Jase and his weird hot-cold attitude. Because, damn it, she was just fine without him.

After Debate, Mari sat with Addison and Zeke outside for lunch. Zeke had on a jean jacket over his school-demanded uniform, and Mari envied the effortless cool he could pull off. She pulled her light, very well-loved Walmart jacket around her body. No one at this table had probably ever stepped foot inside a Walmart. It wasn't a new revelation, just one that slid around her mind.

"Hey." Jase sat down next to her on the bench at the picnic table. "How's it going?"

Mari didn't swallow her tongue but did choke a little on her PB&J, which only increased her embarrassment and desire to sink into a convenient open hole. Thankfully, Jase didn't laugh or ask if she was okay, just waited for her to get herself together.

"The fuck," she said around the remaining choke in her throat. "Surprised me."

"Sorry." He fidgeted with the paper napkin in front of her, picking it up and starting to tear it into little pieces. "Also, sorry for being kind of a jerk this morning."

"Huh," she said, letting his words run around in her head. "So, you do know that word." In the time that she'd been at Atlanta West Prep, Jase Ellison had been a jerk to her way more often than he hadn't, but here he was.

He looked up at her, away from her now-demolished napkin. Blue eyes that she could remember any time of day stared back at her.

"I deserve that." He swallowed. "I had a bad morning, and it had nothing to do with you."

"Well, thanks for being less of a jerk." She turned to her friends. "Zeke, are you going to the football game tonight?"

"Not if I can help it," he said, but was obviously studying what was going on between Jase and Mari. "You?"

"You're going to think I'm such a dork." She laughed, hoping Jase would get the picture that she was done talking to him. "But it's family game night at my house."

"What's the game of choice?" Addison joined them and sat down, ignoring Jase altogether, which Mari appreciated.

"Sometimes, it's a super competitive game of cards, because we can usually all play if my brothers are home. If it's only me and Leo at home, it's Scrabble or Risk or something like that."

"Do you guys do this *every* Friday?" Addison asked, pulling out her own sandwich, but finally looking at Jase and then Mari before rolling her eyes.

No love lost between Jase and Addison, Mari noted. She appreciated that Addison seemed just as bothered by him as Mari was.

"No, just once every so often. We started it when I was locked up in the house a lot of the time because of my cancer treatments." She didn't look at Jase but saw the way his fingers stopped moving. They didn't tap or fidget for just a moment.

"Why couldn't you leave the house?" Addison asked.

Mari was used to these questions. Most people didn't know the ins and outs of chemotherapy.

"Chemo wipes out your immune system, so the general public can be dangerous. I was pretty frail for a while." Mari shrugged around the words. "After my infection and amputation, it was just better for me to stay in, but that didn't stop me from getting cabin fever."

"You couldn't go anywhere?" Zeke asked. "No school?"

"Homebound for a lot of it. I went to the hospital and camp." She didn't think as she said the word, but her heart flipped, tripped, and squeezed. Her skin heated because she knew what was coming next.

"I gotta go." Jase left, and her heart frayed.

Mari just stared after him for long seconds, watching as he ran over to where his friends sat.

"I think Ellison is having a breakdown," Zeke said, pulling Mari back to them. "He's been straight up weird lately."

"I don't know. His ego seems to be intact." Addison rolled her dark eyes, tearing her sandwich into little bites.

"Mari, did you know my mom is on the board for Camp Chemo?" Zeke explained, and Mari read more in his eyes. "She's talked about some of the campers."

Relief filled her stomach, moving into her heart, pulsing around, and filling her whole body. "So . . . you know." She drew out the words, making it clear that she was talking about Jase and his secret.

"Know what?" Addison demanded, obviously irritated at being left out.

"I do. I have since ninth, but it's . . . you know . . ." Zeke raised his shoulders, casually looking over to where Jase had gone.

"Not your story," Mari finished. "That's a decent thing to do." She didn't know of many people who would be able to keep that kind of news, that gossip, to themselves.

"I am going to start causing a scene if one of you doesn't fill me in." Addison glared. "Seriously, I will bang on this table and start singing 'Baby Shark' until you tell me."

"Mari's known Jason for a while," Zeke said, still trying to be evasive, still being a decent person.

"No, I know Jase Ellison. I don't know *Jason*," Mari corrected softly. "I'm pretty positive that the person I know only comes out that one week in the summer."

"At camp? You guys go to summer camp together?" Addison started putting pieces together. "Like, are y'all CITs or something? I know I aged out of my camp this past summer."

"Camp Chemo," Zeke said.

"What's that? I've never heard of it."

"Sure you have." Mari stared at her hands. "It makes the news most summers because it's a camp for cancer kids." She looked around as she spoke, making sure no one was listening. Zeke already knew, but she was breaking her promise to keep Jase's secret.

"Jason had cancer." Addison didn't say it with shock or surprise. Instead, she was squinting her eyes, taking in all of the information. "And you go to camp together."

"We do." Mari nodded her head softly. "But at camp, he's Jase. I don't remember the last time anyone called him Jason. Except for maybe when he was being a pain in the ass."

"So, always," Addison filled in. "No one knows about this, do they?"

"No." Mari carefully destroyed the napkin in her hands, ripping it to small pieces. "And I hate to ask this, but I need you guys to promise to keep this between us."

"It's not our story," Zeke said again. "We'll keep it."

"Are you friends with him?" Addison asked, seeing right into Mari. Seeing that there was more to the camp friendship, at least on Mari's end.

"I was." Mari looked behind her, seeing Jase tickle Lindsay across the quad, flirting so openly that her heart tightened, making it hard to breathe. "Like I said, I don't know this person."

# Chapter Sixteen

Sitting in his AP Psych class, Jase replayed the lunch conversation, drumming his fingers on the desk. He'd left so quickly it had caused a scene, he knew. He should have asked about camp. He'd only drawn more attention to himself. But he didn't want to hear about camp. He didn't want to lie more than he already had.

Mari had turned him into a liar.

The thought struck him, and his fingers stopped their repetitive movement.

Mari hadn't turned him into a liar. That was an unfair accusation.

But he didn't know what to do about these thoughts.

Clearing his head, Jase went back to listening to the lecture in his class. Maybe he should pay attention in here, and he'd be able to figure out what his own motives with Mari were. But instead, he thought of the way that Mari had looked at him, the blankness in her eyes. Like she didn't know him.

With little ceremony, the class ended, and Jase trudged to his last class of the day. He was tired, probably from his early workout. But if he was truthful with himself for just a moment, he'd admit that there was more to it. That waking up each night unable to breathe was not normal. And it wasn't like he knew what to do about it anyway.

In the hallway, Jase saw Mari walking with Lucas. She stopped at her locker, laughing at something Lucas said. And it was that big, full laugh that he'd gotten used to hearing at camp. The one that still sometimes crept into his brain, filling his mind with her smile.

It seemed that she was finding her place in his school.

And he'd never felt more out of place in his life.

Slamming his own locker, drawing the attention of a teacher or two and even Lucas, Jase pushed his way into AP Chem. A headache pulsed behind his eyes, his heart beat in the exact same rhythm, and frustration seemed to cling to him. Jase ached to leave. To go and swim. But he couldn't; his next class was about to start. Instead, his fingers moved over the strap of his bag. Anxiety working a steady beat of one, two, three, four, lifting each finger one at a time.

"You okay, man?" Lucas asked as he walked into the Chem classroom.

"Yep." He wouldn't let himself ask what had made Mari laugh like that. "Just a long day."

"But it's Friday." Lucas smiled. "You going to the game?"

"Can't. Dinner at the club with my parents." Like Mari's family game night, this was his family time. But Jase was sure that family game night would be more fun. He could think of a list of things that would be more fun than having dinner with John Crawford Ellison Esquire, and it included taking the SAT.

"Sucks." Lucas sighed, but didn't get to say more, as Yother called the class to attention.

Jase took notes on how he might explain this Chem lesson to Mari, if she'd let him. Maybe she would make a deal with him: she'd still keep his secret, and he'd help her pass

Chemistry. He looked over his shoulder. Mari was resting her head on her notebook. When she lifted her head up, he could see the frustration etched on her face. The little line between her brows was deep, and she might chew through her lip if she wasn't careful.

Jase went back to his work, making little notes on his paper, figuring out the problems and doing his best to not look at her again.

"Are you meeting Lindsay after dinner?" Lucas asked. "I heard that Chessie is having a party."

"I might make an appearance." He looked over his shoulder again. Jase knew it looked like he was looking at Lindsay, but Mari Manos had his attention. She'd had it since the day she'd walked into this school. And maybe, if he was honest with himself for once, it'd been much longer than that.

The bell rang, springing everyone from the week of school. Relief flooded Jase, the weekend seeming to stretch in front of him with only minor complications and few expectations. He would get through the dinner that night and then maybe go to the party. Maybe the party was just what he needed. Some time with his friends, hanging out, no school.

And there was Mari, putting things away in her locker. Guilt swam through him, moving in his veins and arteries until he had no choice but to try and do something about it.

"Hey." He stood next to Mari's locker in the hallway. "Do you want a copy of my notes?"

"What?" Shock rang clear on her face. She scanned the hallway. "Are you talking to me?"

"Yeah." He shrugged.

"Your notes?" She said it slowly, like he was drunk.

"They might be easier to understand." He felt naked, like the whole school was watching this conversation, watching him trying to win her over.

"Jason! Let's go!" Lindsay pulled at him, pushing him into Mari just a bit. As Mari pitched forward, he instinctually grabbed her around the waist with his free hand like he had a few times before, knowing exactly how to keep her up.

"Stop, Lindsay." Jase shook his arm free from Lindsay's grasp, never letting go of Mari, always making sure she was balanced. She was practically tucked into him, her hair tickling him under the chin. He could feel her breath on his neck. "You okay?" Jase could just see Lindsay studying them over Mari's head. He tried to ignore her, but Lindsay's eyes narrowed with suspicion from across the hallway.

"Dandy," Mari said, pushing him away, putting her hands back on her crutches. "Who knew that I'd get just as beat up in the hallways here as I did in the halls at South."

"Sorry." He smiled but noticed that she didn't.

"It's fine. Go with Lindsay."

She did smile now, but it wasn't real, it didn't reach her eyes. There was no crinkle around the corner of her eyes or a peek at her crooked bottom teeth. She walked away. The sting of rejection settled in him, but he didn't follow her. Again, he watched Mari walk off.

"Were you talking to her?" Lindsay asked, sliding back next to him like she'd never been pushed aside. "I've felt so bad since the whole thing in the lounge." She pulled on him again, her hand going down his blazer to his hand, pulling him through the hall. "I think Lucas should definitely ask her out." Lindsay's eyes lit up. "Or maybe he can do one of those things and ask her to some dance? And we'll record it? Oh! What about your mom's gala? We had so much fun last year. And your mom would die!" The excitement was pouring off of her. "We could get on Ellen or something!"

"Mari would hate that." He said it before he could catch himself.

"Oh, how would you know?" She dismissed him. "I think it would be sweet. Her life has been so hard. A date to the gala and a makeover would be something she might love." Before he could shut down this terrible idea, Lindsay had called over Madalyn, and they were discussing just how they could make this happen.

As they stepped outside the school, the air was finally cool. The humidity of the summer had burned off, and in its place was the perfect fall day. The sky was an autumn blue that could make your eyes hurt with its loveliness. Jase listened to the noise of the school parking lot. People hanging around, discussing movies, football games, and what parties were happening where.

"Jason!" His mom stood at his car in the lot, waiting to hand his keys back to him. "All done." It wasn't that uncommon to see a parent doing the same thing, dropping off keys or having had a meeting at the school with other parents.

"Thanks, Mom." He didn't kiss her cheek like he would have at home, but come on, they were in the middle of the senior parking lot.

"Oh! Is that Mari?" Her voice pitched a little higher, excitement tingeing the words. There were questions all but bubbling out of her, but only one came out: "Is she waiting for the . . . bus?"

Jase looked over his mom's shoulder, and there was Mari, patiently waiting for the same bus his mother couldn't seem to fathom. She was chatting with Addison and Zeke, but after a moment they left.

"Does she take MARTA every day?" Olivia sounded almost outraged. "You can't let her do that."

"What?"

"Jason Ellison, you go over there and offer your friend a ride home."

"Mom, she doesn't—" But the look stopped him.

"We will talk about all of this later."

He was in deep crap with his mom now.

Jase jogged over, knowing his mother was watching him. "Hey."

"Hi." Mari kicked up her foot, standing on the tip of her shoe for just a second before planting her foot back on the ground. "You keep talking to me, and someone is going to figure it out, you know."

"Want a ride?" He ignored her spot-on remark.

"Did you hit your head?" She tilted her head to one side, confusion apparent. "I live on the other side of town."

"I know. I was there on Wednesday."

"What happened to your carefully laid-out rules, Jase—Jason?" she corrected herself.

"I'm being nice, Mari. No one is going to know about . . . you know . . . just because I give you a ride."

"No, I'm good." She looked around him, maybe looking for the bus.

"Mari, my mom is watching," he pleaded, blue eyes drilling hers. "She's going to be pissed if I don't give you a ride."

"I'm doing enough for you." She put in her earbuds then, the kind that still attached to her phone with the little adapter. No Bluetooth or AirPods for her. "Later."

She dismissed him.

# Chapter Seventeen

Friday nights in the Manos house never meant one thing. Sometimes, it was a movie; sometimes, Mari and Leo would go out; sometimes, it was just nice and quiet. Okay, maybe not quiet. Because no one in their house was anything that resembled quiet. Well, except maybe Kris, but even he could be obnoxious if he wanted to win badly enough.

"Mari?" Mama yelled down the hall.

Mari had retreated to her room, trying to process the whole damn day. The MARTA ride home had been blissfully uneventful, but she couldn't help but wonder if she should have accepted the ride from Jase. But she couldn't stand the idea of taking anything from him. Especially when it was just to appease his mother.

"My room!" Mari yelled, putting her book down and sitting up. She'd refused to open up her homework on a Friday. She wouldn't study on a Friday. Even if there was a part of her that felt like she should.

"How was school?"

"Fine." She shrugged.

"You haven't said much about Jase being at your school." Because Karen Manos was Mari's mama, she knew things. She had never explicitly said anything about Mari's long-standing crush, but she knew.

"We don't see each other much." Again with the lies. "I mean, we have one class together."

"Do you see each other at lunch or after school? Is he still swimming?"

Thinking about how to delicately answer this, she twisted a curl around her finger for a nanosecond. "Yeah, he's still swimming. And sometimes, I see him at lunch." She shrugged. She did see him at lunch sometimes. Like today. Or the other day when his friends had been talking about her. "We are in different social circles."

And that was the nicest way to put that Jase Ellison was a complete snob.

"But you have some friends, right?" Mama sat close on the bed, close to Mari.

Mama pushed the same curl off of her face. She was going to have to get a clip or something.

"I do." Mari smiled just a little. "I was going to go out with Addison tonight, but I'm honestly just ready for a night with my book." Even an extrovert like Mari needed a night in to process sometimes.

"We have your appointment at Wilson Prosthetics in a couple of weeks." Mama didn't say anything else, letting Mari think through her statement.

"Yeah, I know. There was a reminder postcard in the mail today." Mari knew that what Mama had really been asking was if she still wanted to go. "It can't hurt to hear what they say."

"It can't," Mama agreed. "But if you're happy at AWP and don't want to do it . . ."

"Do you need me to cancel? Problems getting a sub?"

"No, nothing like that." Mama hugged Mari, holding her

close for a moment like she'd done when she was little. "I would move heaven and earth to make sure you get what you need."

"I know, Mom." What Mari didn't say was she wasn't sure if she needed a prosthesis. But she wasn't sure she didn't either.

Mama left her room, and Mari lay back on her bed, staring at the popcorn ceiling that her parents hated so much. A new prosthesis. It was all she could think about it. Her old one sat in her closet, taking up room, reminding her every morning that she needed a prosthesis to ever hope to *look* normal. Would a new prosthesis be worth the headache? Or would it be just like her other ones? Heavy, tight around her waist, making her feel like she couldn't move? She'd stopped wearing the last one over two years ago—not that she'd used it often before then. She'd worn it to school and then taken it off as soon as she'd gotten home. And since puberty had given her hips, it had become impossible to wear. And now, she wasn't even sure it was something she wanted to try again.

Her thoughts roamed, shifting and turning without much direction, but at the center of it was that possibility of a new prosthesis. Would she be able to walk? Like, confidently and without a hitch in her step, alongside her friends from camp? Noah, one of her friends who had a rotationplasty, rarely faltered. With the right clothes on, his entire disability was invisible (which sometimes led to other problems). She would never admit it, but her heart was a romance novel and she dreamed of holding hands with someone as she walked. Their fingers interlocking as she took steps, laughing and not thinking at all about her disability. She thought about getting married someday, carrying a bouquet, her hands clasped together. She didn't know how to do that with her crutches, no matter how good she was with them. Her hands were always gripped around the handles of her crutches—no way to hold a boy's hand then.

Maybe this was worth it.

Maybe this was the time to do it.

Mari could just hear the murmurs from her parents' room. She stood and crawled over to the air vent just on the other side of her bed and let her ear rest next to it. A few Christmases ago, she'd learned that she could hear their discussions, even if they were whispering, if she pressed her ear right up to the vent. She knew she shouldn't be doing this, but it was how she found out the things her parents wanted to hide from her. This was how she learned about collection agencies and payment plans.

"The videos were impressive." It was her mama talking. "She could carry her children."

"She's sixteen," Daddy answered gruffly. "She's not having children anytime soon."

"Nicholas, she's sixteen, and the stuff with the school has hit her hard."

"I thought she was good at this fancy new school." Her dad sounded more irritated by this.

"I think she is." Mama was using the same tone with him that she used with Mari when she was upset. "But, Nick, she's growing up. This has to be difficult for her."

"I know."

Mari heard the sigh in her dad's voice. She wanted to run in there and assure them that she was fine. That she would be fine forever.

"Can you call the insurance company? Do you think they would cover this?"

"They should. But I don't know how much."

Mari moved away. They were talking about money. And it hurt her in a way she didn't understand really. Her parents would do anything for their children, but Mari knew they had to do more for her. She was the expensive one. The one that needed so much more than her brothers. And she hated that.

She didn't need a new prosthesis. She didn't need it, and she didn't want it. Or at least that's what she continued to tell herself until a crash came from the front of the house, and she heard Leo's laugh, along with the laughs of both of her older brothers, followed by the higher-pitched but just as full laugh of Giselle. Her whole family was home, everyone talking over each other. The noise of her life filled her brain, pushing everything else out.

# Chapter Eighteen

The main dining area of the Atlanta Country Club was dimly lit. Servers who had been working there almost as long as Jase had been alive floated between tables. Friday meant that a lot of families were there before the adults either moved to another event at the club or went out for the evening. When Jase had been a kid, he'd gone home after dinner, where one of his regular babysitters had waited. Now, he typically went out with friends—maybe to a football game, maybe just out.

Tonight, he couldn't seem to focus on anything going on around him. Instead, he sat in his club-appropriate clothing and listened to his parents talk.

"Jason, I couldn't believe when I saw Mari at AWP today." His mom brought him into the conversation.

"Uh." In the last month, he had done everything he could to keep his mom from knowing that Mari was there. "Yeah, she transferred."

"How lovely!" His mom's smile stretched across her entire face. "I love that you are able to keep your camp friendships all year."

"Sure." He didn't deny it, but he'd never really kept in contact with camp friends during the school year. And if Mari hadn't walked herself into his school, he knew that he wouldn't have really kept up with his camp friendships this year either. "I don't see her a lot or anything."

His mom smiled a smile that he'd grown to hate in the last few years. The one that said he was so special and amazing. The one that said she had some memory of his cancer and treatment that he could never access.

"Maybe you could invite her to the club next week."

He nearly spit out his water. "Why would I do that?"

"I'd like to get to know her a bit." Olivia straightened her napkin in her lap. "Margaret mentioned she might be a good person to speak at the gala."

"What?" His heart rate accelerated like he was swimming the last 100 meters.

"Hello, family."

Jase was saved from this conversation going further by his father's appearance.

"Sorry I'm late." John Ellison was imposing in the most traditional senses. He stood over six feet tall, with white hair that had only just started thinning in the last few years and a linebacker's build. All of this helped him in the courtroom. He kissed Olivia before sliding in next to her.

"Welcome home." Olivia smiled, and it was one that Jase only saw when his father was around.

His dad turned to him. "How's school? Are you ready for the invitational?"

"School's fine." Jase shrugged. "And I think we're going to be fine at the invitational."

"Think you'll be able to swim for UGA in the fall?" It was his father's only concern. That Jase attend the University of

Georgia, swim for them, and eventually go to law school, just like he had.

"Potentially," Jase agreed in the easiest way possible. He had never thought about it on his own. College, swimming. It was all part of a plan that had been laid out the first time he had jumped into the club pool and swam across. "Probably."

"Jason, this is your future."

There was a firm sound to his father's voice, and Jase was suddenly sure that his whole life was a cliché.

"You need to be more than potential."

"I've applied, just waiting on decisions." He moved his fingers over the tabletop, lifting each finger one at a time. A tickle slid against the base of his stomach, pulling on his spine with each breath.

The silence at the table stretched, pulling a thin, invisible string between each of them. It was different than the uncomfortable silence between him and Mari. This one was almost painful. Disappointment dripping off of everyone.

"I was telling Jason about some of the plans I've been working on for the New Year's Eve Gala." Olivia plucked the thread with one finely manicured nail, and it resonated right into Jase's overly fine-tuned heart.

"Who is the beneficiary this year?" his father asked, and the conversation turned, but it was just as bad as the conversation about college.

"Camp Chemo." Olivia was delighted, her voice lilting in a way that made Jase both happy and annoyed all at once. "I can't believe that I hadn't thought of it sooner."

"That's perfect." John laughed, the server returning with

his customary highball. "Jason, you should invite some of your friends."

"At least Mari." Olivia smiled, the conversation having settled and the discomfort for them having dissipated, but Jase's own anxiety was still clenching and climbing. "She transferred into AWP."

"Really?" His dad looked at Jase, a face he'd known his entire life sizing him up. "Which one is she?"

"The, uh, you know, uh, amputee." He floundered over the word, unsure which part was tripping him up. "She's been there about a month."

"Oh." And his dad's face morphed then. It sort of slacked, his eyes softening, a kind smile. "Right. I remember her."

"I was telling Jason we should have her to the club one night for dinner." Olivia sipped her white wine. "Margaret mentioned that Mari might be a good speaker."

Jase did all of the things you did when you were uncomfortable. If it had been permissible, he would have ripped his tie off and flung it across the low-lit dining room. Instead, he picked at his food, listening to his parents talk.

"Jason, you should think about preparing some words to speak at the gala," his father began. "It would be appropriate and meaningful."

"I don't really like speaking in front of people." *I will not talk about my cancer in front of people. Period.*

"It's a skill you need to work on then. Develop it. You'll have to do such things for the rest of your life, especially in law school."

*I am not going to law school* was his immediate thought, but

Jase didn't dare speak it out loud. "I don't think it would be a good idea for me to practice at Mom's big event."

"You did a lovely job when you did that speech in middle school, remember?" His mom smiled at him like it was one of the best memories of her life. "You inspired so many that day. They all donated their pocket change for the fundraiser."

Jase remembered things very differently. He remembered the endless teasing, the accusations of making things up, the need to defend himself not only to his peers but even some of his teachers. He could still see the way his teachers had looked at him after that. Like he might fall apart at any moment.

*"Jason, do you need to sit this out?" Coach Criscione asked. "You look a little flushed."*

*"I'm fine." He had smoked most of his sixth-grade classmates in the mile run.*

*"God, Jason, you're such an asshole." Kevin had pushed him hard in the shoulder as he came up behind him, trying out his new favorite cuss word. "You should have to compete in those Special Olympics, not the ones for us."*

*"I'm not disabled." He didn't know if Kevin was referring to the Special Olympics or the Paralympics, the one Noah wanted to compete in. "I had leukemia. It's different."*

*"Yeah, well, you're still diseased." Kevin had laughed, pushing him again. "You should have to go to one of those special schools."*

And that had been the start of it. Jase could still feel the sting of Kevin's words, the hurtful accusations that he wasn't normal or was still somehow diseased. He was none of those things. He was fine. But, for the next three years, he'd spent every day doing his best not to be noticed by Kevin and his group of friends.

He couldn't open himself up like that again.

He wouldn't.

# Chapter Nineteen

"I heard that Francesca Morgan was having a party tonight," Leo said from over his hand of cards. The Phase Ten cards were dealt among all of the Manos siblings and Giselle, who was there with Nick.

Caroline, Kris's new girlfriend, was also there, but they were doing their best not to make a big deal about it.

"I heard something about it." Mari discarded. "Do you know her?"

"No, but Ellie does and mentioned going." Leo discarded a four.

Leo, Mari, and Nick were on the fourth phase; Kris was on the fifth and currently gloating about being in the lead. But Giselle was only on the second phase. And poor Caroline was only on the first. Mari thought she was either letting Kris win or was just bad at this game.

"To an AWP party?"

"To a party," he corrected.

"You should go." Giselle laid down her set of threes and a run of four cards, so she could move on from phase two in the next hand.

"Aren't you supposed to tell us not to drink and to make good choices?" Mari arched a brow. "Or are you telling me to go to this party as my friend and not my teacher?"

"Anytime I am losing to you at Phase Ten on family game night, I am your friend." Giselle flipped her massive amount of curls off of her shoulders, relaxed in the family living room like she might be in her own home, Mari imagined.

"You're her teacher?" Caroline's eyes widened. "And dating her brother?"

"Dating Nick came first." Giselle smiled. "But also, yeah, don't do drugs."

"Also, you're not supposed to drink—and make only good choices." Nick eyed Mari. "I remember those parties from my time in high school."

"You make it sound like you're ancient," Kris teased lightly. "You graduated, like, four years ago." Kris discarded a card, still in the lead, the jerk.

"I am ancient." Nick sighed dramatically. "Plus, didn't I hear you saying that you two were going to the Zeta party at Tech?"

"A sorority girl, Caroline? I'm judging you." Mari laughed.

"I'm a double legacy. It couldn't be helped." Caroline raised her shoulders in defeat. "That being said, are we going?"

"Don't you have to make an appearance?" Kris's brows drew together. "You mean we don't *have* to go to this thing?"

"I probably should stop by, but I promise we don't have to stay long." Caroline looked at her cards before folding them. "And I'm tired of losing. Next time, we're playing Settlers of Catan, and I'm taking you all down."

"Big talk from someone who can't get off phase one," Leo teased. "This means we can go to Chessie's party."

"I don't know." Mari did have a fantastic book on her bed—a teenage girl finding out she's a witch and having to steal back a dangerous spell book—and she wanted to finish it. She thought it was a pretty perfect way to spend her evening.

"Mari, do you want to go to this party?" Leo asked, irritation leaking into his voice.

"Fine." Mari bit the inside of her cheek. Leo would see her interact with the kids from AWP. He would see the way they all still sort of stood off to the side and watched her. But it sounded like some South Side people were coming, and she missed her other friends. "I need to change." She motioned to her ratty leggings and one of Kris's worn T-shirts. "Give me fifteen minutes." She began to move, but stopped short. "Caroline, I'm going to need details later about Kris at this Zeta party."

~

The party wasn't a loud rager like you saw in movies. It wasn't sedate either. It was just groups of people talking, music, food, and drinks. A hum, a vibration of voices and laughter, carried through the large home in the Druid Hills neighborhood of Atlanta. The large brick home was tastefully decorated, Mari noted, not overly stuffy or straight out of *Southern Living* or anything. No one greeted them, and it was apparent that Francesca's parents were nowhere in the vicinity of the house.

"Mari!"

Ellie came around the corner with a couple of other friends from South Side, and for the first time in a month, Mari breathed. Ellie, with her white skin, long blonde hair, and bright-blue eyes that said only that she was incredibly all-American and nothing out of the ordinary. And occasionally, Mari would let herself forget that she was anything other than just like everyone else. That she was just one big dominant gene: brown hair, brown eyes, with the ability to roll her tongue and right-handedness. But then her crutches would catch on something, and it would all come crashing down around her.

"Hello!" Mari let herself be enveloped by Ellie's hug. And with it, a film of tears overcame her. She hadn't expected it, but there it was. Ellie was normalcy. "Is anyone else here?" she said it around a thick lump in her throat. "Brooke? Michael? Emily Grace?"

"Brooke and Michael are in the basement playing some video game, but I think he brought his guitar, which means he'll be singing before long." Ellie tucked Mari under her arm, leading her through the massive kitchen and into the family room where several others were spread out. Chessie had sprung for orange and black Solo cups, festive for the upcoming holiday, over the traditional red.

"Drink?" Leo asked Ellie.

"Sure."

She smiled, and not for the first time, Mari noticed a pretty blush on her friend's cheeks.

"Back in a minute." Leo smiled, a blush on his cheeks too.

"You two just need to make out." Mari sighed, leaning her head back on the plush leather sofa.

"He doesn't make a move," Ellie whined. "Why won't he make a move?"

"Why don't you?" Mari shoved Ellie with her shoulder. "Go on. He's getting you a drink. Go corner him and kiss his face off," Mari urged her friend. "I'll go see if I can find Brooke and Michael."

"Are you sure?" Ellie was practically off of the sofa and following Mari's brother as she asked.

"Yes. Go." Mari laughed, standing herself, slipping her arms into her crutches. "We'll catch up later."

"Okay." Ellie hugged her once more before practically running after Leo.

Mari was alone, but not lonely. She recognized people from several aspects of her life—her former one at South Side and her current one at AWP. It wasn't hundreds of people, and there were some she didn't know. But, following people, she managed to find the basement.

And Lucas.

"Hey." Were her own cheeks heating now? Was it some sort of illness she didn't know was contagious? "So, I lied."

"You did." Lucas smiled, perfectly straight teeth, probably from at least a year of orthodontics, and hazel eyes. He was pale, but where she had undertones of olive, Lucas had undertones of red, light freckles on his face and arms, and light-auburn hair that had probably been red when he was a kid. "But I'm glad."

"Thanks." They moved a little out of the main thorough-fare, and she smiled up at him again. "My brother is around here somewhere, but I sent my friend Ellie after him." She didn't mention that she sent her after him to make out.

"Is he the kind of brother that I need to worry about?" Lucas inched a little closer, almost close enough to touch her. "Like, the kind that threatens to beat up people?"

"No." She laughed a little. "Because my brother trusts me and knows that I'm a capable woman who can choose who she wants to hang out with. We're all pacifists."

"So, I could ask you out next week, and he wouldn't care?"

Mari's face heated in a way she hadn't expected. She also hadn't expected Lucas to just ask her out. "Lucas, I'm still new and figuring everything out here." She had never in her life turned down a date. Then again, she'd never been asked out before.

"I got it." He was cool and not at all upset with her.

And Mari wasn't sure at all what alternate reality she'd fallen in to.

"Hey!"

And there were Lindsay and Madalyn, and Mari no longer wanted to be at this place.

"Mari, you came!" Madalyn said it like they were long-lost best friends.

"My brother wanted to come," she said lightly.

"Oh, your brother came?" Madalyn looked around. "Is he down here?"

"Upstairs somewhere, I think," Mari said. "I have some friends from South here, and I heard they were playing video games down here." She inched away, eager to see her actual friends.

"Yeah, how they ever got here I'll never know." Lindsay smiled over her cup, giving Mari a look that said a lot of things without speaking a single stupid word.

"They drove." Mari didn't smile, didn't raise her own brow. "In a car."

"Wait, can you drive?" Madalyn and her sweetly naïve questions. "Like, or do you have hand controls and stuff?"

"I didn't drive." Mari's lips thinned into a straight line. "My brother did." She didn't feel the need to tell them that she *could* drive. "It's sure fun to run into y'all here." Sarcasm coated her words. "But I'm going to go find my *friends*."

# Chapter Twenty

There was not enough beer at this party. At least, that was Jase's first thought after he filled up his cup and began to slowly meander through the house. Chessie was somewhere, he was sure, but it wasn't like the parties from when they were kids. No parents in sight, no party games, unless you counted beer pong and PlayStation.

He wandered through the house and eventually found himself in the basement where most of the others were at.

"You made it!" Lindsay moved into him, her hand smoothing over his stomach and into a pseudo-hug that was totally just so she could get close.

"Hey, there." Madalyn smiled, her fingers twisted into her hair, curling the strands between them. "You got away from your parents."

"They were doing something at the club with *your* parents." He sipped his drink. "Who all is around?"

"Some kids from South Side." Madalyn motioned with her head over to a group of kids playing video games and another group gathered around a guy playing guitar. "Mari is over there with Lucas."

"He asked her out." Lindsay smiled like she had somehow made the whole thing happen. "Isn't that the sweetest?"

"She said her brother is here." Madalyn looked around the room. "But I haven't seen him."

"You know Leo?" Jase only knew him on the most basic level.

"No, but I figure I'd recognize him."

"How?" Lindsay stared at her friend. "It's not like he'll have on a T-shirt or something."

"I mean, he'll have one leg." Madalyn said it like was the most reasonable thing in the world.

The silence, even from Lindsay, was almost comical. Jase let her sentence roll around in his head. It sort of clinked off the sides, pinging and hitting his thoughts. "Wait." He stopped Madalyn. "Are you telling me you think that because Mari has one leg, her brother does?"

"Doesn't he?" She crossed her arms. "Isn't cancer, like, genetic?"

And life was working out for once. Leo rounded the corner with a blonde girl.

"Hey, man," he greeted Leo.

"Hey." Leo smiled. "This is Ellie. Ellie, Jase Ellison."

"Well, hello there," Ellie said. The recognition in the girl's eyes unnerved him. "Mari's talked about you."

"She has, has she?" Lindsay asked, her arm tightening around him, which just made his skin itch to move.

"Oh." This world was getting too small for him. "Where is she?" Jase pushed at Lindsay, extricating himself from her grip.

"Destroying some friends on the PlayStation," Ellie said, taking a sip of her beer, but she studied him over the rim of her cup.

He didn't like the way she was looking at him, like she knew all about him.

"Right, well, this is Lindsay and Madalyn. They go to AWP too."

"Your Mari's brother?" Lindsay asked.

"Yeah." Leo smiled. "What? Did you think I'd have one leg too?"

"No." Madalyn blushed furiously. "Do people actually think that?"

Jase laughed into his own cup, doing his best to keep Madalyn's secret. "Um, so, Leo, ready for the invitational?"

"Yeah. Sure. Racing against you pampered weaklings will be fun."

"Right, like Dynamo doesn't treat you like kings." Jase shook his head.

"I'm only swimming Dynamo right now because I work there." Leo gave a fake shiver. "Five-year-olds' swim lessons."

"God, wouldn't it be so much easier if teachers didn't give us hours of homework every night?" Ellie turned the conversation back to something that was safer.

Jase understood on the outside that he was lucky not to have to work unless he wanted to, but he knew his parents would never let an after-school job interfere with his swim career.

"Right?" Lindsay laughed. "When do they expect us to sleep?"

"Sleep?" Ellie agreed. "I haven't slept since elementary school."

Jase nodded in agreement, looking around the room, not at all looking for Mari. But she was a magnet to him, and without his permission, his eyes found her. She was sitting on a sofa, Lucas next to her, laughing at something one of her friends was saying. She looked relaxed, like the Mari he knew from summer camp. Her hair was down, curling around her face, just brushing the top of her shoulders.

The party continued on around him, but he wasn't really feeling it. Lately, he hadn't been feeling much of anything. Except that knot of worry he felt in his stomach almost every day. But there was Mari, smiling, laughing, no pit of worry.

"I'll be back," he said abruptly, not at all sure what the group was now talking about.

Lindsay followed after him. "You okay?"

Lindsay's worry was evident, but he was over her neediness, her new clingy behavior. She grabbed him, her fingers wrapping around his forearm.

"Fine." He pulled his arm free of her and took a step back.

"Jason?" She moved closer to him, her eyes pleading. "Don't you want to dance with me?"

"No, Lindsay." He tried to be kind, softening his words. "I think our *thing* has run its course."

"Jason." She got that look, the one that said she was upset. "You don't mean that. I thought we'd at least go to the gala together."

"Linds." He smiled as nicely as he could and ran a hand down her arm, squeezing. "You know we aren't exclusive." He turned to head outside.

"Jason," she seethed, pulling on his arm to stop him. "You are not breaking up with me here, in front of everyone."

"You're right, because we've never been together." It was

probably cruel, but he needed to shed her, to be done with whatever it was they'd been doing that summer.

"What the hell ever," she nearly yelled. "You'll be back."

"Doubtful." He walked out into the night, relief easing its way down his back, his heart calm and not at all the frenetic pace he'd been feeling so often lately.

"Well, that was something." Mari spoke from the shadows, startling him slightly from his own thoughts. "And before you think I followed you, I was out here already. I got a front-row seat to the best non-breakup breakup."

"Just needed air." The sentence explained everything. He shoved his hands in his pockets, refusing to wriggle them. *Don't be a jerk*, he demanded of himself silently. "Having fun?"

"It's nice to see some of my school friends." She crossed her arms over her body, seeming to shield herself from the evening. "But we're getting ready to head out. I have work tomorrow, and Leo does too."

"You work?" How did he not know this?

"Most weekends for a few hours and sometimes after school, but that's harder now since I have to take MARTA home." She tilted her head at him. One of the lights that lit the backyard seemed to illuminate her. "It's a little bookstore in the village, so it's not too grueling or anything."

"And you can read when it's not busy." He stepped a little closer to her, but he wasn't sure why. He needed to keep his distance, not get closer to her.

"I do enjoy a good book." She shrugged. "What's up, Jase?" She stomped her foot in frustration. "Jason."

"It's fine." He wanted to add that she could call him

Jase—that when she called him Jase, he felt something that he didn't know what to do with.

"You run hot and cold with me." She sighed over the words softly, making sure no one else could hear.

He stared at her. Not speaking because so many thoughts were rumbling through his brain. So many words, refusals, acceptances, apologies, and he didn't want to say any of it. "Hey, so Madalyn thought that because you have one leg, your brother would too."

Mari blinked three times as she took in his words. "Wait." She moved in a little closer, so she could still speak softly. "Tell me that again, but slower."

"She literally thought that because you have one leg, your brother would."

"I do not understand how she is doing better than me at Chemistry." She shook her head, her curls obscuring her face, her smile.

"She felt pretty stupid."

"She should." Mari laughed. "I'm starting to realize that she isn't hateful, just really sheltered."

"Has she said something to be hateful?" His spine straightened.

"Nothing more than you have." She was blunt. "You've been a pretty class-A jerk since I came to AWP."

Again, his defenses went up, but she was right. "Yeah," he said instead. "I just can't handle anyone finding out."

"I get it." She nodded. "I sometimes fantasize about not having to tell my life story to people in the first thirty minutes of meeting them."

"You don't have to. No one has to know your life."

"Sometimes, it's just easier. If they know, they'll move on quicker." She kicked up her foot, standing on the toe of her shoe, using her crutches for balance.

He'd seen her do this move a hundred times, something she did when she was thinking or just needed a break.

The headlights from a beige Honda flashed, Leo's head just visible. She moved away then, smiling a little. "I'll see you."

"What about after work tomorrow?" He stopped her, his hand gripping her arm between the cuff of her crutch and the handle. "We can work on Chem. I could tell that you were confused in class today."

"Are you watching me, Jason Ellison?" She smiled, and it was the big one, the one that showed her teeth, but shook her head no.

"Always." It was as truthful as he'd been recently. He watched as she moved toward the car, her body a fluid line of motion, no hitch or stutter on her crutches. "I'll see you after work tomorrow."

"We'll see."

# Chapter Twenty-One

Mari pushed a crate of old paperbacks down an aisle over from the mystery section toward the romance. *Oh, a Nora Roberts I haven't read.* Mari pulled the book, sticking it in the other crate that she pushed around the store specifically for the books she wanted to read first. There was also that science fiction book for Leo about a girl who wanted to go on a space mission and had to compete against the best of the best to do it, but Mari couldn't be sure that he hadn't read it already.

Her cell phone buzzed in her pocket, but it wasn't a number she immediately recognized. Because the store was empty, she took a chance and answered.

"Hello?"

"Mari?"

"Yes?" It was a woman's voice and just familiar enough that Mari didn't immediately hang up.

"This is Olivia Ellison, Jason's mother, from school and camp."

"Oh right. Hi." She sat back against one of the shelves, completely tucked away from where anyone might see her. But she'd hear if someone came in.

"I don't know if Jason has mentioned this or not, but every year I help organize a gala that benefits a charity."

"Right." She'd heard bits and pieces. It seemed that it was

quite the event that at least the parents of her peers at AWP participated in.

"This year, we're raising funds for Camp Chemo, and Margaret mentioned that you would be a wonderful speaker."

"She did?" Mari was a little surprised, but it wasn't the first time in her life that she'd done some public speaking for camp. She would do anything for the place where she felt the most normal.

"And that was before I even knew that you were now at AWP with Jason. Do you think it might be something that would interest you? It's always a lot of fun, a big silent auction, and it's on New Year's, so of course there will be those festivities. I'm going to have Jason invite some of your friends from Camp Chemo—if that's okay, of course."

"Right." Mari usually spent New Year's with her friend Jeff and some of the other Debate kids from South. But maybe being at a swanky party could be a fun change.

"What I'd like is for you to speak for about five to seven minutes. Just talk about camp and how you got involved."

"So, a short cancer story with a lot camp stuff." Mari was already thinking through what that might look like.

"That's it exactly."

"But probably no stories about Jase and glitter or sending unmentionables up the flag pole."

Olivia laughed. "As much as I love those stories, let's stick with the stuff that is really impactful."

"Like one-legged girls doing the ropes course and watching campers finish chemo at camp."

"You are going to be perfect." Olivia sounded almost giddy. "Can I mark you down as a yes?"

There was a brief hesitancy, because how could Mari talk about Camp Chemo and all of its amazingness without mentioning Jase? But surely his mother knew about how he felt about that type of thing. "Sure," she finally announced. Because it was for camp. And she would do it for them.

The bell on the door rang.

"Uh, Olivia, I need to go."

"Of course! I'll be in touch!"

Mari stood up, grabbing her crutches and stepping out from behind the shelves.

"Hi, welcome to Village Books and Gifts. We have a sale . . ." Her voice trailed off as she saw who had come into her bookstore. "Jason Ellison."

"Hey, there." He smiled at her with one of his rare completely beguiling smiles. His eyes crinkled, his full lips turning up, and just the lightest of blushes running over his cheeks.

"This is a little creepy." She moved closer, almost like she was drawn to him. She didn't know why she was giving him this inch. Why was she making it so easy for him to hurt her again?

"What?" He smiled down at her, completely making her breath stop.

"Um, your mom just called to ask me to speak at the gala."

A dark shadow crossed his face, causing Mari to immediately wonder if she'd made the wrong call. "Do I need to tell her no? I thought it might be fun."

"No, no, that's not it," he assured her, smiling again, but it wasn't a full smile, not the one that made her toes curl or anything.

"Well, what are you looking for?" She kicked the crate

with her books up toward the register, leaving the one that she'd been shelving out of right where it was.

"Any books on how best to get a girl's attention?" His words were all sly and full of sweetness.

Mari stopped mid-step and tripped a little, his words stopping her as much as the crate in front of her. And he was right there, like it seemed he had always been since camp. Doing his best to keep her standing and walking. "I think it's in the self-help section," she tried to joke, pushing back from him and where he had caught her. "Thanks."

"Glad I was here." He shoved his hands in his pockets, but still stood sort of close to her. "What's all of this?"

"Perk of working here is I get to pull books I might want to read first and then bring 'em back." It was a used bookstore after all. "I saw a few I wanted and got a couple for Leo. What kind of books do you like, Jase? I can at least help you find something besides your self-help book." Which he totally didn't need.

"Will you think less of me if I tell you I don't love reading?"

She narrowed her eyes at him, because yes, she would judge him a little. Reading was part of her. Something she didn't just enjoy, but something she was passionate about at times. Like camp. It was all part of who she was. "I've judged you for a lot more lately," she said instead.

"I deserve it." He shrugged, thrusting his hands deeper in his jeans pockets. "To be honest, I'm surprised you're talking to me."

The bell jangled as a couple and their toddler came in. Mari stepped away, trying to cool her heart. "Hey, folks. Welcome.

We've got a sale on most of the hardbacks, and if you have your reusable bag, you can fill it for ten dollars."

She turned back to him, hurt still so prominent in her body that it was easy to bring up. "Me too." *Don't be a coward now, Manos.* "In fact, I probably shouldn't be. You're just going to hurt me again."

She could see the way his eyes darkened, a little sadness maybe?

"How much longer do you have at work?" Jase asked across the counter from her. "I was serious about helping you with your Chemistry."

"It's Saturday," she protested. She didn't want his help. She didn't even want to be around him. Because her defenses were so easily shattered by him. She could see the guy who hurt her at every turn now that they were in school together, but she also saw the boy she'd known since she was a kid. How they were one in the same sometimes got all fuzzy in her brain. She could so easily recall the boy who had tended her scraped knee at camp and just as easily see the guy who had sneered at her.

"It is. I'm so glad you know what day it is. Then you know we have, like, two days until our next class."

She looked at the clock on the computer. "I'm off in an hour."

"Great. I'll just hang here and read while you finish up."

Mari helped ring up the family that had come in and went back to shelving. All the while, Jase sat in one of the comfy chairs, reading a graphic novel, but she was pretty sure he was mostly just watching her. She tried to focus on her job, stocking books, cleaning, making sure they had enough of the little gifts around. Mostly, she tried to make sure she wasn't constantly looking at Jase.

Because he still made her heart race.

And she hated herself for it.

~

"Oh." Like a piece of the puzzle, the whole problem made sense all of a sudden. "I guess this step is important."

"Did you finish the pre-lab assignments?" He smiled at her, looking over the work they had done together. "Yother is for real about not letting you do the lab if that's not done."

"I did it, but I'm sure it's not right."

"Let me see it." He took her composition notebook from her, reading over the pre-lab materials for the lab they had next week on thermodynamics.

The Daily Grind was a short ride in Jase's car from the bookstore. Mari's fingers had smoothed over the buttery leather and wondered what his life must be like. She doubted he'd ever ridden the MARTA train even to a Braves game. Probably taking a limo or something if he went.

They sat, their heads together, at one of the couches near the back of the café. There was a floor lamp casting a golden light around Jase, making him look more appealing than she needed. He hadn't said anything about being sorry for his treatment of her. In fact, he'd barely acknowledged they went to school together, other than the fact that he was helping her with schoolwork. It was as if his brain was somehow keeping her separate from his school life, even if she was very much in it.

"Hey, nerds." Davis stopped by where they were hunched over Mari's homework. "I'm out. But I'm working later this week." He gave Mari a high five over the coffee table where their work was spread out. "Tell your brothers to stop by."

"Later." Mari smiled at Davis. "I'll see you."

"See ya." Jase waved as Davis moved out the door. "Meeting?"

"Yeah." Mari doodled in her notebook. "He goes to one at the church around the corner almost every night."

"Yeah, he told me." Jase fidgeted as much as she did. "We text sometimes."

"Oh." She chewed her lip, a little hurt by this information. "So, you talk to him?"

"Some."

He stood and stretched, his shirt rising just enough that she could see an inch of his stomach. Stupid hormones.

"I felt a little guilty when I found out he was in rehab."

"We all did." Her insides still hurt as she remembered that night, the way Tiny and Heather, her counselors, and Grant and Will, Jase's counselors, had all sat around and told them what Davis's parents had told Margaret. Mari could easily feel the sadness, the grief that she hadn't been able to help her best friend then.

"Yeah, but I'd seen him at some parties. I knew about it."

Jase sat back down, not looking at her, probably waiting for her disappointment.

"Jase, I told his parents." Her words were soft, unshed tears clinging to the edges of her vision. "I told his parents a few weeks before camp, and he . . . well, it didn't go over well.

He's told me since then that he's grateful, that I was one of the people in his life to call him on his shit." She swallowed. "But the guilt still sits in me, like I should have done more somehow. Maybe he wouldn't have a record."

"Why didn't you tell me at camp?" He leaned into her then, their heads bent together over the notebook.

"Because I felt guilty." She laughed a little, but it was all sad. There was a pull between them that she couldn't name, this ache that sat inside her chest cavity, and she didn't know if it was because of Jase or because of Davis. "Why did you come to the store tonight?" She jerked back, needing immediate space between them.

"I needed to see you." He stood, seeming to be unable to sit. "I've been a tool."

"Yep." She spit the word. "Why do your friends care so much about me?" She didn't ask why he had let them talk about her that way, like she was a science project and not a real person.

"Lindsay and Madalyn are asinine." He said the words like it absolved them. "Don't let them make you mad."

"They don't," she told him, pulling her bag on both of her shoulders, getting ready to leave.

"Then why are you going?" He looked hurt.

"Because you have hurt me a whole lot more than they ever have." She couldn't stop her quivering lip or the stupid crush of tears stuck in the back of her throat.

"Mari."

His voice dropped, his hands reached for her, and it would have been so easy to let him pull her to him, to absolve him of all wrongdoing with a hug, but she couldn't do it. She pulled away so quick, taking her balance with her.

"Stop for a minute."

"Stop catching me." There was a plea in her voice she hated. "You just drop me later."

# Chapter Twenty-Two

"When I was ten years old, I was diagnosed with osteogenic sarcoma." Mari stood in front of her debate class, note cards neatly splayed in front of her with facts and figures. "I spent the next year in and out of the hospital, receiving life-saving chemotherapy, radiation treatments, and several surgeries." She paused for effect. "And even though both of my parents are gainfully employed with employer-provided benefits, my family soon began to receive bills from various clinics, hospitals, and doctors' offices for amounts that our insurance didn't cover.

"I learned that when my mom would silence her phone and a line appeared between her eyes, that mostly likely it was a bill collector. I watched as other families had lengthy conversations with social workers and billing specialists while their children received chemo. Holding emesis basins while trying to figure out how to pay for all of it." She didn't make eye contact with her peers, feeling like she might as well have been naked in front of them.

"The United States is the only first-world nation to not have socialized medicine. We are not only lagging in development of drugs, but our patients are dying at an alarming rate because they literally cannot afford their medications."

Mari moved into the part of her speech about numbers

and facts. That more people had declared bankruptcy because of medical debt than anything else.

"But it keeps me in Prada shoes." Lindsay laughed, but no one joined her. "What? My dad is a bankruptcy attorney."

"Lindsay," Giselle warned, surprise coloring her words. "Out of line."

Lindsay didn't say anything, instead rolling her eyes and crossing her legs. Mari just stood there, refusing to look at her. She listened as Jocie gave her own opening, talking about how the United States is a capitalist country, how we are a health care destination for many because of the research dollars and drug development that happens because of it.

"Mari, rebuttal." Giselle smiled, letting her know without words that she was doing okay.

"You make excellent points, Jocie. And this would mean a lot more if research dollars were even and handed out across the board, but did you know that childhood cancer only receives four percent of the National Institutes of Health's budget? That there have been three drugs developed specifically for childhood cancer in the last thirty years? But that childhood cancer will kill more children than any other disease this year? Why does this happen? Because children don't have an income, and in our capitalist society, they matter very little to the bottom line."

"But, like, kids don't actually get cancer. Just in books and movies and stuff. It's super rare in real life," Lindsay said again, interrupting her. "Until you came here, I didn't know anyone with cancer."

Mari bit her lip to keep her retort in check. She instead

listened to Jocie argue that childhood cancer was, indeed, rare. And that more children were surviving cancer every day.

It went back and forth, Mari refusing to back down, always stating facts, figures, and a touch of personal story with each instance she could talk.

"And time." Giselle smiled at both of them. "Well done, ladies. Who has questions? Remember, keep it respectful. Both girls offered personal information."

"Mari, is the reason you don't wear a prosthesis because of the money stuff?" Phillip asked curiously. "If it's not too personal."

"No problem." She smiled even as her stomach clenched. "They are expensive and, from previous experience, not something I've gotten a lot of use out of. Knowing that, I can't ask my parents to fork over money for what might become a really expensive doorstop." She thought of the one in her closet.

"But wouldn't it be easier?" he asked again.

"Not for me." Mari didn't mention tomorrow when she would meet with Wilson Prosthetics. Tomorrow, she could potentially have a different answer altogether.

"Cool."

"Jocie, do you really think that we should keep with the private insurance?" Zeke asked, seeming to know the answer.

"No way." She laughed. "My dad is a trauma surgeon at Grady Hospital. He knows all too well the failures of this system and rails against it all the time."

"If it's such a bad system, why don't y'all move to Canada or something?" Marcus asked sincerely.

"You're assuming that everyone has the financial means to make that kind of move," Jocie said easily. "And that people with fragile medical histories are always accepted by countries with national health care."

"Also? I like living here," Mari said defiantly. "That doesn't mean I can't want our country to do better—to be better."

"Mari, you talked a lot about how childhood cancer is under researched and that chemo drugs are expensive and stuff," Lindsay began. "But I saw a documentary, and my mom said that Dr. Oz said that cancer is caused by sugar. That if everyone just cuts out sugar, they won't get cancer."

Mari sighed because she'd heard this tall tale more than once. "There have been several peer-reviewed medical studies that prove those claims are fictitious."

"The documentary had a woman who had completely recovered from cancer just by doing that," Lindsay said.

"There have been cases of spontaneous remission before." Mari wanted to roll her eyes. "And those are the lucky ones, but I've literally seen parents try this, and their kids still die. In fact, I'm really tired of this myth being perpetuated in random internet memes and false medical attributions. It's hurtful to those of us who have had cancer. It's, like, victim blaming or something."

"Oh, did I hit a nerve?"

"Lindsay," Giselle warned again. "Back to the topic at hand. Not cancer and what might or might not cause it."

"If your parents couldn't pay, then they should have planned better." Lindsay held her chin strong, not backing down. "It's not fair that my parents' taxes have to foot the bill for so many people who just didn't get the right kind of education."

"What?" Mari's soul began to whither a little.

"Lindsay, shut up." Addison stepped in before it could get any uglier. "You're just resentful, and it's not a good look on you."

"That's enough." Giselle interrupted. "Mari, Jocie, well done. Lindsay, see me after class." And she moved the class along.

But Mari could still feel the words. Each time they repeated in her brain, they were seared into her skin. She could practically see the words rising on her skin in angry crimson. They hurt like physical burns.

When the bell finally rang, Mari ran from the classroom—needing to get out of there before anyone could say anything else to her, defending or not. She needed space, to be away from these people who had never felt what it was like to be called a charity case. To be told you only got something because of your disability. To have no idea how much harder she had to work to prove her worth to this stupid and ridiculous world.

And to have no idea what it was like to secretly hate parts of it all.

She knew that her amputation had saved her life. But she also hated it at times. She relished in the moments when people would forget.

Because she didn't think of it constantly, every time she reached for her crutches or apologized when someone tripped over them, she remembered. And wasn't allowed to forget.

# Chapter Twenty-Three

Jase would never admit that he was looking for Mari. But he'd walked past her classroom, something he did most days now, but wouldn't admit it was so he could walk with her after class.

"You were out of line." Ms. Austin was laying into Lindsay, who wouldn't even look at the teacher, instead typing something on her phone.

"Whatever. You're only saying that because you're dating her brother," Lindsay replied.

Mari.

She'd done something, again, to Mari.

It wasn't too hard to find Mari once he realized she was probably somewhere she could be upset in peace.

Mari sat on the bench just outside the library door, her face in her hands. The shaking of her shoulders told him that she was crying.

"Oh hey." He didn't think twice as he sat, pulling her into his arms and holding her. "It's okay," he soothed, but he also felt woefully inept. He'd seen Mari cry a few times. Once, this past summer, he had held her much like this as she cried when they found out Davis was in jail, a result of his destructive behavior. But she was always so strong. He'd never seen her taken down by words.

"Shh." His hand moved in circles over her back, trying to comfort, trying to help her feel better.

"God, she's awful." She sniffed into his shoulder and neck.

He could feel the hot tears on his skin. Knowing that Lindsay had made her feel that way made him angrier. He gripped her a little tighter, his fingers flexing into her.

"I wish I could be like you," she said softly, pulling away from him, but not looking him in the eyes. "I wish that no one knew."

"Oh, Mari." He tilted her chin up. "You don't mean that."

"I do." She sniffed, wiping at her face. "I hate that it's part of my life story, that people feel like they are owed an explanation. That I don't get a choice of who knows this stuff about me." She gulped in a breath. "Maybe tomorrow will make it all different."

"What do you mean?"

"I have a consultation with a new prosthetist." She bit her lip.

He didn't know what she was expecting from him. Surprise moved over her face as he took her hands, squeezing, his heart breaking a little. He had only hurt Mari before now.

In this moment, he promised to do better.

Jase didn't say anything about the prosthesis.

"I know you only see the terror in people's faces when you tell them your story, but I see the after. I see the astonishment when you do the impossible."

"I don't do the impossible," she whispered hotly. "I live life as someone who is disabled. That is not worthy of any praise."

He didn't say anything because he knew it'd upset her

more, but Jase disagreed with that entire sentence. She always seemed to do the impossible to him.

"What are you going to do when everyone finds out?" Mari's eyes were bright with unshed tears and sadness. "Because people will."

This stopped him. His immediate reaction was to say they wouldn't find out, to defend the position that he'd held for so long. But he looked at Mari, seeing what she bared for the world on a daily basis.

"I don't know," he answered honestly. "But it's like you were saying: it's not anyone's business."

"I guess at least I get to be in charge of the story." She looked at him. "Like in *Hamilton* when they talk about who tells your story. At least I get to be in charge of that."

"What happens when you don't?" He took her bag, pulling out her lunch and handing her the PB&J that she brought every day.

"When I first got to South, there were a ton of rumors." She laughed sadly. "Everything from a car accident to me being hit by a train." She offered him half of her sandwich. "At least I get to control the narrative."

Jase took a small bite, letting the words roll around in his head. What did it mean to be in charge of his story? "I'm not even sure if my leukemia is part of my story."

"I have no idea what that's like." Mari said the words almost mournfully. She took a bite and swallowed slowly. "But I bet it's nice."

# Chapter Twenty-Four

Bodies slid through the water. The smell of chlorine burned Mari's nose. She watched them swim. She tried to focus on Leo because she should—he was her older brother. But instead, she watched Jase Ellison. And she tried to keep her cheering for someone other than her brother to a minimum, but she couldn't do it.

She studied the way Jase eased through the water, nearly like a water snake, all coiled muscles and deliberate strokes. Each time he'd come up, she could instantly see that squared jawline, those taut shoulders, defined muscles in his arms and continuing down to his legs.

Now she couldn't be around him without her breath shortening and her heart feeling heavy in her chest. Her stomach would curl anytime he looked at her or if he got just close enough for her to feel the electricity jumping off of his skin.

She could still feel his arms around her as she'd cried today. And for once, she wasn't completely embarrassed by her own emotions. She could feel the way his skin had felt against hers. The way they had shared a sandwich. She didn't know what was going on there, but she liked it. She wasn't going to rock the boat.

"How's Leo?" Giselle sat next to her on the bleachers.

"Warming up." Mari motioned with her head to where her brother was shaking out his limbs.

The first race the boys had together was the 400 free. Mari shoved her hands under her one leg, refusing to bite her nails like she wanted to. Talk about being torn. Her brother, her best friend, was racing against someone who was rapidly becoming more important. Much to her own disappointment, her rabid crush had seemed to return all in one afternoon, because he'd shown her kindness.

The tone, a blaring horn sound, signaled, and the lithe bodies of the guys competing dove into the water. It was a flurry of water and movement. Each stroke pulling them toward the wall, their bodies contorting, twisting, sliding as they swam. It was loud—people cheering, bells ringing, coaches and teammate encouraging, and of course, the sounds of kicks, splashes, and arms and hands cutting through the water at a nearly painful velocity.

Mari's eyes moved from lane three to lane five, trying desperately mark where each boy compared to the other, pushing and pulling. God, why couldn't there be a tie in swimming? But after the first turn, it was like Jase lost his breath. His strokes grew choppy, and his body began to fight the water, like he was punching it to keep him alive, not to help him win. Leo, on the other hand, only hit his stride. His body slid through the water, coasting on the way it flowed beneath and around him. Each breath was measured and pushed him forward.

And then it was over.

Leo's hand slapped the wall, his head popping up, and then, immediately after, was Jase. No anger on his face. Instead, just a little frustration, maybe some disappointment. Leo stopped

Jase as they climbed out the pool, a good-natured handshake, maybe some jokes or something, and then they both moved to their benches. Mentally preparing for the next race.

"That was close." Giselle looked up from her phone where she was texting Mari's brother. Both Nick and Kris were at basketball practice or conditioning or something that had to do with athletics.

"At least I have a couple of moments to breathe before they compete against each other again."

"You've known Jason for a while?" Giselle led into the question.

"I have." But Mari didn't further explain, keeping her promise about his health history.

"He came by my classroom today. I think he was looking for you." Giselle's dark-brown eyes said everything. "Did he find you? After your showdown with Lindsay, I'm sure a friendly face would have been nice."

"He did. And, it was," Mari assured her. "But before I go any further with this conversation, I need to know if I'm talking to Giselle or Ms. Austin, my Debate teacher."

"Oh, totally Giselle. Now spill." She was practically giddy with excitement.

"Jase and I . . . We've had a thing . . . I don't know . . . a flirtationship? Since back in the summer. It imploded when I first got to AWP, but things have changed." Mari smiled a little, looking up and over to where Jase was currently standing next to the pool, a towel slung over his well-defined shoulders as he cheered on Lucas. "We almost kissed." She didn't say it was over the summer at camp.

"Almost?" Giselle seemed nearly as frustrated as Mari had been.

"It was interrupted." Mari shivered at the memory of Margaret appearing over Jase's shoulder, a very knowing smile on her face.

"Not by one of your brothers, I hope."

"No, thank God!" Mari laughed.

"I guess we'll be grateful for that." She patted Mari's knee. "So, was Jason helpful today? Or did it just make you feel worse?" Giselle turned into teacher mode almost. "I wanted to rip Lindsay a new one, but I had to have some shred of decorum in the situation."

"She's just . . . young." Mari offered in forgiveness. "And she's not the first person to say that kind of thing to me."

"Still, it shouldn't have been said in my class."

"Jase—Jason—was helpful. And he reminded me of some things."

"So, it's all good?"

"It's going to be great," Mari said with false bravado. She had no idea what any of this meant. "And I'm going to get that A I need in AP Chem. I'm almost caught up."

"I never had any doubts." Giselle patted her knee once more. "Looks like your boys are up."

Both Jase and Leo stood third in line for their respective relay legs. Mari was thankful that Leo had switched off of anchor for this one, but still wished he wasn't racing directly against Jase. Her heart beat so fast that she thought it would eventually break through her sternum and just pulse there on the bleachers in a bloody mess. As they loaded the starting blocks, shaking their arms, watching for their signal to dive in, Mari's blood pressure soared to what had to be unhealthy levels. She could feel each flutter of her pulse in her neck. The throbbing nearly burst when Jase dove in two whole seconds before Leo.

They both cut through the water like selkies. Bodies gliding, twisting, and rotating in full lines, their hips and legs working in a complete circuit, and Jase was just a hairbreadth ahead. It was so close that Mari could barely tell who would win. Her breath was caught in a scream that wouldn't come, and her heart was pounding furiously.

And then, almost in tandem, the anchor swimmers for both South Side and Atlanta West were diving in. Leo and Jase popped up like synchronized swimmers, watching for the briefest of moments while in the pool. They climbed out, and Mari watched the interaction between them, all smiles, friendly rivalry. South Side would never have the money that AWP had, but their team was just as dedicated, and they pushed just as hard.

And in mere breaths, Atlanta West Prep won the relay.

~

The boys climbed out of the water, the last heat done. Mari cautiously crutched out of the pool area to the lobby. Pools were still treacherous, even with her fancy crutch tips and pretty decent balance.

"Hey, gimme ten minutes." Leo dripped on her in the lobby.

"Ugh, towel off." She laughed. "You did great tonight."

"Good enough."

"And you're already going to be swimming for Tech next year," she assured her brother.

"Then, when I swim against Jase at UGA, it'll be an even more bitter rivalry. Am I taking you home, or are you planning on using your AWP connection to get a ride in a fancy car?"

"Shut up." She laughed. "I'm sure I'll ride home with you, so don't leave me."

"We'll see." He slugged her in the shoulder, because she was just another sibling, and ran off toward the shower.

Mari shook her head and walked out of the lobby to the parking lot and the just-turning-cold air. Parents were filing out, some still milling around, waiting for their kids. Mari smiled and nodded at those she knew. She found it kind of awkward that she couldn't wave and walk; it would have been easier. A head nod would have to suffice. She stood underneath one porch covering, scrolling through various social media apps to keep from having to interact with the adults present. Her fingers were beginning to ache from cold, and she tried to flex them to work out the burn. She should have remembered her gloves.

"Hey. You okay?" Jase stepped into her space, taking it up and her breath with it.

"Fine," she assured him, a flutter of warmth filling her stomach knowing he had noticed her hands were bothering her. "It's just cold, and I forgot my gloves." She gave him the most winning smile she could that still hid her teeth. "Great race." Mari's heartbeat pushed so loudly against her throat she thought that everyone could hear it.

"Thanks." He was all humble pie, mixed with just a touch of Kanye.

If she told him what she really thought, that he was gorgeous and graceful in the water, then he would throw up all over his new tennis shoes. "Were you okay during the 400?" is what she asked instead.

"Just lost my breath." Jase took another step, invading her space just a little bit more. "But Leo is going to be a powerhouse at Tech."

"Maybe," Mari checked her phone for the time. Leo would be coming out soon, and they were going to have to book it home if they wanted to get some of Mama's baklava before Nick and Kris ate all of it after their practice.

"Got a hot date?" Jase asked.

"Only with Mama's baklava."

"I have heard amazing things about your mom's baklava. Maybe we should ditch Leo, and I'll take you home."

They continued to stand under the stingy streetlight in the parking lot. His blond hair was long but not shaggy, pulled into a stubby ponytail. Mari wanted to know what those little hairs would feel like under her fingers.

"You don't want to drive across town for baklava." Mari smiled, but she sort of hoped that he would.

"Are you kidding? I'll drive a lot of places for baklava, and if it's your house . . ." Blue eyes that looked darker in the night smiled down at her. "I will absolutely drive across town for it."

"Let me text Leo." She typed as quickly as she could with aching fingers. "And if we hurry, we might even beat Nick and Kris and get the ends. Those are my favorite." Mari tried to fight the excitement in her stomach.

"I like the way your eyes turn gold when you're excited." He moved half an inch closer, a hand touching one of the curls in front of her face. "I'm glad you came."

Her heart moved into a triple beat.

"In my head, it was all for me and had nothing to do with your brother."

"You have groupies." She'd lost her own breath. This was such uncharted territory.

"I tried to send them home when I saw you."

"Aren't you presumptuous, Jason Ellison." They were flirting. She knew this. And she would not stop for anything.

"Confident?" He raised a brow. "And call me Jase."

"Jason."

"Hey, Mom." He stepped back, ending Mari's internal debate on if she should try and touch him. His mom stepped into the middle of the conversation to give Jase a peck on the cheek. "I didn't think you could make it."

"We finished the meeting for the gala early." She breezed a smile in Mari's direction. "Mari, it's lovely to see you. We are so excited that you're going to speak for us."

"Mrs. Ellison." Mari didn't smile too wide. She studied Jase's mom almost like she was a tourist. She knew her on the most basic of surface levels, from camp pick-up and drop-off, but nothing more than that.

"Are you here to cheer on Jason?" There was a tone. It was as cool as the saucer-sized diamond on Mrs. Ellison's ring finger.

"Partly." Heat pulsed in her cheeks.

"Mari's brother is the guy from South who beat me at the 400."

"Oh, he's good." Mrs. Ellison smiled, perfect teeth, white and straight.

"He's swimming for Tech next year," Mari bragged, openly

proud of her brother's accomplishments. "My other brothers play basketball there."

"Are you athletic as well?" Mrs. Ellison's interest was clearly piqued. "I know that Noah Sanders is, but I didn't know if you were too."

"Mom, I'm going to run Mari home. I'll be back by nine." Jase cut into the conversation, sliding an arm around Mari's shoulders, coming into her, seeming to want to protect her from the conversation that was about to happen.

"Of course, sweetheart." Mrs. Ellison sipped her fizzy water.

Mari always thought that it was stupid to pay that much money for something that tasted like bitter cherries.

"Homework?"

"Done," Jase assured her, with his most brilliant smile.

"Mari, I would love to talk to you more about what would make you the most comfortable for your speech. Maybe Jason could bring you by the house one afternoon and we can discuss."

"Oh sure." Mari smiled, but also knew that it could all be covered in an email. Olivia Ellison really wanted to dive more into Mari's life.

"Mom, you're keeping me from baklava." Jase started moving, pulling Mari along. "And Mari's hands are popsicles."

"Go, go! Don't let me keep you from that!" She laughed at them.

Mari smiled at Jase, feeling the warmth wrap itself back around her insides, curling into puffs of crush and happiness.

"Thank you." She smiled. "And thanks for earlier today."

He opened her door before moving around the car to climb in on his side.

"Sorry that Lindsay was out for blood." Jase pushed the button to start his car, his brows drawn together in question and concern.

"She really hates me." Mari shook her head. "Also, thanks for not asking about the consultation I have tomorrow."

"For the new prosthesis, right?"

"Yeah, but like I said, it probably won't mean much. There's just not a lot they can do without a residual limb. But this place is supposed to be the best for amputations that are my level."

"I've never seen you use one."

"No, I've had a couple, but they've never worked for me." She shrugged. "I don't know if I want to try it again. It's a lot of time and money."

"What do you mean?" Jase pulled out of the parking lot at AWP, starting the drive from one end of Atlanta to the other. He turned on her seat warmer, upped the heat, and pointed the vents at her.

"If I want a new prosthesis, it will involve lots of trips to and from the prosthetist for various fittings and fabrications. Then there would be PT, which could be a few times a week, and because I am so unathletic"—her laugh was full of self-deprecation—"I'd need to start working out, at least getting my abs and lower back in some sort of shape. It takes a lot of muscle and energy to use a prosthesis."

"What's going to happen tomorrow?" Jase glanced at her.

She held her fingers up against the vents, trying to warm them, to heat the arthritic pain out of them.

"Here." He tossed some black gloves at her.

"Thanks." She smiled, pulling them on. "Tomorrow will just be a consultation. They'll try to sell me on all of the new technology and why I would be better off wearing a prosthesis."

"Sounds like a car salesman," Jase said. Mari thought his voice had an edge of concern, but she wasn't completely sure.

"Some can be a little pushy. Especially because of my track record of not wearing one."

"What do other amputees like you do?"

"Whatever, but some of us don't wear a prosthesis." She shrugged. "But my level is rare, even in the amputee world. I think we're something like half of one percent of all amputees."

"Why is that?"

"The more residual limb a person has, the easier it is to be fitted for a prosthesis, and the better mobility and stuff. That's why a lot of people go for the rotationplasty—better mobility."

"The surgery Noah had, right?"

"Yeah, where the surgeons make the foot the knee." Mari described how the surgeons were able to remove the affected knee and reattach the person's foot where the knee had been, facing the foot backwards. This way the person would still have a functioning knee in their foot. "It shortens your limb and looks different, but it gives great range of motion."

"Why would you do that instead of a limb salvage?"

"You're just full of questions tonight." Mari smiled.

"Sorry, am I being insensitive?"

He looked genuinely concerned. In the dark, Mari couldn't see his eyes, but the line of his mouth told her everything.

"No, it's fine. You can ask me and not worry about being judged. People have lots of reasons for making different surgical decisions. With a limb salvage, there are more limitations on what you can do physically. Most sports are off the table."

"And Noah would never go for that."

"It's his story." She shrugged. "I don't mind you asking me questions; it's the way you learn. It only bothers me when strangers demand to know something really intimate."

"Like Lindsay and Madalyn."

Even in the dark, she could see the regret in his face.

"Yeah," she answered honestly. "I've been with Mama in the grocery store, and people have stopped her to ask what was wrong with me and stuff."

"With you right there?"

"Yeah, they talk around me." Mari rolled her eyes. "Like, because they amputated my leg, I can't comprehend questions or hear them. It's ridiculous."

"What do you do?"

"Depends on how I'm feeling that day." Mari laughed. "Sometimes, I'm a bitch, but it's intrusive."

"No one gets the right to your life that way."

"You get it." Her insides warmed. It wasn't something she'd expected.

He looked at her, the car conveniently stopped at the red light near the fire department. "I think I'm beginning to."

# Chapter Twenty-Five

Jase thought about Mari's words as he drove home. Her house had been filled with loving chaos and noise. Neighbors floated in and out. Her older brothers had been there and had no problem letting him know they were watching him.

"Jase." Nick—who, at six-foot-four, seemed to tower over him—stood close. His plate had several treats, including the much-coveted baklava. "Thanks for bringing Mari home."

"She mentioned there would be baklava and that if she wanted any, she would have to get home before y'all." Jase's own plate was empty, but he was holding Mari's while she floated around, chatting with the neighbors.

"Mama loves this tradition." Nick's affection for his mother was clear. "They've done this open house almost every year, not even taking off the year that Mari was sick."

"A chance to give out treats before the holidays," Jase reasoned. "Makes sense."

"I'm not going to grill you or ask your intentions with Mari." Nick turned the conversation so abruptly that Jase's brain had a hard time catching up. "Because she's perfectly capable of taking care of herself."

"But?"

"She's still my sister."

There was a lot not said in those four words. And Jase heard each unspoken statement.

"I got it." Jase wasn't nervous about her brothers or their sort-of implied threats. He'd been serious today when he'd made his promise. He was done hurting Mari.

But now, on his way home, he thought about his conversation with Mari that day and the one on the way home, her confession about going to the appointment at the prosthetist. He couldn't imagine feeling like you owed some sort of explanation for your life to the whole world.

And he knew that was part of the reason he kept his secret.

He didn't want to owe anyone anything.

~

"Morning." Jase leaned against the locker next to Mari's. Her eyes were bright and maybe just a shade darker than normal. Could brown eyes change color that way?

"I brought you something." Her cheeks flushed a little, just lighting up her face.

"And what's that?"

Mari rummaged through her bag and pulled out a little brown bag tied with a pretty ribbon, his name written in some fancy script on the front. "Here ya go."

"What's this?"

"Mama said you looked hungry and for you to eat all of this baklava and some other leftovers."

He took the bag, but with his free hand, he flipped Mari's hand over, her palms roughened and callused from her crutches. His thumb swiped over one of the calluses, thinking about how the years of walking this way now showed up on her body in different ways.

"They're ugly." Her voice wasn't soft so much as just a lowered volume, like she was embarrassed that she even felt that way.

"From your crutches?"

"Yeah, it's why at camp I wear the bike gloves."

His heart stopped when she mentioned camp so casually, something she'd never say out loud to him in the halls of AWP. No one was around, he assured himself. No one could hear.

"Of course." He ran his thumb over it again, but this time it was so he could watch her pupils dilate a little, her breath catch slightly. "Speaking of gloves, did you bring mine back?"

"Shit," she muttered. "I set them out so I wouldn't forget, and I still forgot."

"Maybe you wanted to keep me close." He still hadn't let go of her hand, flirting shamelessly.

"Or I was in a hurry to catch the bus this morning."

"I could drive you, and then it wouldn't be a problem."

"Jason Ellison." She blushed prettily. "That is impractical and inefficient."

"Most definitely, but I wouldn't have offered if I didn't want to." He pressed his thumb gently in the palm of her hand, then moved it in a small circle. "Maybe I'll just have to stop by to get my gloves."

"Not today." She was whispering now. "Because I have . . . that appointment."

"How do you feel?" He slid in a little closer, seeing anxiety build in her.

"God, like my stomach is going to turn itself inside out."

"That's quite the visual." He brushed a curl off of her face, just wanting to be closer to her. "Haven't you done this before?"

"Yeah, but it was at the children's hospital. This is with a larger prosthetics company. The guy who is doing the consultation is supposed to be, like, the best in the world for hard-to-fit amputees."

"It's all new."

"Yeah."

"You'll be fine." He wanted to assure her more, to promise her some sort of miracle, but he didn't have one.

"Sure I will." She smiled, but it was that brave smile she often wore around people who didn't actually know her.

"I won't be there, but I'm only a text away."

"I can't text you while you're in class."

Ever the rule follower, that Mari Manos.

"I promise to respond only if I'm really bored or already know what they are teaching me."

"You're impossible."

But she laughed, and that made him feel better about all of it.

"But you like me." He turned his hand, pressing their palms together, linking their fingers.

"Yeah." She breathed the word on a smile. "I do."

# Chapter Twenty-Six

Mari tried to remember her Chemistry notes, because that was a hell of a lot more fun than sitting in a generic waiting room and waiting to be called back. It was basic, except for the random posters hung on the walls. She tried not to be offended, but in each one an amputee stood wearing their prosthetics, sporting medals or standing on the tops of mountains.

In her brain, she knew it was perfectly reasonable, given that they were in a prosthetics office waiting to see a guy about a leg. That, of course, there would be pictures of people using their super-cool, ultra-hi-tech prosthetic limbs. But to her it felt like an implied *You can't live a fulfilling life without one of these.*

And Mari didn't think that was true.

Because her life was pretty fulfilling, and she didn't wear one.

"You okay?" Mama looked at her, dark-brown eyes full of questions, concerns, and maybe just a little hope.

And that tiny hope in her mama's eyes is what made Mari smile reassuringly. "I'm totally great." She said the words on a promise. But she wasn't fine. She was worried and concerned and nervous, and she really didn't need to be missing Chem.

"Mari?" A young woman in a set of green scrubs called her name. "I'm Wren, Scott's assistant." She was young, like probably just out of college, with dark-brown skin and hair twists that brushed her chin. "Let's go chat."

Mari stood, grabbing her crutches, and her mom followed close behind. Mama patted Mari on the shoulder, squeezing as if to say, *See, it's just talking.* And Mari tried to hold on to that thought.

*Just talking.*

~

"So, like I said, I'm Scott's assistant, but really, I run the show." Wren smiled, and Mari saw that she had two little crooked teeth on the bottom. Just like Mari did.

"Don't we always?" Mari smiled, but it wasn't big enough to show her whole smile. Nerves warred against her other emotions, battling and winning at every corner.

"I know you're here for the clinic, but let's talk about your past prosthetics and experiences." Wren took out her laptop, ready to go. "When was your amputation?"

"Five years ago." Mari knew these questions; the answers were all in her instant-memory recall. She answered them at almost every new doctor's appointment she went to—even the dentist needed to know all of it. "I was diagnosed with osteogenic sarcoma when I was ten. I had a limb salvage and then contracted antibiotic-resistant bacteria. Because of my suppressed immune system, the docs knew this was the only option."

"Was your tumor located on the femur?" Wren typed more notes.

"Closer to my knee, but the infection was widespread, and they needed to do a hip disarticulation."

"So, no residual limb." Wren nodded like all of the pieces were falling together for her. "Which has made fitting you difficult."

"Yeah." Mari breathed the word, still feeling a little jittery and nervous. Her hand itched to text someone, but mostly Jase, to help distract her. But she didn't. Some part of her felt like she needed to give this place, this woman and her boss, her full attention.

"How many prosthetics have you had?"

"Mama?" Mari didn't really know.

"One full prosthesis and then two new sockets and a couple of components here and there."

The questions continued. When was her last socket, the part that attached to the residual limb or body? What kind of socket was it? Soft? Hard? Suction? Pin-and-lock? Did she have a hip joint on the prosthesis? Had they ever tried any other socket besides the traditional bucket seat, the one that wrapped up and around the user's body?

"Okay. Let's talk about you." Wren put the laptop down and smiled at Mari.

"I thought we had been." Mari felt a smile lift on one side, unsure of what they wanted from her.

"That's your medical stuff. I want to know about you. Tell me about your life. School? Significant other? What do you do for fun?"

"Oh." Mari didn't understand her feelings right now. The nerves were gone, like she'd expected, but she was uncomfortable with the feelings just under her skin.

Was that hope?

# Chapter Twenty-Seven

Jase had never really paid attention to the fluorescent lights overhead before. But today, they seemed to be eating into his brain, sucking his entire soul through his eyeballs. Or maybe he was being just a touch dramatic. He kept looking up to where Mari should be sitting at her table with Madalyn and Lindsay. But she wasn't there, and she hadn't texted at all since she'd left school right after lunch.

"You look lonely," Lucas teased.

"Yeah, yeah." Jase had stopped listening to the Chemistry lecture. It wasn't like Yother was going to light the table on fire . . . again.

"You two are getting awfully close, though." Lucas was clearly trying to pry out what was going on between Mari and Jase, but Jase didn't give an inch. "Mom said Mari was speaking at the New Year's Eve Gala. Your mom must be over the moon that you're dating the speaker."

"We're not dating," Jase said quickly. They weren't. Hell, it was still new that Mari would even speak to him after what he did. "We're just friends."

"Right." Lucas nodded, but it was all sarcasm. "Which is why you look like a lost puppy. Is your mom in major gala mode yet?"

"You know, every year I think I'll be prepared for her

moods during this time, but I never am." Jase laughed. "I have no idea why she does this to herself. At least once a week, she swears that she won't host this again, but come February, she'll miss it or something."

"Do you have pictures of sick kids at cancer camp all over your house?" Lucas laughed. "My mom came home and hugged me for, like, an hour after the first gala planning meeting."

"Huh. Yeah." Jase didn't lie. His skin began to crawl, and instinctually, he looked to Mari's spot. *Screw it*, he thought as he took out his phone, texting Mari.

**Jase: You okay?**

The little typing box popped up, but she never responded.

"My mom then went a little extreme and, like, cleaned our fridge and pantry of anything she might have heard caused cancer in kids. And got rid of all of the non-organic cleaning products our housekeeper uses."

"Do you need me to bring you some Oreos or something?" He wanted to change the subject. Before Mari had come to AWP, he never would have given it a thought that his mom might have talked to his friends' parents about his cancer. She was just as removed from it as he was.

"Dude, do you have some?" Lucas practically salivated the words. "Like, I will pay you good money."

"I'll see what I can do for you." Jase laughed. "Sorry my mom has traumatized yours."

"I think it was the pictures of little bald kids." Lucas laughed. "I told her to get a grip, but she got all sniffly and stuff."

"Geez, what did my mom tell them?" Jase's heart started to pound, pulsing and pushing against his sternum, bordering on painful. His pulse knocked at his veins, the increase in rate so fast that spots formed in his vision.

"Dude, you okay?" Lucas's voice was now all concern. A hand went to Jase's shoulder. "You're stupidly pale."

"Yeah." Jase said the word, but couldn't seem to catch his breath, the spots blurring his vision.

"Uh, Mrs. Yother." Lucas clearly didn't believe Jase at all and for good reason. "I think Jason needs some water."

The teacher came over, tilting Jase's face up to hers. "What's going on?"

"I'm just a little dizzy," he confessed. "I'm fine. It'll pass."

"Lucas, help him to the nurse," Yother demanded instead.

"I'm cool," Jase insisted, but he didn't try to stand, knowing without a shadow of a doubt that his feet would never make it.

"Humor me," the teacher insisted. "Either he escorts you, or I call for the nurse. Your choice."

"Fine." Jase stood, not moving until he was certain the floor wasn't going to rise up and smack him in the face. His pulse still raced, spots still danced, and his heart still thrummed so hard that he thought it would break his chest. He only left the room because he wanted his classmates to stop looking at him. If he wasn't there, they couldn't see him. He prayed they'd forget about this whole thing.

Slowly, they walked through the hall. Jase refused to let Lucas help. Instead, he let his hand trail along the wall, the lockers. "She's being overly cautious," Jase insisted.

"You're the color of paste," Lucas said. "Panic attack?"

"That's all I need." But Jase didn't deny it.

They walked slowly down the hall, Jase still refusing any help.

His pocket vibrated.

And the thought of Mari only made his heart race more.

And not in a good way.

# Chapter Twenty-Eight

"Mari, how long has it been since you wore a prosthesis?" Scott Wilson, a tall white guy with perfectly straight teeth and a dude-bro haircut, sat with her in the exam room now.

"I don't know. Three? Four years?"

"And she's never worn it consistently," her mom interjected.

Mari sent her mom a look, irritation slinking into her stomach, like she was being told on for not doing her homework or studying for a test.

"I'm sure you know that most people with your level of amputation don't wear a prosthesis."

"So I've heard." She didn't know why, but she didn't like Scott Wilson. She'd liked Wren, and maybe if she was the one in here doing this part, Mari'd be more interested, but instead, every hair on the back of her neck was up.

"Do you want to walk without those things?" He nodded to her pink forearm crutches. "As fashionable as they are."

She was fairly certain he was being just a little sarcastic.

"My crutches are fine." She leveled him with her eyes. "What I'm interested in is what you can do for me. Can you fit me with something other than a bucket seat? Is it comfortable while also offering stability? Do I have to take it off to pee? Is it going to add major inches to my hips and waist?"

Scott straightened and then smiled. A smile that said Mari

was a challenge and someone he was interested in taking on. He had no idea who she was or what she wanted. "Change into your shorts, and we'll see what we can do" was all he said, leaving the room.

She changed into the nylon athletic shorts and wondered briefly if she should have shaved her bikini line this morning when she'd showered. But pushed the thought aside. Waiting, she saw the text from Jase and finally took a moment to reply.

**Mari: I'm not sure why I'm here.**

But didn't get a chance to wait for his reply, Scott knocked on the door, announcing his entrance. Mama sat off to the side, sending her a look that said to be a little more open minded. But right then, Mari didn't have a lot of open mindedness.

Scott had her stand up between a set of parallel bars, just like the ones used in the Olympics by gymnasts, except lowered to a level where she could use them like crutches. "I'm sure that you're aware that the human body is not meant to walk on its shoulders."

"I've heard that before." Mari gritted her teeth. She should really just thank the guy for his time and go. "But my leg didn't seem to know that when it contracted a deadly infection."

"Ha." He laughed, but it was all for show, not at all truthful. "I'm going to examine your tissue and stump."

"I'm not a tree," she said automatically. Shouldn't a guy who worked in prosthetics know that the correct term was residual limb or residual tissue? "Dr. Lee, my surgeon, said she tried to leave me with a healthy amount of residual tissue."

"I see that." Scott Wilson pushed up the open leg of her shorts, his gloved hands feeling around her residual tissue and the empty hip socket.

Mari focused at a spot on the wall, feeling extremely naked while still being fully clothed. She wanted to make a joke about him having to buy her dinner first, but her mom was in the room. And it would probably make them all feel more uncomfortable.

So instead, she took in a deep breath and stared straight ahead. His hands moved around her tissue, which was essentially her butt, and she definitely wished she'd shaved her bikini line this morning as he tested the flap of tissue that would have been her inner thigh if she'd still had a leg. Dear God, this was . . . embarrassing wasn't the right word, because it was completely professional, like any other medical procedure.

Uncomfortable.

That was how she felt.

Uncomfortable.

"I can't really know what kind of socket we can offer you until I get a test socket."

"Huh?" His words pulled Mari from her thoughts. "A test socket?"

"Mrs. Manos, do you have time today for us to get a test socket?" And all of a sudden, Mari was no longer in the room. "It would take a couple of hours."

"Yeah," Karen answered, looking at Mari for approval. "You don't have work today or anything, right?"

"Yeah," Mari agreed but wasn't sure she wanted this at all. "What kind of sockets are you thinking?"

"Let me go get the casting materials, and we can chat about potential components."

~

"How's this feel, Mari?" Scott pulled on a tube of elastic around her residual tissue. Tissue that was currently encased in a plaster cast.

"Tight." She laughed, never letting on just how uncomfortable this whole situation was. She was half naked, feeling pretty grateful that she'd thought to wear nice-ish underwear that morning. She was half naked, and dude-bro Scott Wilson was lined up pretty directly with her genital area.

"Is it too hot?" Scott tried to pull tighter on the rubber tubing. It was making an indention in the plaster that went around the flap of tissue of her "inner thigh" and up over her hip bone. The plaster was warming as it hardened.

"It's okay." Mari held on to the bar in front of her, gripping it tighter in her fingers.

"I'm going to need a few more hands in here." He smoothed his hand across Mari's backside, pressing out the wrinkles in the plaster.

She knew it was completely professional but hated it. She didn't want to be in this position. She didn't even want to be here.

"Wren? Carter?" he called out into the hallway.

The prosthetist office was part regular medical building and part autobody shop. There were pylons, or tubes of metal used to make tibias and femurs, and plaster of Paris, the white stuff that used to be for casts and was currently slathered around Mari's butt. There was a set of parallel bars for you to take steps once they had the prosthesis on you. There were wrenches, hammers, and hex keys scattered around the room, along with saws, pliers, and other tools.

Wren and another young guy who must be Carter came

into the room. Wren smiled warmly while the other guy looked at her with the same look that Scott had. That look that she was a problem to solve, some*thing* to be fixed, instead of some*one*. He didn't really acknowledge her, instead diving in and putting his hands on her. Around her.

"She has so much residual tissue," Carter commented, pulling tighter on the tubing currently used to help make a deep indention onto the plaster of Paris.

"Dr. Lee knows what she's doing." Wren smiled at Mari. "She did you a great service leaving us so much to work with."

"She does." Mari didn't add that originally, she'd had a whole leg. Now, just a little tissue remained of that leg.

"Are we going to fit her in a bucket?" Carter smoothed the casting around her good hip.

He was definitely here for the uniqueness of her amputation, not at all concerned with the person it was attached to.

"I'm hoping we can fashion a modified suspension socket or a bikini socket," Scott explained as he stepped away. "If we can get the tissue to pull into the suction, then we can treat this like a traditional above-the-knee socket."

"What about a hip joint?" Carter took over on the pulling.

Mari felt like she was being pulled in two. Or at least like part of her butt was being squeezed off.

"We'll have a locking one. She won't have to control it."

They continued to speak around her. She didn't even have to be there. She was just the body they were going to attach this new part to. They were Dr. Frankenstein, and she was just the greatest experiment.

# Chapter Twenty-Nine

Being home was nice. Granted, all Jase had gotten out of was that afternoon's conditioning. After putting his head between his knees and drinking some Gatorade, it was determined that he'd had a panic attack. Jase didn't know if that was the case or not, but it meant he got to leave school twenty minutes early and go home.

"Are you sure you're okay?" Olivia Ellison doted on him, giving him more Gatorade, some snacks, and whatever else she thought he might need. "You're doing too much." She sat down on the couch with him, pushing his hair off of his forehead. "Maybe you need to see Dr. Johnson, have some blood work done or something."

"Mom, I'm fine. Probably just tired." *Or having a breakdown.*

"Well, I'm going to cancel my appointment this afternoon and just make sure."

"Don't do that." *Dear God, do not do that*, his brain pleaded. He wanted to spend some time by himself, maybe thinking or doing his absolute best not to think.

"Are you sure?"

"I am very sure." He smiled, hoping to reassure his mother. She didn't worry often, but when something like this happened, she did. And if he wasn't careful, he would end up in the doctor's office for blood work before the day was done. "I just got dizzy, and the nurse at school overreacted."

"With your medical history, it's bound to happen."

Jase had heard of the phrase about blood turning cold, but he'd never experienced it until this very second. His blood froze in his veins, a little sluggish, allowing him to feel every pulse and pump of it through his body. "Why would the nurse know my medical history?"

"Don't be silly, sweetie. We have to disclose important information to the school. It might not be something you think about, but your treatment could impact you down the line, so it's something your school has always known about."

"Huh." He let that rattle around in his head with the facts and knowledge that were being revealed each and every day. "You don't, like, tell strangers on the street about me, do you?" He tried to make it sound like a joke, but his heart was still thrumming with frozen blood.

"Of course not." She smiled at him, brushing at his hair once again. "It's your story to tell, not mine. That was something the old Child Life Specialist and the hospital's psychologist went over a lot with us when you were transitioning to the cancer survivor program. I have a very different story as a mom of a cancer survivor, but I can never understand what it's like to be a cancer survivor. I can never speak for you.

"It's been years since I've been to the hospital support groups or anything. Other than when you go to the clinic or camp, our lives are blissfully untouched by cancer." His mom finished her speech, still looking at him like he'd done something amazing.

"Truthfully, I don't even remember it." He shrugged. "Like,

it's not something I think about at all." He paused, thinking about it for another minute. "Mostly, I remember it just being my life. I remember playing with the nurses and with puzzles. I don't remember bad things or pain." His fingers began to twitch with anxiety as he pushed the limits of his memory. "Maybe just the nervousness of not always knowing what to expect."

"I have your Beads of Courage in a shadow box." Olivia smiled. "I'll see if I can find it for you. It's got other things, like some hospital bracelets, a lock of your baby curls before they all fell out." She laughed over a memory. "I asked if I could keep your port, but the surgeon told me absolutely not."

Jase lightly touched the spot on his chest where the port had been placed under his skin. "It was right here."

"Yeah, they used them to give you all of your chemo and to do blood draws and stuff. It saved us a whole lot of grief and kept you from getting collapsed veins."

"I still don't like shots."

"The docs and nurses told me you wouldn't remember much. I wrote down a lot of it if you ever want to read it."

"You did?"

"Of course." She ruffled his hair, standing up. "Just in case you did want to know someday. I need to get going. Your color is back, so I'm going to leave you, but rest. Don't do your homework or anything."

"Not a problem," he promised as she left. Jase thought over her words, thinking about what she had said about reading through his mother's memories.

He wasn't sure if he wanted to know.

Because what if it changed everything?

# Chapter Thirty

The party was loud. Or maybe it just sounded like it was too loud after being at home for the past few days—strict orders of his mother since the weird panic attack. Jase refused to think of it as anything else. He should have stayed home or maybe gone to a movie. He should never have come to the party. There weren't enough people here to necessitate it being this loud. The party had started at 7:00, and it was just barely 7:15, but trick-or-treaters had been out since 5:15. His neighborhood was mostly finished, with parents handing their youngsters off to their babysitters, dressed to go to their own parties.

Jase: Can we talk about how terrible Halloween parties are?

Mari: Grant Park is guaranteed to be still rocking until at least 9:30.

For some reason, his random texts now went to Mari, not Lucas and definitely not Lindsay.

Mari: Are you feeling better?

Jase: It was so stupid. I'm fine.

Even as he typed out the text, he felt like he was telling a lie. Because even right then, he was exhausted. His pulse was thrumming, and his heart seemed to be echoing in his chest.

"Hey." Lindsay slid up to him. Her costume, a ritzy store shopping bag, was clever. A play on the whole "bag lady" theme. "Let's dance."

"I'm good." He sipped the tepid beer and, not for the first

time, wondered why no one could keep it cold so it was at least somewhat decent.

"What is your problem, Jason?" Her face turned ugly. Her long, blonde hair was pulled into a high ponytail, but the extensions she'd had put in meant it still brushed near her lower back and over his arm and stomach as she whirled. "Lately, it's like you are above everything."

"I'm not a snob," he sneered, at the same time recognizing that he did, in fact, act like a snob sometimes.

"Then why don't you want to hang with me anymore?"

"Because it's over." He didn't want to sound mean or hurtful. "We had this discussion at the last party."

"So you just want the handicapped girl?" she snarled.

Her eyes had that glassy look they got when she was a little high. And when she was a little high, she got nasty.

"Don't be mean," he said. "This has nothing to do with Mari." But even as he said the words, he tasted the lie.

"Whatever." She tossed her long hair again. "Do you really think I haven't noticed that you smile at her in the hallways or find reasons to talk to her after school?"

"I'm being nice."

"Sure." She rolled her eyes. "What could you possibly have in common with someone like that?"

*More than you know.* "She's not an alien." He felt his brows draw together.

"Whatever." She pushed him, knocking him back a bit, his drink spilling on his T-shirt, which read, "This is my costume." "You're only interested in her to make yourself look good. Just so you know, they don't ask if you took a pity date on college apps."

"You know, I've always known you were mean." He really thought her harsh words had more to do with her hurt feelings than her actual thoughts about Mari.

"Whatever, Jason. Go make the little handicapped girl feel good about herself. Everyone will know that it's just a pity date."

"God, Lindsay, I'm not dating anyone."

"Right, because it's not like you can take her to the gala or anything. It's not like she can dance."

The words snarled around them both, purposefully angry and mean, and Jase was glad that Mari was nowhere around to hear them.

Jase took a step toward Lindsay, lowering his voice as he spoke clearly. "Lindsay, you are mad at me because I'm not interested in you. You do not get to be hateful toward Mari because you have some misplaced anger. Do better." And with that, he turned, leaving the room and the party.

Jase walked the short distance to his car. He found a wrinkled polo in his backseat and changed shirts, not wanting to reek of beer.

He drove through the city without really having a destination in mind, but then there he was, standing in front of the wide front porch of a little blue bungalow. He was passed by two kids—one dressed in a dinosaur costume and the other, a bat—as he climbed the few steps and rang the bell. He shoved his hands in his pockets, completely unsure of what in the hell he was doing there. Then Mari was standing the doorway, still holding the candy bowl.

"Well, that's a costume." Mari arched a brow at his jeans and wrinkled polo, his letterman's jacket slung over his arm. "High school athlete?"

# Chapter Thirty-One

"And you are?"

Jase came a little closer, all but touching her, and her breath stuck somewhere around her throat.

"Fashionista?"

She could feel her breath as it moved in a rapid pace between her heart and lungs. In what weird alternate universe had she slipped into where Jason Ellison stood on her front porch, the faintest hint of beer on his clothing? Not that she should be so close that she could smell him . . . but she could.

"Social outcast." She smiled and moved so he could come in. And wondered why she hadn't bothered to change into something a little less grubby after school, why was she wearing her old yoga pants, with her hair piled on top of her head?

"I don't know of any social outcasts that look like you, Mari." He sat down near her book on the couch like he had done it a thousand times, like he had grown up coming in and out of her house.

"You just haven't studied us enough." She sat next to him, but made sure there was space between them. "Didn't you have plans? Weren't you at a party? Or something?"

"I was, but my car drove itself here." He picked at one of the loose threads on the couch. "I don't know. I just didn't want a lot of noise."

"But going to the club for dinner with your parents didn't appeal." She nodded knowingly. "I get it."

"I sort of knew you would."

His smile wasn't full, but it was sincere, just filling his face and making him that much more attractive.

"You don't mind me hanging out?"

"Not if you don't mind helping with candy detail." Mari welcomed a little company. Halloween falling on a Friday and staying home made her feel like a social pariah, but with Jase here, it was a little more acceptable.

"I've never given out candy before." He shrugged off his coat, laying it over the back of the couch. "Should be fun."

"It's been busy." And on cue, the doorbell rang. "Come on."

They handed out the candy, making appropriate comments on costumes, and Mari talked with neighbors as they came and went.

"So, how did your prosthetics appointment go?"

Mari knew he'd been curious but had been kind enough not to bring it up at school. She stood next to the door, waiting for another kid to come get their candy.

"Weird." Her brows drew together with the memory as she moved back to the couch. "Like, I really liked one of the people, but the head doctor guy made me feel . . . odd."

"How?" he asked, rising to give the candy this time.

"Well, it's just so strange anyway." Mari paused as he finished with the trick-or-treater. "The guy is literally in my very personal business." She didn't want to say that Wilson had basically been eye level with her vulva. "And then he called in more people to help, and it was like I wasn't needed, just my amputation."

"Are you still thinking of getting a prosthesis?"

"Yeah, because we've already done a test socket. Why not see?" She shrugged. "But it was all so weird-feeling to me. It always makes me wish that I hadn't gotten that infection." She could remember all of it. There had been pain with the limb salvage, but it had worked. Her leg had still been there. It still would be, if she hadn't had the infection.

"What happened?" He touched her hand, drawing her attention there.

"You know this story." She laughed a little, trying not to sound so depressing. "I got an infection."

"I get the one that's coated in 'It saved my life, so it's fine.' Tell me what really happened."

"There were a lot of complications, but mostly, I had no immune system, and my body just couldn't do it. It was either amputate, or I was going to die."

"How did your parents tell you?"

"They didn't." She looked from their hands, which were still touching, to his thoughtful blue eyes. "I was so sick that I was out of it. I didn't know I'd had surgery until I woke up a few days after the fact."

"Holy shit," he breathed.

"Yeah." She smiled weakly. "I was pretty mad for a while, but it's not like it could be changed. So here I am."

"But you don't let it get you down."

"I am not an inspiration," she said quickly, knowing what he was thinking. "If you look at me like those people who don't know me, I'm going to make you leave."

"Ah, the look."

"Right," she said. "Don't give me the look."

"God, I hate it."

"Is that why you've never told anyone at AWP?" she asked tentatively. "Because you don't want the pity look?"

"When I transferred to AWP in ninth, I made a choice not to tell anyone."

Jase touched her fingers, his moving over hers in little taps, like she'd seen him do on tabletops often.

"My whole middle school career, I was . . . harassed . . ."

He trailed off, but Mari saw more. She stopped his fingers and held on, waiting for the rest of the story.

"I was . . . bullied, maybe? For something I didn't even remember. So, I made a choice. I couldn't change it."

"You made a choice." She studied their hands, the way she was holding his.

"It was so much easier to forget," he confessed. "I feel like a tool complaining about this with you."

Another trick-or-treater came to the door, but their conversation barely paused as Mari handed out the candy.

"Don't." Mari's heart bled a little for the younger Jase. The one who felt like hiding part of himself was his only option. "We all do what we can to cope."

"But I've heard the assholes. You brush it off."

Mari stopped next to the arm of the couch, staring at him for a moment, his face more handsome than she even remembered.

"Not always." Her own issues bubbled just under the surface. "I didn't the other day." She could still feel his arms around her as she'd cried. "They get to me too. What do you remember from when you were on treatment? Anything?" she asked as she sat back down, unintentionally (or totally intentionally) closer to him.

Jase looked up from the couch to her, his skin lit by the lamplight in the family room. It was golden, like the way the sun looked when it set out over the lake at camp. His eyes seemed bluer than they had before, but she suspected she was getting sentimental, as her crush resurged each time they were alone together.

"I remember being scared." He said the words slowly, thoughtfully. "I guess now I would say I was anxious, but I didn't have the vocabulary then. I remember throwing up in the car on the way to the clinic." He bit his lip. "There was an old, abandoned hotel on the corner not too far from the hospital, and it was like a marker for me. When I'd see it, I'd feel nauseous and typically got sick by the time Mom was parking her car."

"I remember that building. They demolished it a few years back for the office park." She nodded thoughtfully. "I wonder if the office park makes other kids sick."

"Did you get nervous when you saw that building?" Jase touched her hand then, but not with his tapping, just his palm lying flat over hers. If either of them curled their fingers, they would most definitely be holding hands.

"It did at first. Like, when I first got sick and I wasn't sure what was coming at me with each visit." She stared at their hands and then looked up at him. "But after a while, the hospital, the clinic . . . they became my play place."

"You were ten?" He picked up her hand, holding it in his, his thumb moving over each knuckle on her hand like he did when he tapped his fingers.

"Yeah, I didn't get to attend most of fourth grade because I was in and out of the hospital. Low counts, all of that."

Another ring of the doorbell, and this time Jase got up and doled out the candy.

"If we turned out the lights, we could eat the rest of the candy." He sat back down and immediately picked up her hand again.

"They ring it even if the light's not on." She laughed. "We even put up signs that say we're out of candy, and people still ring it and just hope."

"Persistence."

"It pays off." Mari smiled. Butterflies in her stomach were dancing. "I mean, I wouldn't have finished the ropes this summer if you hadn't been so persistent."

"I just wanted to be close to you, and if I had to hang thirty feet in the air to do it, so be it." His cheeks hinted at red over the words, a little embarrassment and humility on his face. "I got to touch you, and we did the ropes. It was a win-win for me."

A smile pulled at the corner of her mouth. "Jase, why are you here?" She whispered it, because she couldn't seem to talk at all, her mouth dry.

He leaned in, his eyes level with hers. "To see you." He said the words softly before taking her face in his hand, lifting her chin up to look her in the eyes. "I didn't ask last time, and I should have."

"Ask what?" She wanted to curl into his hand, to feel it cup her face.

"Can I kiss you?"

His mouth was so close she could feel the warmth of his

breath on her own lips. The surge of lust that shot through her was so strong she nearly shivered from it.

"Really?" Why was she doubting him? She should just say yes already.

"Yeah."

God, it was spoken so softly. His gravelly voice filled her entire soul. They both started to lean in, warm breath fluttering over her lips and making her insides drip with anticipation and want.

The doorbell rang.

"I can ignore it," she said, her eyes laser focused on his mouth.

"Me too." His fingers stroked the side of her cheek, down under her jaw.

A tilt of her head, a tilt of his. Mari could practically feel his lips pressed to hers.

The doorbell rang again, followed by a persistent knock. "Your light is on, and Jase's BMW is out front. Let me in!" Davis bellowed.

"Shit," Jase muttered, his hand falling from her face to her side. Their foreheads pressed together, heat simmering between them. "Someday, this will come back to bite him in the ass."

"Absolutely." Mari swallowed hard over the knot of downright lust in her throat.

"Come on!" Davis called. "It's cold!"

Mari stood, her body still tingling, her arms a little wobbly in her crutches. She took a deep breath, attempting to clear some of the fog from her brain as she opened the door for Davis. "To what do we owe this surprise?"

"Grant Park is more fun than my neighborhood." Davis came in, took off his coat, and hung it up like he was making himself at home.

Mari glanced over his shoulder to where Jase was still sitting on the couch, a faint red blush on his cheeks. Their eyes met, and no words were needed.

"Mari was just telling me how she was going to personally beat us at Capture the Flag this summer."

Davis sat on the other sofa, laughing, completely oblivious to the fact that he was now in the same category as Margaret.

# Chapter Thirty-Two

Things with Mari had changed. Even Jase knew this. Part of his brain said he should back off, let things cool down, to stop nearly kissing her. But the louder part of his brain told him to stop thinking so damn much and just kiss her already.

He sat at the breakfast table, eating a bowl of ridiculously sugary cereal and looking through his Instagram feed.

"Morning, Jason." His dad sat down next to him.

John Ellison was dressed in gym shorts and a T-shirt, a sweat band around his head that always made Jase laugh—but only on the inside.

"What's your training schedule like today?"

"Mom told me to take today off." And he hadn't been planning on swimming today anyway.

"Fair."

His dad smiled, and Jase's heart warmed.

"You were out last night?"

"I was in Grant Park, helping Mari give out candy."

"You've been spending a great deal of time with her," his father noted. "Your mom has said that Mari's the speaker for the gala in a few months."

"Yeah." But he didn't acknowledge his father's insinuation that something was going on between them.

"It's nice that you make the girl feel good."

There was an implied *but* in the sentence. Jase wasn't going to give his dad the satisfaction of saying it.

"Just remember that you're going to college in the fall. That Mari, however lovely, is not right for you."

"We're not even dating." But maybe they were? He might not have bought her dinner, which he needed to fix, but he was seeing her a lot.

"Good." His dad picked up the business section because he was a complete stereotype of himself and started to the garage. "You should work out today. Get in some conditioning before swim picks back up."

"Yeah, maybe." He was not at all going to do that.

Jase: Lunch?

Mari: At work. Sorry 🙁

*Sink or swim, big guy.*

Jase: Dinner then?

There was a pause, but the three little dots indicated she was typing . . . or at least thinking about typing.

Mari: Sure

Jase: It's a date.

# Chapter Thirty-Three

The Daily Grind was busy, but not full. People were getting their coffees and drinks to go before heading out on a Saturday night. A date should have meant picking her up from her house, meeting her parents again, all of that. But Mari had suggested meeting at the Grind. He was pretty certain her brothers were around, and she didn't want to deal with them.

Jase glanced around the shop. Mari wasn't in sight, and he didn't see her stuff at the end of the bar where they usually sat to study and pester Davis.

Lindsay: Wanna hang?

Jase didn't even think of replying. He didn't want her to see the potential three dots or to even know that he'd read the text. He'd been perfectly clear with her.

"Mari here?" Jase sat in his normal stool and waited for Davis to hand him his Coke.

Lindsay: Do you think I don't know you're ignoring me?

"Not that I've seen, but she might have been held up at the store or something." Davis slid the drink to his friend. "What are y'all doing here on a Saturday when you could be anywhere else?"

Lindsay: Jason, come on. The crip can't be that entertaining.

"Uh, we're meeting to go get dinner." Heat raced up his cheeks, tingeing even his ears with pink. He could feel it. "Hey, um, what do you do when the girl you kind of dated is being clingy?"

**Lindsay: Fine. Whatever.**

"I went to rehab, and that got Alexis off of my back," Davis said, referring to his ex-girlfriend, a girl he used drugs with a lot, Jase remembered. "But let's go back. You're going to dinner with Mari?" He leaned over the bar and carefully placed the drink on a coaster. "Like, a group of friends from AWP is going to dinner and you're giving her a ride?"

"Nope." He took a deep breath. Davis was probably the best person to tell this to. "I'm taking her out."

"Like, on a date?" There was mild surprise in Davis's eyes, but also a hint of a grin, just waiting to give Jase a hard time. Then Davis's brows shot up. "Wait, she's not . . . the clingy girl you're talking about, right?"

"No, no. It's my kind-of ex . . . Lindsay. She's texting me all of a sudden. I called off our thing, like, last month, and she's been trying extra hard to connect again." His phone continued to buzz with messages from Lindsay, messages he was not even going to look at.

"Did you tell Lindsay you were taking Mari out?" Davis asked as he walked away, swiping at a table with a rag.

"No." His brows drew together. "But Lindsay always seems to know everything. She's been giving Mari a hard time."

"But I'm sure you've been helping Mari deal with that." Davis moved over to where Jase was sitting. "I mean, I'd love to go to school with Mari. Or just anyone who went to camp with me."

Jase only nodded because he didn't want Davis to know what an ass he'd been to Mari. He still didn't want anyone at school to know he'd had cancer, that he'd known Mari for years, that he went to camp.

**Jase: You on your way? Need a ride?**

He texted Mari. He didn't know why, but this interrogation from Davis and the incessant texts from Lindsay were starting to rankle his fraying nerves.

"How's everything?" Jase asked, wanting to turn the conversation to something he thought of as safer. "Everything" was his not-so-subtle code for "your sobriety"?

"Okay." Davis's shoulders sagged. "I'm tired today, and that makes it a little worse. Like, when I'm tired, I feel sad, and I remember getting high, and it made me happy."

Jase nodded, listening to his friend's words. "Is that how it all started? You wanted to be happy?" His fingers picked up one at a time off the table, and his brain unconsciously counted each one. One. Two. Three. Four.

"It didn't start out that way." Davis sighed. "I didn't get high the first time as some sort of coping mechanism or anything. I did like that I could get high and forget all of the . . ." He searched for the word. "Stuff that was always around me."

"What do you mean?"

"Like, eventually people stopped referring to me as the guy who'd had cancer, and instead, I was the guy who was a stoner or whatever."

"And you preferred that?" Even as he asked the question, Jase could see the reasoning. Hadn't he just talked about it with Mari? It was about being control of your own story.

"I preferred not being special." Davis smiled, but it was sad and didn't meet his eyes. "It's hard, you know? Always having to own this thing that you had no choice in."

Jase did know. It was why he had made the decision to keep his cancer history a secret when he'd transferred to AWP. He didn't want it to be part of who he was. A lens that others saw him through.

Davis went back to serving customers, giving Jase more time to think. He knew exactly what Davis meant, being special, being recognized only for one thing and not anything else. Jase wondered if he'd ever be willing to risk the curated life he presented to AWP. The words that Davis said crawled around in his brain, little ants scratching in his skull, demanding he think about them. He raked his hands through his hair, gripping at the longer strands and feeling the pull on his scalp, like he was trying to physically pull the uncomfortable thoughts from his brain.

Where was Mari? He wasn't sitting at this stupid place because he didn't have better things to do on a Saturday night. He checked his phone, and damn it if there weren't twenty-two texts from Lindsay sitting in his notifications.

**Jase: Mari? You okay?**

He wanted to ask if she was having second thoughts, to find out if work was holding her up. She probably had a good reason for being late. She wouldn't stand him up . . . would she?

There was no response. No little dots to indicate that Mari had even seen it.

"That accident was no joke," a male voice said, catching Jase's attention.

"There was an accident?" Davis picked up easily. "Where?"

"Over on Memorial. A car was T-boned. There was an ambulance and everything."

Without a backward glance, Jase left the Grind. He didn't

wait to hear more. His heart rate told him everything he needed to know. The pounding, the ache behind his breastbone was more than enough proof.

He couldn't breathe.

Jase shook his head, trying to clear the thoughts. His brain was being ridiculous. *It wasn't Mari. It couldn't be.* And yet, she was never late . . .

Jase whipped his car down the side streets of Grant Park, hitting Memorial Drive. He was stuck in a traffic jam, cars stopped both ways. A notification from his phone said there was a car accident up ahead.

Of course there was. He stretched out his body, trying to see around the traffic jam. He couldn't.

Jase's heart rate continued to climb. He debated parking right there and running to the accident, but what little sense he had left stopped him. *It couldn't be Mari. It couldn't be Mari. It couldn't be Mari.* The worlds were on repeat in his brain like the most sacred of prayers.

His car inched forward, and he heard the wail of an ambulance—either coming or going, he couldn't be sure. Dusk having almost come and gone, it was getting darker by the minute.

Then, in an instant, the accident scene came into view. Jase's mouth went dry, and it was as if sand filled his mouth, and with each impossible breath, he inhaled the tiny particles.

There was a beige Honda Accord rolled onto its side, crushed on the front end and crumpled on the other.

"There are lots of those cars," Jase whispered around the sand. "Just because it looks like Mari's doesn't mean it is." *It couldn't be Mari.* He inched his car forward some more to where the police were talking to several people.

There was Leo. He sat on the ground, his head in his hands, holding his phone to his ear. Jase wasn't sure that he even signaled as he whipped his car into a parking lot, jumped out, and ran to Leo.

"Son, you can't be here." One of the policemen stopped him.

"Come on, I know him." Jase motioned to Leo. "Was anyone else in the car?" His heart thudded the word "Mari" with each beat. His brain pleaded for the policeman to say no.

"I'm afraid I can't answer any questions."

"Come on!" Jase's voice rose. "That's my girlfriend's brother over there. Was she in the car?"

"Jase?" Leo walked over.

"Leo, where's Mari?" He barely noticed the sort of glaze that was in Leo's eyes, the light burns around his arms, the shock clearly all over his body. "Was Mari with you?"

"Yeah." He shook his head, and his hands trembled. "They took her to the hospital."

"Are you done with him?" Jase demanded. The anger was now acute fear.

"Yeah, we'll be in touch." The cop looked at both of them. "Are you taking him to the hospital?"

"Yes." Jase put an arm around Leo, leading him to Jase's car. Leo's adrenaline must have been wearing off. He was starting to sink. He shook so violently it was like he had an uncontrollable fever.

"Come on, Leo." Jase poured him into the front seat of his car. "Where did they take Mari?"

"Children's," Leo managed. "I made them promise to take her there."

"Was she conscious?"

"Mostly." Leo looked down at his shaking hands, shoving them under his legs. "Her arm was hurt."

"Okay." Some of the sand loosened in his throat. Mari was sort of okay. She would be fine. "I think you need to be checked out."

"Our car is totaled." Leo breathed the words. "It was too old to be worth much, but it was ours."

"It's why you have insurance" is all Jase could think of. He'd already had his car in the body shop twice, and both times, it had been because he'd been driving carelessly.

"It's good I can walk to the pool," Leo said in some sort of shock. "I'll find rides to Dynamo." He kept prattling on about swimming and MARTA.

Jase didn't know the way to the hospital all that well. He only had to go once a year, and his mom always drove. But he managed to find the ER parking deck with its multiple levels, each one brightly painted. He knew that at some point, this lot had been the main one for the hospital. Swinging into a spot, he waited for Leo, who was trembling less but still rattled.

They took elevators, traveled through a maze of hallways, and eventually made it to the emergency department.

"Jase." Heather McNeil, Mari's camp counselor and the Child Life Specialist, helped him take Leo. "Karen called me as I was leaving." She explained her presence in the ER when she was typically in the cancer clinic.

"How's Mari?" He breathed the words.

"Grant's with her now." Heather mentioned Jase's camp counselor, who was also the ER doctor. "I've let Dr. H know." Dr. Henderson was Mari's oncologist. "Why are you here?"

"I was supposed to be meeting Mari. A guy at the Daily Grind said something about a car accident and . . ." He shrugged his shoulders, letting that fill in the rest. Leo was now being wheeled away by a nurse. "I saw Leo."

"He's lucky you were there," Heather said, her eyes moving toward the triage area where Leo was being taken. "Their parents are on the way."

"Heather, did you see Mari?" He needed to know if she was okay. He needed the reassurance that she wasn't unconscious or hurt too badly.

"Just for a minute before they took her up for films." Heather squeezed his arm affectionately. "She was in pain but tried to make a bad joke and was concerned that her crutches made it in the ambulance."

"Okay." That was good. That meant Mari was talking, worrying about something. Heather led him to one of the chairs, handed him a water, and told him she'd be back in a minute. The edge of the adrenaline faded, the fear that something terrible had happened easing. Now shame crept in, sliding over him like an itchy sweater. God, why had he been so mean to Mari? His head fell forward again, staring at the hard floor below. The small lines between tiles blurred through unwanted tears. Shame, fear, relief—it all mixed inside him and filled his entire system with just too much.

Carefully, he texted his parents to let them know what was going on. But Jase still couldn't look up. Couldn't look at the faces of the other families in the waiting area.

"Hey." Heather came back, sitting next to him. "It's okay. She's fine."

"Yeah," he murmured. "I'm such a jerk."

"Jase, you're not a jerk." Heather patted his hand reassuringly, stopping his ever-moving fingers. "It's not your fault someone ran a light and T-boned them."

"Yeah, I get that." Sensation tickled his fingers, begging him to twitch, move, do something. "On the outside, but . . ." He was full of only half-explanations.

Heather nudged him with her shoulder. "So, you were meeting Mari."

"I've been tutoring her in AP Chem," he lied, still feeling too much. "She's had a hard time keeping up in our class."

"Mari is at AWP now?" Heather seemed both excited and a little startled. "God, you two must be in trouble all the time."

"We're at school." Jase's brows pushed together. He didn't want to talk about the way he'd treated Mari at first. In fact, he was trying to forget about it altogether. She had deserved more than the shit he gave her. "God, I need to apologize." His head fell back against the wall, and his feelings of shame and sadness washed over him. Would his apologies ever be enough? He still felt guilty.

"She's back from CT," Heather assured him again. "I'm not supposed to let you back until her parents are here, but they're stuck in traffic near Lenox Mall. I'll talk to Grant and see if I can get you back." She pulled out her phone and texted someone.

"Is Leo okay?" Jase went back to staring at his fingers, moving each of them slowly.

"Getting checked out now," Heather reassured him, still looking at her phone.

"It was a bad accident." He still couldn't believe the condition of the car, the dazed look on Leo's face, all of it.

They fell into silence, and for Jase it was like a warm hug

at the moment, not uncomfortable or draining. It allowed Jase's brain to run around without distraction. Heather, in her infinite Child Life Specialist wisdom (or maybe just from knowing him) seemed to know that he didn't need to talk, but her presence was very much appreciated. Jase could taste unshed tears, could feel his heart pounding still from the adrenaline. And he hated the useless, defenseless feelings coursing through him. Anxiety poured out of him, his fingers working their magic counting over his knee, tapping his worn jeans with each thump.

"Jase?" Dr. Grant Johnson appeared in a doorway. "I've cleared it so you can see Mari."

# Chapter Thirty-Four

Mari's head hurt. But she'd been told she didn't have a concussion, which was handy. She did have a nasty broken arm that was going to require surgery later that day. And she had enough pain medication that she was almost certain she was floating. Or at least not completely tethered to the ER gurney. She lifted her hand, the not-broken one, and watched the way her fingers drifted and almost caught up with each other.

Yeah, she was completely stoned on these meds.

She didn't get whatever Davis had from drugs. She wasn't in control of her body right now and that bothered her more than it could ever appeal to her.

"I've got a visitor for you." Heather spoke softly, coming to Mari's side. "Your parents are stuck in traffic, but I found this guy and took pity on him."

"These meds are brilliant." And if Mari hadn't been sure before, she was absolutely sure now that she was stoned because there was no way in hell that Jase Ellison and his really fantastic eyes would voluntarily be at the hospital. "Because I swear it really looks like Jase."

"It is me." He smiled a little; it did not reach his fantastic eyes. "I have fantastic eyes?"

"That was an inside thought," she mumbled, only mildly embarrassed, more irritated that not only was her body weird, but her tongue and brain weren't cooperating. "I guess I ruined our date."

"Date?" Heather asked, the interest dripping.

"You should leave," Mari said to Heather. She wanted to smile, but it was weighted down by pain medication. "That sounded mean."

Heather only smiled, patting Mari's foot, which was covered by a thin sheet and the hospital-grade quilt. "I'll bring your parents as soon as they get here," she promised. "I want to go check on Leo because he could probably use my knowledge as an actual professional."

"He thinks you're cute but that you play with dolls all day." Mari betrayed Leo quite easily. "Oops."

"I heard nothing. And I'm way too old." Heather smiled a little as she left. "And way married."

"How is she way married?" Mari asked, forcing her eyes to Jase. "You look ridiculous."

"I thought I was fantastic."

With her delayed senses, his face said the words out of sync with his voice. She hated this feeling. She squeezed her eyes shut, demanding that her brain wake up.

"Are you okay?" He rushed forward, scanning her form.

"I hate pain meds." She wanted to shake the feeling off. "I feel like I'm tied up. I don't like not being able to control what I say."

"It's okay. I won't use it against you if you won't use it against me."

He still seemed to be looking for blood or other major wounds. But he had calmed a little, bringing a chair closer to her bed.

"You didn't tell me I had fantastic eyes," she grumbled. "Don't sit there."

"You want me to leave because I haven't complimented you enough?"

His head tilted, and to Mari, it wasn't quite as slow.

"No. Here." She moved her body over tentatively. "If you're not going to hold anything against me, I'm going all out."

"I think this is against the rules," he said, but still came and perched on the side of the bed.

"No," she whined again. "Here." She demanded he sit in bed with her. "I was in a car accident, and I want you to hold my hand and tell me I'm pretty."

Jase laughed, and it made Mari smile. His shoulders stopped trying to touch his earlobes, relaxing a little. "You're pretty." His voice was soft in the way that it had been at camp, in the way that it had been on Halloween.

"You're just saying that because I whined." She pulled at him. She was cognizant enough to know she was completely exploiting this situation to get in some snuggles. With the arm that wasn't in a sling and a stabilizer cast, she pulled him closer, making him all but hold her.

She could feel his rumbly laugh through his chest as she wriggled herself closer to him. She sighed a little when his arm tightened around her, officially holding her.

"Mari, I've always thought you were pretty."

"Well, I've always thought you had fantastic eyes." Her brain cleared slightly, haze and fog lifting just a little. "How did you know I was here?"

"You were late."

"And I am never late."

"And some people were talking about an accident . . . And I don't know. I left just in case."

He twirled a curl around a finger. She could feel the gentle tug on her hair, and she buried her face in closer to his chest.

"They wouldn't let Leo go with me." She closed her eyes. "I think they thought I'd had a traumatic amputation, and I kept telling them that my leg was already gone."

"When I got there, the cop kept trying to make me leave."

She could feel his fingers in her hair, winding around the curls and letting them loose.

"I told them that it was my girlfriend's car, and then I saw Leo."

"You saw Leo?" She lifted up her head, blinking slowly. She tried to grasp the first part of his sentence, but all she could think about was her brother. "Was he okay?"

"Yeah, I brought him here. He was shaken and mostly concerned about you. Heather said he was getting checked out right before I got to come in here."

His voice paused, but Mari was focused on the sound of his breath moving through his chest. How was this more comfortable than any pillow?

"Did you miss the part where I told the cops you're my girlfriend?"

"No." That's what he'd said. Those were the words she'd been trying to understand. Even to her own ears, there was a smile in her voice. "But you said you wouldn't hold my ramblings against me if I didn't hold yours against you."

"I was terrified," he admitted slowly, his voice that deep gravel that had fueled so many of her daydreams. "And when Leo told me you were at the hospital, it was the scariest."

"I just really broken arm." Words rolled around in Mari's head like rocks or tumbleweeds unable to be stopped. "I think I missed a word there."

"That's okay."

Mari moved a little, tilting her face to look up at him, unable to really grasp that Jase Ellison was here. He was holding her, playing with her curls. It was all the things she'd ever wanted. "Will you remind me of this when I'm not doped up?"

"Only the good parts." He smiled, the one that was all softness and care. "Like where I apologize for being a complete jerk when you first got to AWP."

She felt him move hair off of her face, his fingers tucking it behind her ear.

"You were a total douchecanoe," she agreed.

"I'm sorry." He grimaced over the words before shaking his head a little. "And you have been way more gracious than I deserve."

"It's because I'm a good person." She smiled, but pulses of pain began to hum in her arm, down her forearm into her fingers. She wouldn't let stupid pain ruin this perfectly amazing moment though.

"One of the best."

Jase didn't bother with the pretense of pushing hair out of her face, running a finger slowly over the tip of her nose and just brushing that sensitive skin just above her lips. Mari's eyes drifted closed on their own, but she wasn't surprised when his warm breath drifted over her mouth. It was as simple as breathing, this kiss. Just warmth and the slight tug of his mouth on hers. A tripping in her heart, a lovely spread of heat over her body, perfect.

"Will you do that again when my brain isn't fuzzy?" she whispered when the kiss broke. "I want to remember it."

Jase laughed a little, still caressing her face, his eyes reflecting exactly what she was feeling. "Absolutely."

But he didn't kiss her again, as much as she wanted him to. Instead, he tucked her against his body, cuddling her close.

"It's been a hell of a day, Mari."

"One I'll remember forever." And it was for all of the right reasons.

"I'm sorry for being such a douchecanoe."

He said the words into her hair, the heat of his voice on her scalp causing goose bumps in the best way.

"You're forgiven." She said the words because she knew him well enough to know that he needed to hear them. "Just keep helping me pass AP Chem . . ." She paused before smiling at him in a dopey way. "And kisses."

"Anything else? Now's the time to make demands."

"Just . . ." Her brows drew together, she felt them move against his worn shirt. "Don't make me feel like that again." It had to be the meds making her weepy when she was lying in his arms.

"That won't happen again."

The emotion behind his words filled her tired and broken heart.

"That, I can promise."

# Chapter Thirty-Five

"Jase." Grant came into the room where Jase was ensconced with Mari. She'd fallen asleep fifteen minutes before, her head still tucked into his chest, his fingers unable to stop running through her hair. "Mr. and Mrs. Manos are just outside, talking with Mari's orthopedic surgeon. You might want to extricate yourself before they come in here and think that she needs another surgery." He laughed a little, giving all the grief he could. "And you should also know this is very much against hospital policy."

"I don't know what you're talking about." Jase spoke softly as he gently moved Mari off of him, immediately missing her weight, her warmth. "I have been sitting in this chair the whole time."

"Right. That is exactly what I saw." His camp counselor laughed.

Jase wasn't used to seeing him in scrubs with his serious doctor face on. Usually at camp, Grant sported some strange facial hair just for the occasion and gave Heather as much of a hard time as he could. "I know you. I know that you are just a very tactile person."

"Oh absolutely." Jase shoved his hands in his pockets. "Will you let her know that I stayed until her parents got here?"

"Of course." Grant's smile softened. "Camp Chemo makes

friendships that those on the outside can only ever imagine. Aren't we lucky to know such a place?"

Jase's throat closed. This day was too much for his brain, his heart to handle. He just nodded, looking back at Mari, her eyes a little tight even in her sleep, pain apparently seeping into her. "I should go."

"I think her parents would like to speak to you, if you can wait a bit." Grant was all doctor now. "And Heather said something about needing extra hands since Davis is at the Daily Grind today."

"She makes Davis work on Saturdays?" Jase nodded, but his stomach was tightening, his fingers itching to move, even in his pockets.

"Not usually. She was here today for a seminar for parents whose children are moving into the long-term cancer survivor program. Too bad it happened earlier today. You could have been a model patient example."

"I'll go find Heather." Had his parents attended a similar seminar? Had there been a survivor there to talk to them? His gut tightened at the idea of being on display like that. People asking him questions and wanting to talk about his cancer experience. He had nothing to share. And that was the end of it.

~

Helping Heather meant scrubbing plastic toys with a bleach solution and wiping down all of the gaming controllers with wipes, de-germifying them as much as he could. He wore a pair of medical gloves to keep his own hands from getting irritated by the cleaning solution.

"Huh, you're even worse at this than Davis was when he

started." Heather took a paper towel and dug into some crevices on the toy that Jase had obviously missed. "And that's saying something."

"Thanks." Jase knew that she was trying to make him feel better. A pretty big part of him wanted to forget that today had happened, that he'd said so much to Mari, confessed so much. Kissed her.

There was silence, only the sounds of them washing the toys. There was a buzz, and Heather checked her phone. "Mari's asking for you." A brow raised, and *that* question was all over her very expressive face.

"Oh." The heat in his cheeks probably said everything, so he didn't elaborate further. "Is she still in the ER?"

"They've moved her to a room on the floor." He saw her brows go together, something concerning her.

"On One West? The Hem/Onc floor?" Jase's heart thudded painfully. They didn't put kids on the Hem/Onc floor for busted arms and orthopedic surgery.

"It's probably just because her nurses have heard she's here and they want her." Heather gripped his shoulder. "She's fine." The words *no cancer* weren't said, but implied in the way only another survivor could understand.

But the fear in his gut was real.

Jase had never worried about cancer before. He had never worried about relapsing or even thought that his annual checkup could come back as anything other than completely normal. But now, those words seemed to be revolving and jerking through his brain at a whiplash pace. Jase felt sick to his stomach.

He didn't say anything else to Heather, leaving her in the

playroom at the clinic and making his way through corridors over to the inpatient unit. He had no memories at all of ever being admitted to the hospital. He doubted there were even nurses who would claim him as one of their favorites or something like that.

Approaching the nurses' station slowly, he saw a nurse he recognized from summer camp. "Uh, hi. Sarah, right?"

"Jase, nice to see you." She smiled from where she was doing something at her computer. "I'm betting you're here to see Mari. She just got moved in at 1656."

"Is she okay? I saw her in the ER but didn't think it was serious." He wanted to know what he was going in to. What was the atmosphere going to be? What was all of this going to mean?

"Dr. Johnson—Grant—knew she'd be most comfortable here." Sarah smiled supportively. "And we had room for once."

"Sure." This did nothing to ease his stomach or the anxiety that boiled inside of him. "Is it safe for me to go in?"

"Yeah, I'm done with her until they come to get her for surgery."

"Okay."

He followed the sign down the hall where he'd been told Mari's room was. Her name was plastered in writing on the doorplate. A sign that read "FALL RISK" on the door let everyone know that she was supposed to have help getting out of her bed. His smile was wry.

Oh, he could only guess how much that pissed her off.

He knocked lightly, seriously hoping he didn't catch her at a bad moment.

But was there ever a good moment in the hospital?

"If it's not Jase, send them home," he heard Mari practically yell. Her mother's laughter was full and not something he expected from someone who had just found out that her daughter was in a car accident. "If they would take that ridiculous sign down, I could walk to the door myself."

"Mari, hush." Her mom laughed, opening the door. "Good. It's not one of her brothers who she has offended."

"It's Jase!" Mari sighed from her bed, looking at him.

He hadn't thought it was possible, but she was more out of it than she had been in the ER.

"They've given her pre-meds for her surgery this evening." Karen laughed a little. "She's stoned."

"You should record this. You could probably go viral or something," Jase said, his shoulders lowering as tension slid off of him.

"I could be internet famous." Mari didn't slur, but her words were slow and loud. "Hi." She sighed.

"Hey." He crossed over to her, but didn't get too close. "I hear they're working on your arm tonight."

"Damn carpenters," she cursed. "Sorry, Mama."

"It's fine. You only dropped the F bomb when Dr. Lee came in."

"She expects it from me." Mari laughed loudly. "She knows I hated her guts for a while."

"Dr. Lee did Mari's amputation after she got the infection," Karen explained. "Mari told her to F off one time."

"No, Mama, I told her to get the fuck out of my room." Mari corrected the story, not even faltering over the curse. "She deserved it."

"Oh, Mari." Her mom laughed. "Jase, do you think you

could keep her from getting out of that bed for a minute? I want to call her dad and brothers."

"Mama thinks some stupid sign is going to keep me in this bed." She was so loud that now everyone in the hospital probably knew.

"Hush," her mom said again, still laughing a little on her way out. "Behave until they come to get you."

"Hello, Jason." Mari smiled, her face all serene and a little dopey. "I'm so happy to see you." She started to get up.

"Stay there." He stopped her, putting a hand on her shoulder. "Your mom gave me one direction and that was to keep you in bed."

"Well, I didn't tell her about you kissing me earlier and how well that worked, but I bet it'd keep me here again."

"Mari, I said I wouldn't do that again until we're sure you'll remember it. And you definitely wouldn't remember it now." He sat on the edge of her bed again, smiling at her clearly medicated self.

"That's okay. Doesn't mean we can't do it."

"It definitely means we can't do it." He pushed at her curls, just touching her face in a gentle caress as he did.

"Fine." She huffed, her eyes were already closing a little. "Mama's worried. She's always afraid when I get hurt." Now her words were softer, but still drunk sounding.

"Cancer makes all parents worried."

# Chapter Thirty-Six

Mari's arm thrummed with a little pain. It was mostly uncomfortable from the cast. But at least she was at home now.

She wasn't allowed at school until the logistics were all figured out. This break meant she couldn't put pressure on her arm, which meant she couldn't use her crutches. Hopping around her house was one thing—she could get from place to place easily enough—but it wasn't like she could hop around AWP.

So, a wheelchair was supposed to be delivered any day. Dr. Lee promised it would be a small-framed one, not one of the geriatric hospital-issued ones. Mari found all of this very ironic, considering she'd left South Side because she would not agree to use a wheelchair. And now, here she was. At least the arm break hadn't happened on school property.

She scrolled through the Netflix menu, but had watched every true-crime documentary out there. She picked up the book she'd been trying to read all day, but it didn't hold her attention. She briefly thought of making her way upstairs to her room to rifle through the pile of unread romance novels she'd acquired from work just before the accident, but it seemed like too much effort.

Today was the first day her mom had gone back to work in her kindergarten class, leaving Mari to rest and be bored by herself. She scrolled through countless TV shows, not really wanting to have to focus on anything, just wanting noise to sleep to. She settled on a baking show that was suitably entertaining enough that when she eventually fell asleep it wouldn't be interrupted by a car chase or overly dramatic music. Plus, she'd always wanted to learn how to bake a rough puff pastry.

~

For two whole minutes, Mari was able to concentrate on scrolling through her social media and then switched to a random game. But after losing twice in forty-five seconds, she put her phone down. Her brain couldn't focus on anything for longer than two minutes, it seemed. Mari hadn't been outside in three days, and her brain was starting to wither and die from lack of actual non-screen stimulation.

She was going to implode on herself any minute. She was sure of it.

Jase: Tell me what you need?

Mari: Aren't you in class?

Jase: It's boring.

Mari: I need the AP Chem notes and any notes from APUSH.

She had been attempting to stay caught up on her school work with the help of her computer and very good . . . friend? Boyfriend? She didn't know what to call Jase these days. He was at her house almost as much as her family, always being helpful, bringing things from school or delivering one of the meals his mom had set up.

But she wouldn't complain about him stopping by.

Jase: When is your wheelchair supposed to be delivered?

Mari: After Leo gets home. Mama didn't want me here alone when they were delivering it.

Jase: I'll be by as soon as I'm done at swim.

She was voice-dictating a reply, letting him know that it wasn't necessary, that he had to be tired, when his own reply popped up on the screen.

Jase: I can't wait to see you.

His affection, his attention—it was enough to make Mari melt into a puddle of warm, fuzzy girl. She'd never had this type of attention before, and there wasn't one part of her that didn't love it, revel in it. But she also knew that it was going to get to be too much. Jase wasn't super human, and he was going to get exhausted from the pace he had been keeping. Between swim, his classes, and now his time with her, she didn't know when he was sleeping or doing homework.

Addison: Speech is literally the worst now that you're not here. Do you have an ETA?

Mari grinned a little, still remembering when Addison had called her the afternoon she'd been discharged from the hospital.

"I just got a very interesting text message," Addison had begun.

"It must have been," Mari said, "for you to actually call me and not send a message or Snap."

"Well, when Jason Ellison texts and says that Mari has broken her arm and that I should call her, I do. Because my very first thoughts were not so much about the concern for you or your arm, but about how it is that Jason Ellison knows this."

"Oh, you know, he's just really on top of the gossip." Mari laughed.

"How could I forget?" Addison said. "How's the arm?"

"Very much broken, set with a few pins, and casted in a very charming navy-blue fiberglass." Mari sighed. "But it's still attached, so I guess for me that's a win."

"Yes, you do need the appendages that you have remaining to stay. But I think not breaking them should also be added to the list." There was a pause. "How'd it happen?"

"We were T-boned by a person who was way too involved in a bidding war on their phone."

"They forgot about the hands-free law, huh?"

"Appears that way." Mari tried to think of a good hands-free pun she could make now that one of hers was out of commission, but couldn't quite find it. "Jase heard about the accident. He got there after I'd been carted off to the hospital, but Leo was there."

"Jase was a knight in shining armor?"

"Don't give him that kind of credit. I can rescue myself." Mari laughed, but he was the bright spot in all of this damage. She hadn't wanted to go into all of it with Addison right then. She didn't have a name for what was happening between them, and until she did, she just wanted to hold it close. To protect this little relationship.

Mari picked up her phone to respond to Addison's text message.

Mari: New wheelchair is getting here today, so hopefully early next week. We're still figuring out transportation and stuff.

MARTA was still an option, but she would be completely dependent on the Access buses; the trains would be harder to navigate in a chair, especially a chair she was going to need help pushing. The logistics of how to do all of it was starting to make her head hurt.

Mari: I'm going to watch Netflix because I can. Send any love notes via Jase.

Addison: Braggart.

~

*Dreams are good*. That was the only thought Mari had, but this dream in particular was lovely. Someone was stroking her head, and when she turned her head, she could smell the familiar scent of Jase's detergent. In her sleep, they were snuggled together on the nature dock at camp, her favorite spot that no one really knew about. Unable to stop herself, she snuggled in deeper. The faint rumble of his laugh was so real that she could have sworn that he really was there and she wasn't dreaming.

"Come on, princess."

Her eyes opened. She was on the couch, Jase kneeling down next to her, his smile warm and sweet and a little amused. "This is better than the dream."

"And what exactly were you dreaming about?"

"Camp. It's my happy place."

"Even if I always beat you at Capture the Flag?" He still stroked her hair, a thumb moving over the shell of her ear.

"You cheat." She pouted a little, knowing she should sit up, be normal, but this was too nice. "You picked me up before I could get to the flag, and you know that's against the rules."

"Want to know a secret?" He leaned in a little, his breath warm on her cheek.

"Sure." Her heart hitched with his closeness, still not used to this change in their relationship.

"I only did that so I could hold you."

"Nuh-uh," she argued, laughing just a little, leaning in just a little. "You didn't want me to win."

"That was an added bonus." He rocked back a little, cooling off the tension glowing between them. "I come with gifts of homework, food, and my fantastic personality."

"And humbleness." She went to push up, not thinking about her arm, putting all of her weight on it. Pain sparked through her, a sharp intake of breath sticking in her lungs.

"Hey, you okay?" He was beside her, helping her up instantly.

"Just got so wrapped up in the idea of your brilliance that I forgot I have a broken arm." And damn, did it hurt. She hadn't taken any serious pain meds since leaving the hospital, despite having a prescription for them. In reality, she knew that what had happened with Davis wouldn't happen with her, but it had freaked her out enough that over-the-counter pain relievers were all she was taking.

"Want me to get you something?" He slid next to her, still holding on, his hands at her waist.

"Nope. Just hang here for a minute." She breathed, willing the pain away. "Aren't you supposed to be at school?" Her brain finally clicked enough to realize that not even Leo was home yet.

"Eh, it was full of useless knowledge today, so I skipped out and headed this way."

Mari knew she should be irritated, but it was too nice having him here. "Aren't I lucky?"

"Also, your brothers have been hovering around." Jase leaned in close to her ear. Soft wisps of his words flitted over her ear. "I had more time with you alone in the ER."

"You wanted me alone?" Most of her brain cells fogged over with a haze of want.

"Yeah." He said the word but stared at her mouth. "Are you on any pain meds?"

"Nope, clear as a bell." She couldn't stop the quirk of her mouth to one side, a glimmer of a smile for him, remembering her demand that he kiss her again when she would remember.

"So, it's a good time to kiss you again?"

"The best." She said the words as he leaned into her, his mouth on hers, a sweet kiss that caused the butterflies in her belly to dance and swing while simultaneously making her heart rate triple its pace. She could feel his fingers grip into her, just pressure on her skin, a tightening. She didn't remember wrapping her non-casted arm around his neck, but the feeling of his hair under her palms, through her fingers, heightened the whole of this kiss.

"Thanks for remembering," she whispered, her breath still a little ragged. "I will definitely remember that."

"I'll make sure that you have more memories." He smiled, pulling back, but not breaking contact all the way. "I did actually bring your homework. And I thought we could work on AP Chem, since you'll have to do the test online this week."

"God, you're responsible."

"One of us needs to be." He kissed away the wrinkle of her nose. "I only have two hours until I have to get to the pool."

"Okay." She smiled, unable to stop it. "Then studying it is."

~

Mari watched Jase trot down the stairs of her house, Leo passing him on the way in.

"Thanks for helping with the Chemistry!" she called, wanting to staunch any questions that might be coming from her loving but nosy brother.

"Chemistry, huh?"

"Is that what they're calling it these days?" was inferred by Leo's arched brow, something both of them had perfected over the years.

"I'm still just barely hanging on to a low B." Which was true. And she was afraid that she was falling more and more behind with each passing day. "But he also brought dinner."

"I guess he isn't completely useless." Leo stood by cautiously as Mari hopped back to the couch. "I know that you have no problem getting around, but you hopping now makes me a lot more nervous than it did when we were kids."

"I just don't do it as much as I used to." She shrugged.

"Why is that?"

Leo sat beside her, flipping through Netflix, but both of them knew he was going to pull up either *Voltron* or *She-Ra*. His hidden geek was the best side of him, Mari thought.

"Weight distribution after puberty," she said. "Boobs make hopping harder, and not being stick-thin makes it harder on my knee."

"I did not need to think about your boobs." He grimaced.

"You asked." She laughed. "I also got a little taller, so I was falling from a higher place." There was a beat of silence as they watched the cartoon, neither commenting on much of anything, having seen this particular episode a few times already. "I hope this wheelchair dude gets here soon." Mari broke the silence. She hated waiting for things like this.

"It'll be fine," Leo assured her, seeming to sense her anxiety building.

"I don't know why these things makes me anxious." Mari's brows drew together as she chewed on her lip.

"Fear of the unknown. You know it's not going to hurt or anything, but it's not something you're used to."

"Yeah." She nodded. "I guess." And anxiety was definitely hanging out in her belly now.

They were watching *Voltron*, but Mari was actually working on her homework that Jase had brought. She could do the reading, but writing out her work was a problem. She'd been dictating it to her computer or doing her best to type it out, but exponents and the like were just such a bitch to type.

Mari had checked the time for the fiftieth time in the last four minutes. The guy was officially late. And that was only making Mari more nervous. She tried taking herself through some steps. It wouldn't be that hard. She just had to sit there, let the guy figure out how tall she was, what kind of support she needed, her wants for this wheelchair.

There was a knock, and Leo rose to get it, squeezing her knee in assurance.

"Is Mari here?"

"Holy shit." Mari stood up, her anxiety melting off of her in a giant laugh. "Kelsey, what in the hell?"

"You don't think Dr. Lee is going to let someone else help you with this, do you?" Kelsey was Mari's physical therapist from the hospital. She had been one of the people who helped pull Mari out of the hospital bed after her amputation. Now Kelsey was also a counselor at camp, running the dance activity, and basically being a nuisance.

"I didn't know this was in your realm of things."

"I do it all."

Kelsey smiled, but Mari got the feeling that she was doing this just for her.

"But I wanted to make sure you got the right stuff. I know you better than some joker from Durable Medical Equipment."

"Mari?" Leo was backed against the wall, just sort of looking at the two of them. "I take it you know each other."

"Kelsey's my PT from the hospital and is a counselor at camp," she explained.

"Nice." Leo smiled. "You're the one Mari referred to as Satan."

"Only a few times," Mari clarified.

"I make my patients work." Kelsey laughed. "I'm used being called names."

"Mari, I'm going to get a jump start on my homework before I have to go to work." Leo grabbed his bag on his way toward the hallway where their rooms were. "You okay?"

"Yep." She smiled, relaxation easing over her, through her. "He's a good brother," Mari said as Kelsey got out some materials for them to go over.

"I am not here to discuss your brother, who is obviously a good guy." Kelsey immediately began to write things down. "I need to know what's going on. How in the world did you break your arm?"

"Car accident." She rolled her eyes. "I guess at least it wasn't something stupid like tripping or falling out of the closet."

"How have you been getting around? I have a loaner chair for you until yours gets here."

"Hopping or using one crutch, but I've mostly just been going from the couch to the bathroom or my bed and back. I go see Dr. Lee later this week, and I'm hoping she's going to release me back to school."

"Then let's pick you out an awesome chair." They began going through the pamphlets, Mari immediately saying no to the standard silver or even black chair. Thankfully there was no cost difference when it came to colors, so she opted for bright pink with black accents. She kept the push handles because she might need them, but still wanted the sleeker design. She didn't add a lot of luxuries or anything, knowing that her insurance probably wouldn't cover the whole thing and this was only a temporary situation.

"I don't know why Dr. Lee is insisting on me keeping a wheelchair when we could just rent one." Mari grumbled a little.

"Come on," Kelsey said. "I know for a fact that she explained to you that this is a good idea for a lot of reasons. What if you have another accident? Travel? A wheelchair is just another mobility aid. It will aid you in getting around in ways your crutches might not."

Mari didn't reply. She was trying really hard to see it that way and not as a waste of funds.

With the logistics of her new chair decided on, Kelsey brought in her temporary loaner chair, which was quite similar to the one she would get: black instead of pink, with light-up front wheels.

"Let's go test this out," Kelsey stated, a gleam in her eyes.

"What? My house isn't really that big." Mari laughed.

"Then let's go out. We'll walk over to that coffee shop where Davis works."

"How did you know that Davis works at the Daily Grind?" Mari's brow arched. She felt like she was being expertly maneuvered into something, and in this wheelchair, it was a literal movement.

"I have my sources. I also know that you've been cooped up for a bit. Let's go."

For about a half a second, Mari thought about complaining about not being dressed or needing to touch up her makeup. Jase had already been to her house that afternoon, and from the kisses they'd shared, it didn't appear that he really cared what she looked like, so why would anyone else?

"How are you going to get around the halls at school?" Kelsey asked as she pushed Mari down the uneven sidewalk.

"I'll use my foot. The floor is level, so I can pull myself around with my foot." Mari had at least figured that one out. "And I'll use those accommodations in my 504, leaving class a little early, making sure the teachers know I might be a little late if I've got to stop and pee between classes." Mari enjoyed the crisp air. Grant Park was showing off its beautiful fall colors, the trees in full glory. She hadn't realized how much she'd needed this until she was out the door.

Kelsey turned around, backing into the coffee shop with Mari. But, as she turned the chair, the first thing Mari saw wasn't the usual group of college students and locals. Instead, there was Mary Faith, Noah, and Paige. The more she looked, the more she saw another familiar face from Camp Chemo. Tiny and Heather, her two counselors, were passing out coffees that Davis handed them. And there was Jase, paying for something with a little smile on his face as she came in.

"What in the world is all of this?" Mari laughed, her soul lifting for the first time since she had broken her arm. Worries and anxiety melted off of her in a wave, leaving behind just joy.

# Chapter Thirty-Seven

In the four seconds it took Mari to take in everything, Jase decided he would do whatever was humanly possible to keep that look on her face. Her smile was bigger, her eyes brighter, happiness seeming to radiate through her.

"What is this?" she asked again as Kelsey wheeled her to the corner, where everyone was congregating.

"I think a gathering of people is usually considered a party," Noah said glibly, his smile filled with sarcasm and a lot of teasing. "Only you could break your arm."

"I know, right?" Mari laughed, accepting hugs from her various friends and camp counselors. "I need to know how all of this happened."

"Jase talked to Heather, and she got me in on the wheelchair fitting." Kelsey smiled. "And the rest just sort of fell together."

"You." Mari grinned, looking at Jase, her eyes filled with something that he couldn't quite pin down, but it filled him with warmth.

"It's not enough that you bring dinner and homework, but you coordinate parties too?"

"I'm resourceful, and text chats are amazing." He brushed off her compliment, a little uncomfortable with the adoration. Instead, he sat down, pulling a chair close to her, and slid her overly sweetened coffee to her.

"This is wonderful." Mari grinned again, taking in her friends' faces. "Thank you."

"I knew you were bored." Jase shrugged. "And really, homework can only be so entertaining."

"Tell me of the outside world!" Mari demanded. "I've been limited to the computer and my phone for close to two weeks."

Conversation flowed. Jase listened to his friends and held his breath a little each time someone came into the café. He'd picked the Grind for two reasons: It was close to Mari's house, and it was too far out of his school friends' comfort zone for them to ever come down here.

He didn't want to have to worry about who might come in, who might look at this group of people—two amputees, some adults, and even though you might not see Mary Faith's or Paige's scars, they didn't look like Jase's other friends.

"You know, if you wore a prosthesis, this wouldn't be such a pain in the ass," Noah started.

Jase didn't have to be touching Mari to know that her back instantly went up. He didn't understand the slightly antagonistic relationship between Noah and Mari.

"She doesn't have any residual limb," Kelsey butted in. "You have a rotationplasty. Those are like the two most opposite types of amputations out there."

"But she could use one," Noah pushed again. "Like the guy on my soccer team."

"You have to know that prosthetics aren't for everyone." Mari sipped her drink, but Jase knew she was simmering. "And I would expect you to understand that."

"I gotta admit, I think you're doing things the hard way." Noah stared at her. "I think you like the attention."

"I like attention for *who* I am, not *what* I am." Mari looked at Jase, then back at their friends. "I shouldn't have to be the happy cripple to be palatable to society."

"The happy cripple?" Mary Faith asked.

Jase didn't know MF (as she was called most of the time) very well. She was the same age as Mari, but didn't look much older than her early teens, her body still small and underdeveloped from treatment.

"You know, the 'the only disability is a bad attitude' person." Mari rolled her eyes. "To quote Stella Young, 'No amount of a positive attitude has turned a set of steps into a ramp.'"

"Inspiration porn," Paige interjected. "I wrote a paper on it."

"What's wrong with being inspiring to people?" Noah's dark brow furrowed. "I know I get a lot of sponsorships and stuff because I'm happy to talk about my handicap and how it doesn't stop me."

"Disability isn't a monolith," Mari countered.

Jase just listened. He'd never thought about any of this, never heard of half the things they were talking about.

"And if you're going to be a speaker and educator, you need to stop using the word 'handicapped.'"

"God, more political correctness." Noah shook his head.

"Words are important," Paige said. "Personal choices and all that."

"Look at that. The abled person over here is more with it than you." Mari smiled over her drink. "But I'm done with this."

Noah didn't say anything for a beat, and Jase wondered if he was going to double down on his stance.

"You're right." Noah grinned across the table at Mari. "But I really enjoy these arguments with you."

"I don't know why." Mari leveled Noah with her eyes. "I always win."

The conversation shifted to other things. Jase didn't bother to stop himself as he reached out, taking Mari's hand, tracing the knuckles.

"You did this," Mari whispered to him, her smile big, her eyes shining.

"It wasn't anything." He shrugged. "But you can kiss me later as thanks."

The pretty blush that filled her cheeks made him smile. It wasn't often that he could ruffle her. "That, I can do."

"How's swim?" Davis looked between the two of them like he was deciphering something he didn't have all the information for.

"Fine." Jase rolled his shoulders. "My dad is on me about swimming for UGA."

"And?" Noah asked. "You're going to, right?"

"I don't know," he said plainly. "I'm still planning on going to UGA, but I don't know about swimming." He was tired.

"Parents' dreams for you are hard to shake." Heather moved into the conversation, putting on her Child Life hat. "But it is your life."

"But they are paying for college." Davis laughed. "I feel like, as much as it is our decision, it totally isn't."

"Yeah, my friend said her parents wouldn't pay if she wanted to major in theater." MF bit into a chocolate macaron.

"And mine would never allow me to major in something that doesn't have a skill attached." Paige sighed. "I guess it's a good thing my college fund went to major hospital bills and neurosurgery."

"How are you going to pay for college?" Jase heard the words slip out before he could stop them. He looked at Paige, a little embarrassed that he was asking such personal information from a friend.

"Loans and scholarships," Mari answered for her. "It's how my brothers are at Tech and how I'll go to college too."

"Tech for you?" Tiny asked. "It's a family tradition."

Jase had always liked the fact that Tiny's nickname was the exact opposite of her, coming in at close to six feet tall, with long blonde hair. Jase had been going to camp so long that he remembered when she went by Eleanor.

"I doubt it." Mari shrugged. "I could probably get in, but the campus is bigger, and I have to think about that type of thing."

"Where then?" Jase had just assumed she'd follow her brothers. "Break major ranks and go to UGA?"

"If I can't get around Tech, what makes you think I can get around UGA?" She laughed. "I'm looking at smaller schools, maybe even a women's college or community college for a couple of years. It'll be cheaper, probably."

College and real-life decisions were all compounded with difficulty, cancer still pulling more challenges through the fabric of their lives. It was something Jase had never thought about. Certainly, he'd never had the campus size or cost of a potential school get in the way of his decision.

"Jase, fill me in on this gala," Paige said. "I got my invitation and stuff, but what's gonna happen at it?"

He didn't choke on his Coke, but it was close.

Of course. It was almost Thanksgiving. The invitations had gone out earlier this week. And why wouldn't his mom invite everyone from camp? He couldn't breathe around the beating of his heart. The force of his blood pumping through him made his head ache.

"I think it's gonna be fun." Mari looked at him as she spoke and smiled at their friends, but he saw the fear in her eyes. She squeezed his hand, trying to calm him, but he wanted to run, to go away and never think about any of this.

"Gonna throw around some of those big words you like so much, Mari?"

Noah was teasing, no one seeming to notice Jase. And God, he wanted it to stay that way.

# Chapter Thirty-Eight

Kris held on to the back of Mari's loaner wheelchair, pushing her down the sidewalk, Mari trying as she might to not be bumped and jostled with each crack and tree root that interrupted the way. She pulled her coat closer to her, straightening the gloves she still had from Jase. She was fidgety and anxious about a lot of things today: She was now using a wheelchair, which was going to cause mass hysteria from most of the AWP student body—they'd barely gotten used to her crutches—and she was dating Jase Ellison.

And she wasn't sure which one was going to bother her fellow students more.

"Hey." Kris sat next to her on the bench as they waited on the platform for the next train to arrive. "You okay?" He hadn't shaved that morning and was sporting a five o'clock shadow at 7:00 a.m. Mari was sure that Caroline probably found it rugged and handsome, but Mari thought a good shave would help him out.

"Sure." She didn't smile, because Kris would know. He always knew. Leo was Mari's confidant, but Kris just knew her. He had never needed words from her but knew what she needed. Her brothers were some of her favorite people out there.

"Whatever." He pushed her lightly on the arm. "What's going on?"

"I'm behind in Chemistry again."

"So, all of those homework 'sessions' with Ellison weren't that beneficial?" he said, a perfectly raised brow right in her direction.

"He did help. I'm just behind." Her blush gave her away in every way.

"Want me to see if Caroline has some time?"

"Seriously? Isn't she busy being a rocket scientist?"

"Her grad program gives her some time off," Kris teased. "I'll talk to her."

"Thanks." Mari looked down the platform, hearing the rumbling of the train that would take them to the Five Points station, where they would change trains, then navigate their way to the North line. At the Midtown stop, Jase would be waiting for her. A compromise, considering he had wanted to drive her to and from school every day.

Kris pushed her onto the train, not afraid to take out people's ankles as they came on or off the train. It was an every-person-for-themselves type of fight.

Mari locked the brakes on her chair, and Kris stood near her, holding on to the pole as they hurtled to the next stop.

"She's too pretty to be in that thing."

Mari's head jerked up when she realized that someone was addressing Kris.

"She should find someone to, like, buy her a leg."

"*She* can hear you," Mari spoke, not loudly, not screeching, but just with her normal voice.

"Girl, you need to get out of that thing. No guy will want to be with you in that."

"Hold up." Kris moved between this random dude and his sister. "She doesn't have to do anything. She can speak for herself just fine, and you have antiquated ideas about women."

"Thank you, Kristopher." Mari glared. She wanted to rant about this ignorant jerk's ideas on everything. But instead, she kept quiet. She didn't want to incite anything. Mari had discovered that most people really hated being corrected by a disabled girl—especially dudes who looked like this one, with his preppy popped collar and sunglasses on indoors. She now went to school with enough of them to know it.

Thankfully, the rest of the trip was completely nonconfrontational. In fact, no one said or did anything to her, except occasionally moving so Kris could move. It was an easy trip up to Midtown.

Mari shifted uncomfortably in the loaner wheelchair as she waited for Jase at the station. Kris had grabbed the bus headed for Tech. She didn't mind waiting, but she was still unsure of things in her wheelchair. Only having one foot and arm to propel herself with made her feel like she couldn't move efficiently. It took her longer, and she was tired before the day had even started.

And people talked to her differently. Like she was a child and couldn't possibly understand things. Another layer to her disability that Mari wasn't sure how to deal with.

"Hey." Jase appeared, running to her with a smile that made her heart flutter. "Sorry I'm late."

"It's fine." And it was, but it didn't get rid of the feelings of weirdness coating her. The anxiety was building and building.

"Can I push?"

He always asked. It was like he had read some wheelchair etiquette book when she'd gotten it or something.

"Sure. I'd appreciate it," she admitted, sliding her foot onto the pedal. "I can do it in buildings and stuff, but out in the world it's hard to navigate with one leg and one arm."

"Are those my gloves?"

She could hear the smile in his voice.

"They look familiar."

"I couldn't find mine this morning?" She said it as a question, not wanting to admit just how much she liked wearing his.

"Maybe the Christmas fairy will bring you some new ones."

"Don't you mean Santa?"

"Christmas fairy, Santa, same difference." He leaned down, speaking right next to her ear, goose bumps crawling up and down her arms. "I am so glad you're back."

"Well, I'm glad that one of us is," she said as they stopped in front of his parked car. Instinctively, Jase took her bag and put it in his car while she got up and folded the chair so it could more easily fit in the back. "I sort of liked my days of watching enough Netflix to rot my brain." She hopped into the seat, smiling at Jase as he climbed in. "Plus, I had my very own tutor."

"I'll still do that." He leaned into her, sliding his hand into her hair, cupping her cheek and kissing her softly over the center console.

She blushed again. "Good morning."

"Morning."

Because he was a thoughtful boyfriend, he handed her coffee in a travel mug.

"This is why I was late."

"You are the best human being ever." She sipped the coffee, noting that he had gotten just the right amount of sugar and cream (which was a lot) for her.

"Ready to do this?" He pulled back onto Peachtree, moving through the morning commuters to get over to their school on the edge of the perimeter that wrapped around the city. I-285 signified the difference between those who could say they lived inside the Perimeter and those who lived in the dreaded suburbs outside the Perimeter.

"I am now." She sipped again, feeling an inch more settled, still a little anxious, but it was resolving with each sip of her perfectly made coffee. Because a good friend, boyfriend or not, made it easier.

# Chapter Thirty-Nine

Yanking at his school-issued tie and blazer, Jase ran toward the locker rooms. If he didn't hurry, he was going to be late for warm-ups, and then he'd have to stay after. That would mean he wouldn't see Mari before she got her ride home. So, he ran.

By the time he barreled into the locker room, spots were forming in front of his eyes, little tinges of yellows, blues, and purples swirled and swished as he wrenched open his locker, shoving some clothes in and hurriedly pulling out what he needed.

"Dude, get a grip." Lucas snapped a towel in his direction. "Bartlett is running late."

"Miracles happen." Jase breathed, pushing air from his lungs, demanding that his heart rate slow and for the spots to disappear. He did not have time for whatever shit this was.

In the end, he still beat Bartlett out to the warm-up area of the pool deck. He was used to—comfortable with—the feel of slick tile under his feet. Jase began stretching, his body still tight from sitting in desks or at tables during the day. His arms hung in front of him as he bent over, as though he'd touch his toes, stretching his spine in the process.

More damn spots.

He pulled up slowly, knowing that if he did it too fast, those spots would turn into a full-on blackout. His heart pounded.

He could feel the whoosh of his blood through his neck—not a painful feeling, but one that he was sure he wasn't supposed to ignore.

Jase completely ignored it.

"Into the pool!" Coach yelled as he walked into the natatorium, clearly irritated by whatever it was that had held him up, which definitely meant that today's practice was going to suck out loud.

Jase was doing his absolute best, but he couldn't breathe. The water wasn't working with him. Instead, it was like his body was forcing through the water, not gliding with it. His arm reached over his head, pushing and pulling his body through the water, but as his head lifted to the left side, it was like he couldn't breathe at all.

His heart hurt.

It was a literal pain in the center of his chest, like a rock over his heart as he tried to pull his way through the water.

Jase didn't stop. He couldn't. He was in the middle of the swim lane, his body twisting, fighting.

God, he couldn't breathe.

He barely touched the wall, his heart thundering, the pain something he couldn't grasp. He gripped the wall hard, the knuckles on his hands turning a bright white. Spots danced and spun before his eyes, and if he hadn't known better, he might have guessed he was still under water, drowning.

Jase couldn't breathe.

This time, there was no straw. Nothing was bringing air into his lungs.

"Ellison?" Coach Bartlett squatted in front of him, irritation dripping like the water off of Jase. "You're supposed to be in the middle of drills, not holding on to the wall like you're going to pass out."

Jase nodded in agreement, but he couldn't talk.

He couldn't breathe.

"Son?" The coach dropped down more, irritation changing to concern in an instant. "Out of the water." He didn't give Jase the chance to argue; he gripped his arm, practically hauling him out of the pool. "Do you have an inhaler? Is something going on?"

"No." Jase wheezed the word. Spots danced, his heart hurt, and he could feel the blood being forced from his heart, but it never reached anything else. "Okay." He wanted to say he was okay, but the words stuck. He coughed instead, sitting on the side of the pool, others still moving through their drills, but he couldn't.

"Take five. Then find me in the office."

Shit.

He sat for a minute, willing his heart to work right, to beat normally and at a much slower pace. But it thundered, pulsing between his eyes instead of in his chest. Standing slowly, his ankles and knees feeling like they might collapse at any moment, he counted his fingers, the tiles on the floor, the steps to the mats that would prevent him from falling on the hard floor.

He dried off in the most cursory way, slinging the towel around his neck, and walked toward Coach Bartlett's office just off of the gym. Still counting, he frantically willed his breath to even out before he got all the way into the office.

"Mrs. Ellison, thanks for taking my call." Coach eyed Jase from where he stood behind his desk, the phone pressed to his ear. "I'm worried about Jason."

No amount of counting was going to make his heartbeat slow down now.

Shit.

# Chapter Forty

Jase hated the posters in this room. There were children with smiling faces, bald heads, and Beads of Courage. There were families smiling, a teenager with a knit cap sitting with his sister. Another poster for Camp Chemo and the upcoming gala. All of them motivational in their own right.

And it made the skin on Jase's spine itch.

"Why am I here?" he grumbled, doing his level best to not sound like a put-out teenager, while also sounding like a put-out teenager. "This is ridiculous." It was the Friday after Thanksgiving, and he should have been out with his friends or sleeping off all of the dressing and pie.

"Don't think we haven't noticed how run-down you've been," Olivia said, filling out all of the required paperwork. "With the incident at school before break and the one around Halloween, I thought it best to get you checked out."

Jase mentally cursed Coach Bartlett and that stupid phone call. Until this morning, when his mom had informed him that he had a doctor's appointment, he'd really thought that she had forgotten about the whole damn thing.

"Why the oncologist, Mom? Why not my GP, like a normal person?"

"Because, son, you are different. I want to make sure they

check your counts and run some tests on your thyroid and other things that could have been impacted by your chemo."

"I had chemo ten years ago." He wanted to clench his teeth. "I don't even remember it."

"You cannot compete at the level you need to be for college if we're not making sure your body is working right." She leveled him with the mom-gaze. "And late-term effects from your chemotherapy are real. Just because you haven't felt any before now doesn't mean they won't happen."

"Mom, the work on the gala this year has warped you."

"Humor me, then." She got up to return the paperwork.

Jase wanted to cross his arms and pout, but he didn't. He stared at his phone, wondering just what he would say to his friends. "You should have told me we were coming."

"So I could listen to you complain like you are now? No thanks. We're lucky they are open today. Most places aren't, since it's right after the holiday." She sat back down. "Don't you want to be your healthiest?"

"Yeah, but that doesn't mean running to the cancer clinic every time I get the sniffles."

"Please. You know I've never been like that." She softened, though, reaching out and taking his hand. "But I have noticed you've been pale. You've lost weight, and you're tired. And you go to college in less than a year. Let me mother you just a little longer."

"Jason?" A tech stood in the doorway. "Come on back."

He didn't smile. He was being rude, and he knew it. But this was ridiculous. This was unimportant and a complete waste of his time. Of course he was tired. He was swimming, doing his best to stay on top of his grades, and attempting to have something resembling a social life. Add to that the fact that his girlfriend had a broken arm, lived across the city, and couldn't drive at the moment—it meant he was on the road more.

"Dr. Henderson has ordered some blood work, a couple of X-rays, and an echocardiogram," the tech explained, wrapping a blood pressure cuff around his arm and slipping a pulse-ox monitor on his finger.

He watched his pulse rate climb and then hold steady at 101. Just nerves. It was just nerves.

"Dr. Henderson." Jase said the words with a groan. "Come on, Mom." This was all total overkill.

"It's not my fault that Dr. V retired, and we now have to see Dr. Henderson." She glared at him, telling him to be grateful and quiet. "The survivor clinic isn't open today, and Dr. Henderson agreed that you should be seen."

Jase groaned internally, completely sure that Dr. Henderson had only agreed to this because his mom raised a ton of money for the clinic. They all had to know this was excessive.

He didn't flinch when a bright-blue tourniquet was tied around his arm, just above his elbow, and the nurse felt around for a good vein. On the count of three, she slid the butterfly needle into his vein and then deftly untied the tourniquet. Dark-red blood flowed into the green-topped cylinder. She filled up four tubes before removing the needle and replacing it with a gauze pad.

"Batman? Frozen?"

"What?" Was the nurse speaking a different language?

"For your Band-Aid." She smiled at him. "Sadly, I don't have any for the teens. I could probably just tape it if you want."

"Batman is fine." He did smile a little then because who wouldn't smile when offered a Batman Band-Aid?

"Head down to radiology. They've got the orders for your X-rays and the echo." The nurse smiled. "Then come back and let the front desk know you're here. We'll get you in a room."

"Will Dr. Henderson have any results by then?"

"He's put a rush on the labs that can be done in house, but a few will have to be sent off." She patted Olivia on the arm. "But don't worry. He always seems to know what he needs to know."

Jase followed his mom. And his fingers itched to text Mari and tell her about this stupidity, but he didn't. She was with her family, school holiday and all, and he didn't want to tell her . . . didn't want her to know. He didn't want her to worry, because she would. Because she probably knew more than he did about what this might mean.

"Hey!" Davis jogged over from where he was walking down the hall and met Jase right in front of the radiology suite. "Jase, unusual seeing you here."

"Hey." Olivia was signing him in, and he didn't mind unloading on his friend. "Mom's got it in her head that I'm sick or that I have some sort of side effect from my chemo."

"Parents like to do that." Davis nodded in understanding. "It's part of the reason I hid out so much when I was using. I knew Mom would drag my ass in here in two minutes if she thought I was sick."

"Well, that, and drugs are bad," Jase teased, immediately wondering if he'd crossed some unspoken line. "Sorry."

"No, you're right. For me, they are bad." Davis shrugged with acknowledgment. "X-rays?"

"Yeah, Mom swears I've been coughing."

"Did she forget that you were a swimmer and probably drinking a gallon of pool water a day?"

But Jase could see the way Davis studied him. It was the same way others who knew, who understood how cancer worked, would look at him. Checking his color, the exhaustion on his face, his clothes a little baggy, even though he'd noticed that his socks were leaving tighter marks around his ankles. Those things that for every other teenager in the world said that they were overworked and not taking good care of themselves. For Jase, those things said that he might have relapsed and could die.

"It's all pool water, for sure." He laughed but didn't mean it.

"I can hang for a few minutes." Davis walked with him into the waiting area. "Heather won't skin me if she thinks I am helping a patient."

And the stupid hospital bracelet on Jase's wrist said he *was* a patient.

"Shouldn't you be home enjoying leftovers?"

"I'm here a couple days of the week. Part of my probation."

"Right." Jase sometimes forgot that Davis had more than just his job at the Daily Grind.

"When I'm not at the Grind, I'm either here, a meeting, or school."

"And sometimes home," Jase said. "But I hear ya. I feel like if I'm not at school, I'm with Mari."

"But that's a good thing, since you guys are dating or whatever," Davis reminded. "And I know she has three older brothers who like to give you a hard time, so I don't have to."

"It is nice to know that she's well liked and stuff." Jase

laughed a little. "You don't have to hang out with me if you have real work to do or real patients who need you."

"It's cool," Davis assured him. "I get it, man. This is the last place any of us wants to be."

And that was the truth.

# Chapter Forty-One

"And that is how you win!" Caroline crowed. "I knew I could take all of you guys at Settlers."

"I'm still not sure I completely understand what happened." Mari laughed. "Something about the robber and victory points, and then you did something else."

"We'll play more. You'll get it," Caroline assured her. "Family game night is my favorite."

"Only when you win." Kris rolled his eyes at her, but the affection was clear.

Mari liked Caroline. And not just because she brought new and interesting games to game night, but she was a burst of energy. Always moving, always talking, and giving Kris just enough of a hard time.

"I can't compete." Giselle laughed, stealing a chip from the bag Nick was holding. "I don't know any confusing games that I can bring."

"I'll teach you how to play For the People next time we have six hours to kill." Caroline was very into her random board games that took hours and hours to play.

Mari didn't have confirmation, but she was pretty sure that Caroline had probably met Kris at one of his D&D get-togethers. (Mari was only vaguely aware of what D&D was; her geek cred ended at books and some Marvel comics.)

"Can you teach me some chemistry instead?" Mari flopped back against the couch. "I'm struggling."

"Over your break?" Caroline asked from her space on the floor. "Are you sure?"

"Mari's an overachiever and breaks out in hives if she's not the favorite student in every class," Leo teased playfully, not really meaning any of it.

"Heck, at this point I just want to be comfortable that I probably have a B and could get a three on the AP test," Mari said.

"I got a three and did just fine." Nick shrugged.

"Oh, only a three?" Caroline was smarter than Mari's brothers, and it made Mari ridiculously happy. "Go grab your things, and I'll meet you in the kitchen. I love poring over chemistry reactions."

"Kris, your girlfriend is just north of our nerd standard," Nick said as Mari hopped over to where she'd left her bag on Tuesday before the long Thanksgiving holiday. "Mari, where's your regular tutor? You know—the one I'm constantly catching you . . . um . . . studying with."

"Nick! Are you telling me you walked in on Mari making out with Jason and you DIDN'T TELL ME?" Giselle smiled almost too brightly for this to be good. "This is choice news here."

"It's so weird with you being her teacher," Nick confessed. "Like, I don't know what's going to get her in trouble and what's fine."

"As long as it happens outside of the four walls of AWP, it's all fair game," Giselle reminded him as they stood, gathering their things. "You can tell me more about it while we're fighting the Black Friday crowds to the movie theater."

"You know, Nick, you could learn to knock, and then none of this would be a problem," Mari reminded him as they left. She grabbed her computer and Chemistry notebook and tried to not get a headache before they even started.

"Do your brothers give you a hard time?" Caroline asked as she sat at the table with Mari. "I only have a younger brother."

"Sometimes, but it's usually with love." Mari shrugged. "Being the youngest and the only girl means I'm a bit more of a target. But they also know I can handle myself."

"Yeah, Kris has said as much."

They stopped talking for a minute, working on the thermodynamics lab Mari was going to have after break. When Caroline explained it, it was like it all made sense. The chemicals and the potential reactions all worked. Granted, Mari had probably been distracted when it had been Jase explaining things . . . He was more and more distracting lately.

"Yo, where'd you go?" Caroline tapped on the table, jerking Mari back to the current time and place. "Are you stuck?"

"Uh, no. For once, I kind of get what's happening." She smiled. "Tell me what my brother is like at those sorority mixers."

"Mostly, he stands in a corner and waits for me to be done. He's not a party person."

"That's a really nice way of saying he's antisocial." Mari loved her brother, even if he was the exact opposite of her. "How he ever found you is still a mystery."

"Oh, *I* found *him*." Caroline laughed. It was full, loud, and not the least bit restrained. "I saw him across campus one day and made it a mission to ask him out."

"You asked him out?"

"You think he'd ever ask me out? We'd still be smiling at each other if I'd waited for him to make a move."

"I knew he couldn't have done this on his own." Mari shook her head, laughing just a little.

"Will you two stop talking about me like I'm not actually just in the other room?" he called out. "It's real obnoxious."

"Caroline, I think we're in for a beautiful friendship." Mari laughed.

"I think I've figured out why you're struggling with Chemistry," Kris said, walking into the dining room. "You talk too much."

"And from the sounds of things, making out with your tutor," Caroline said.

"Stop," Kris demanded. "I will not think of my baby sister that way."

Mari laughed, listening to them tease and flirt. She liked Caroline, and she really liked making her brothers just a little uncomfortable with her new relationship with Jase. She was going to meet him later that day at the Grind and couldn't wait to show him how prepared she was for the next lab. Maybe they could do more of that making out and not so much Chemistry.

# Chapter Forty-Two

The room was cold. Jase stood, wearing a hospital gown and not much else. Vulnerability moved over him like little bugs that tickled and unnerved him with each skitter. He stood in front of a giant plate, his arms stretched up over his head, a lead blanket around his waist.

"With the little ones, I tell them to line up with the stickers on the plate," the X-ray tech, a blonde-haired white woman with superheroes all over her scrubs, explained.

"Got it." Jase lined his chest up, reaching to hold parts of the machinery above his head.

"Closer." She pushed him a little closer, his body now touching the cold metal plate. "Great." She adjusted the camera that would take the X-ray, lining up crosshatches on his chest.

Jase briefly wondered if "X" did indeed mark the spot. What would they see in there? Hopefully, just his lungs, his heart, nothing of consequence. But it didn't change the fact that whatever his mother had told Dr. Henderson, it had been enough to warrant an appointment, X-rays, and labs. Jase couldn't help but think about when Mari had been in the hospital, the way his gut had turned when she'd been put on One West. Was he going to be put there next?

"Okay, Jason, I need you to hold your breath," the tech instructed.

He stopped breathing, counting one, two, three.

"Okay, breathe."

He could have held his breath for at least twenty more seconds if they'd needed him to.

"Okay, we're done with that one." She came back into the main room from the little area where she had snapped the X-ray. "Face that wall and the frog over there."

"Arms up or down?"

"Up." She pushed an IV pole in front of him for him to rest his hands on. "Last ones, and if these turn out good, you can change back into your clothes." She escaped back to the little room, where she was protected from the radiation that would flow into him, the radiation that allowed the doctors to see exactly what was going on inside him. "Hold your breath."

Jase imagined she said it so often that she got bored with it. That this phrase was something she said over and over all day. There was the whirring sound of the machine firing the radiation and the snap of the picture.

"All done," she chirped.

Jase dropped his arms. He tried to read something in her face, to see any of the results, anything that might tell him what had been seen or not seen in the X-rays. But she had the same smile, the same look in her eyes. Radiology people were experts at not giving anything away. They were the best secret keepers. They had seen it all.

"Dr. Henderson wants you back in the clinic. I'll make sure he gets these." She smiled again, and Jase wanted to hate her.

Back in the lobby, Davis was gone. Jase sat next to his mother, re-dressed in his favorite worn UGA T-shirt and gym shorts, even in November. He was tired but didn't close his eyes or even let his head lean back against the wall. Jase did not want Olivia to see—it would just solidify to her that he needed this.

"Jason?" a man called, holding a clipboard. His beard was white, and he looked like he could be the reincarnation of Santa Claus.

"Do you want me to come?" Worry crossed over his mom's face as she asked.

"This will only take about thirty minutes, Mom," Santa explained. "If you want to grab lunch."

"Okay." She tightened her hold on her purse and kissed Jase's forehead, like she'd done for as long as he could remember. "Text if you need me."

"I'm fine." He wanted to roll his eyes but didn't, because of the concern reflected in hers. He would humor her some more, and then they could laugh when all of this was over. It would be totally funny later.

This room was nothing like the X-ray room. There was a gurney, a computer with lots of nobs and controls, and some things hanging from the ceiling to entertain babies. A TV was up above, and he knew from his previous echos that sometimes he could watch movies.

"I'm Austin, and I'll be doing your echo today." He asked for the pertinent information—name, birthdate—and explained what he would be doing. "Just take off your shirt. If you get cold, I can have you put on a gown, but truthfully, they don't offer a ton of warmth," Austin explained as Jase sat on the gurney. "Lie on your right side for me, arm up above your head."

He followed directions and wondered if he was going to get to watch anything on the TV like he had a few years ago or if, since he was older, would have to suck it up and be bored. Honestly, something to distract him from all of this would have been welcome. He thought about asking, but his pride was enough to keep his mouth shut.

"This will be cold." Austin smeared the top of the wand with some clear jelly and then pressed it to Jase's chest.

It was more slimy than cold, sliding on his skin, pushing into his breastbone. It didn't hurt; there was just pressure and slime. On the screen, Jase saw a picture appear and assumed it was his heart, even if it looked wavy and weird. He watched with bored fascination as Austin moved the wand around and continued to gather moving pictures of Jase's beating heart.

Austin did things with one hand on the computer, moving a ball-mouse around, marking things on the screen, capturing images. He kept this other hand on the wand. "I'm measuring the thickness of your hearts walls," Austin explained. He talked a little about what he was doing, but for the most part it was just Austin, the sounds of the wand, the occasional sounds of Jase's heartbeat through the computer, and Jase's own thoughts to keep him entertained.

~

Jase had very few memories of the clinic exam rooms. He didn't have a single one of his time getting chemotherapy or sitting in one of these rooms with a bald head. Instead, to him, these checkups were like every other checkup kids got, just as normal as going to the pediatrician. He'd never noticed his mother's anxious and tight face, the way her foot tapped on the hard floor, until now.

Jase refused to sit on the exam table, instead sitting in one of the chairs next to his mother. He didn't look at his phone, afraid of what he might find. It was a Schrödinger moment for him: if he didn't look, he wouldn't feel bad for ignoring Mari. Because he knew it would be Mari who had messaged him.

"Mr. Ellison." Dr. Henderson came into the room with a smile, but not the silly one he had at camp. "I don't get this pleasure very often."

"Dr. H." Jase couldn't help but return the smile. He was southern, and some manners had been drilled into him. He wanted to make a glib comment about only seeing the doc at camp or something, but didn't. He just sat there, his fingers tapping out the familiar, soothing rhythm on his knee.

"Dr. Henderson, thank you for seeing us." His mom's voice was tight, like she was expecting the worst.

"I'm glad you brought Jason in today."

With those seven words, the color drained completely from Olivia Ellison's face. Her fingers clenched tightly around the phone in her hand, and the small smile dropped right off of her barely lined face.

"Is everything okay?"

Those three words had been humming in the back of Jase's head since they had pulled into the parking lot of the hospital. He didn't think about the way he had actually been feeling, the tiredness, the shortness of his breath, the spinning of the room at night sometimes, his times slipping in the pool.

"We've been monitoring Jason for years now for late-term effects or effects from his chemotherapy that are not immediate," Dr. Henderson began, his eyes filled with concern and warmth. "The cancer survivor program here has been on the forefront of medical science with the way that we treat childhood cancer survivors, their lives and outcomes so different than adult cancer survivors. With children who had leukemia as children, we typically see issues in their memories, growth and development, and bone issues. Jason has always been typical."

The *until now* was implied, even if it was only in Jase's own mind.

"But we do check our patients routinely for potential heart problems. He had an echocardiogram three years ago, and everything was fine. It is not as common in patients who were treated for ALL, but it happens."

"And here we are." Jase didn't mean to speak at all, but the words fell from his lips.

"Let's get you on the table." Dr. Henderson motioned for Jase to sit on the exam table. "How are you feeling, Jason?"

"Fine." He didn't throw himself to the ground and have the tantrum he wanted to have. He stared straight ahead and refused to look at the doctor. "This is a waste of time."

Dr. Henderson didn't agree or disagree. Instead, he strapped a manual blood pressure cuff around Jase's arm and began to take his BP. "How are you sleeping at night?"

"Fine." That was a lie.

"How many pillows are you sleeping on?"

"I don't know." Another lie.

"Are you waking up at night? Short of breath?"

*Shit.* "Maybe a few times."

"Dr. Henderson?" Olivia said his name like a question.

Dr. Henderson moved his stethoscope to Jase's chest, listening to the beat of his heart, the rhythm that was too fast and uncontrolled, flapping like a trapped bird. Jase tried to breathe evenly, to slow his heart with will alone.

"Based on Jason's echocardiogram today, there is a little concern. Lie back." The doctor helped him lie back on the raised head of the exam table. His cool fingers pushed at the collar of Jase's undershirt, studying his pulse as it moved.

"Your white count is elevated, too, which tells me there's an infection of some sort. But your ejection fraction, which is your heart's ability to pump blood, has dropped significantly from your echo three years ago." He manually checked Jase's pulse in both wrists, counting the little blips under the thin skin.

"Not a relapse?" His mom's voice was hoarse with all of the possibilities. "His white count at diagnosis was astronomical."

"Nothing like that." Dr. Henderson patted Jase on the shoulder, all assurance and guidance. "But your system is run down, and your heart is not happy right now." He motioned for Jase to get off of the table.

"Does Jason need to see a cardiologist?" Olivia opened her phone, ready to take numbers or whatever it was that Dr. Henderson was about to unload on them.

"I've spoken to Dr. Jefcoats, the cardiologist on our long-term cancer survivor program, and she wants you to be fitted for an event monitor."

"A what?" His pulse skipped and slid to a halt.

"An event monitor, or mobile telemetry unit, is a little device that you'll wear with a few electrodes attached to your chest. This way, we will see when and if anything irregular happens"

"How long will I need to wear this?"

"A month."

"A month?"

Dr. Henderson gave him a look that said this was important. Like, maybe life-or-death important.

"Jason, for the next month, you are to take it easy—no major physical activity, early bedtimes, lots of rest and hydration, and wearing your monitor," Dr. Henderson began to explain.

"But I'm swimming. I have meets!" Tension and terror began to skim over his back, over his neck, his ears. "I can't just not swim. I won't be able to qualify for state and colleges . . ." He drifted off, aware that both the doctor and his mother were staring at him with pity.

"It'll be okay, Jason," his mom started.

But the panic had set in, filling his gut, his brain.

"I have to swim."

"Jason, you have to rest and take it easy." Dr. Henderson offered kind eyes, the eyes that said, *I'm sorry to disrupt your life.* "If this is just a reaction to an infection, you will be back in the pool in no time, but if this is cardiomyopathy, that's a different set of issues to deal with. I'm sending you over to the cardiac lab to get fitted for your device, but the cardiology team agrees we need this data. It will help us to see how much of this is caused by the infection and how much is something potentially caused by the chemotherapy from years ago," Dr. Henderson reassured him.

"But I'm still benched." It wasn't a question. Jase shut his eyes, frustration burning and digging underneath his skin.

"For a month."

Dr. Henderson said the word like it was no time, like it

was nothing. But that was weeks of practice, meets, Jase's rank slipping each time.

"What can I do?" Jase gripped his hair, wanting to pull until it all came out in great chunks. At least the pain distracted him from the rest of the world.

"School and home. At least the first week or so. Nothing else." Dr. Henderson smiled a little. "I know that'll put a crimp in your social life."

He heard his mother continue to talk. Words were being said, but a loud whirring sound filled his brain, a near-constant buzzing in his ears covering the words and even his own thoughts. He knew he should focus on something. He should listen to what was being said. Surely instructions were being given, but his brain was filled with wasps and bees.

The drill continued as his mom helped move him from the exam room to an elevator, then another floor. It was all blending together. He needed to pay attention. He needed to focus. He needed to fucking swim. His brain couldn't focus on anything, because he needed the pool, the water, the relief of being anywhere else.

"Jason." His mom's hand was on his arm, finally clearing the buzz and bringing him back to the room. "Jason, pay attention."

She was soft, soothing, and instantly, he could feel her brush a hand over his bald head. He could see the love in her eyes, and she promised the "owie" would be over soon.

"Right." His voice came from a tunnel to his ears. "Right."

They were in another exam room, and another nurse was placing electrodes on his skin. He wasn't even sure when he'd taken off his shirt again.

"This sticker goes just below your collar bone, right side." She pressed the cold sticker to his chest.

The sticker seemed to pull and pucker his skin when he moved. He wanted to rip it off.

"This one, on your left on the bottom of your rib cage." She pressed hard again, then proceeded to hook a little black box, like a microphone pack, to the wires coming off of the sticker. "Your shirt will cover it most of the time."

"What about showers?" he asked as she switched the pack on, the little lights coming to life.

"The stickers can get wet, but you should let your skin breathe a little. Take off the stickers and replace them every day."

"But no swimming," he managed to say at last, sliding his shirt back over his head. He didn't need a mirror to see that the top electrode poked up just above his shirt line. "Can I move it down a little?"

"No, it needs to be right there to catch any arrhythmias. It's not that noticeable. Promise."

"Sure." But he knew that it was. He knew that people would immediately notice it and would ask questions.

Jase just didn't know how he'd answer them.

# Chapter Forty-Three

The Grind was packed for once. Students studying or, more appropriately, drinking lots of caffeine so they could stay up for hours that evening to continue to study . . . or party. Having spent a significant portion of her afternoon studying with Caroline, Mari definitely felt more confident. But the lab on Monday was going to be a significant portion of her grade.

She had still missed a week and a half of school with her stupid broken arm. And it had definitely put her behind again, but at the moment she was feeling pretty good. Between Jase and Caroline, she could get back. She just needed to work a little harder.

"Hey." Davis slid onto the stool next to her.

"Aren't you supposed to be on the other side?" She slid her pencil behind her ear, grateful for the break.

"I'm not on the clock quite yet. I left my meeting early and came on to work."

He smiled, and Mari thought once again that not many people in the world could pull off an "all on one side of your face" smile, but that Davis did it with aplomb.

"Nice. I could use the distraction while waiting for Jase to show up." She checked the time on her phone and saw that he was not only officially late but hadn't left her any sort of message to say what might be holding him up. Mari brushed it off as he must be driving, but there was worry in the back of her head.

"I saw him at the clinic this afternoon."

Davis said it so offhandedly because obviously she would know that Jase had been at the clinic today. She would know this because she was Jase's girlfriend, the one he shared things with, especially things like that, because she would understand.

"Oh," she answered, too surprised to say more.

"Yeah, he was getting some X-rays before seeing Dr. H." Again, Davis said all of it like of course she would know this.

"Right." But Mari's heart tripled its beat. Jase didn't see Dr. H. Jase was in the long-term cancer survivor program and saw Dr. Miller. His oncologist had retired years ago. Jase didn't see oncologists in the traditional sense anymore. Because he was cured. He was a survivor. Why had he seen Dr. H?

Mari checked her phone again.

Nothing.

Not a text.

Not a missed call.

*Nothing.*

But the door opened, and there he was, walking into the Grind, his face pale, wan, maybe even a little pinched. How had Mari missed the dark circles that were bruising his eyes? How had she missed the fact that he seemed to be barely functioning?

"Hey." She hopped to him, not caring who watched and who might see. She just needed to get to him, and maneuvering the wheelchair was too much to think about. Once in front of him, she reached up, touching his chest, his face—something that, just weeks ago, she would have never done. Then her hand moved over his heart, needing to feel the beat, the strength under her hand. Instead, there were wires. Electrodes. "Hey," she said again. Tears were too quick, stupid emotions and exhaustion. Fear. She hated to admit it, but the fear was so big now that it filled her gut, her belly, holding on to her with a sick vicelike grip.

"Hey," he said in return, cupping the side of her face, exhaustion so clear on his form. "It's been a shit day."

"I've been worried," she confessed, leaning on him as they moved out of the center of the café over to the couch against the wall, tucked away in a poorly lit alcove. "Davis said you were at the clinic." The words hurt in her mouth.

"Mom surprised me with a visit." His head fell forward, strands of his long hair falling over his face. "Come here." He pulled at her, fingers pushing into the soft flesh of her waist, tucking her around him, his breath warm on her neck and ear. "I didn't know how much I needed to see you."

His words were hot on her skin. And she wanted to revel in them, to curl around him, kiss him senseless. But she needed to know what had happened.

"What happened, Jase?" She pushed his hair out of his face, the blond strands tangling in her fingers, his blue eyes dull instead of filled with their usual spark. "What's with your new gear?" God, she wanted to make this funny, but nothing about it was.

"It appears that I might have cardiomyopathy."

The words stuck. She could see how he tasted each one, the bitterness in his breath.

Mari bit her lip, her broken arm starting to throb for no other reason than the intensity of her feelings needing to go somewhere. She was frightened now. It was the kind of fear and terror that was only felt when you found out a friend wasn't okay. And that had happened all too often.  Too often, she got the messages that someone had relapsed . . . that someone was in the hospital . . . that someone had died. These were feelings Mari knew intimately—the fear, the grief, the despair.

But her heart constricted when she thought of any of this touching Jase. She could live with the everyday side effect of her cancer: her amputation. But Jase? Could he?

"What does that mean?" she asked softly, almost hesitantly, because what if the answer was really awful?

"My heart's not pumping the way it should." Jase blew out a breath. "Or something like that. I had a hard time following everything Dr. H was saying."

"So, you'll wear this through break, and then they'll see it's fine." Mari wanted to beg, to plead for that to be the truth. "It's no big deal."

"No." Jase stopped then, not saying anything for a second.

Mari wanted to beat it out of him, to demand that he tell her exactly what was going on.

"I'm benched for the next month."

"Fuck." She whispered the word. "What about your meets?"

"Doesn't matter." He shrugged finally.

"I guess it's good your admittance isn't tied to swimming." She tried to find the right words. "We'll get to spend more time together."

"Right." Jase rolled his eyes, pulling away from her so quickly that it nearly threw her off the couch. "Because this isn't something I've been working for since I was seven years old."

"I'm just trying to find the positive." Her words were soft, but her heart was now hammering, pushing at her neck.

"There isn't one." Jase stood, pushing his hands into his pockets as he stared down at her.

"It'll be okay." She tried to calm him. "We've seen this before. It will be fine."

"I get that you want me to join your little club of scarred cancer kids, but that's not me."

"Whoa, Jase." She stopped him. "It's okay to be upset, but you don't get to be a jerk."

"Sorry." He sat down again, a deep sigh pushing out of his clearly exhausted body. "I-I—" Words didn't seem to be working for him.

His head fell forward, and Mari watched as the unstoppable Jase Ellison broke.

"Jase." She didn't know what was the right move here. Did she wrap him up, calm him? Trusting what little her instinct was saying, she gathered him close, his face buried in the space between her neck and shoulder. There were tears. She hadn't expected those. She didn't offer words of wisdom or promises of "It's fine." Instead, she let him get this out. God only knew how long he had held it in.

He didn't stay there long, instead scrubbing his face with his hands, seemingly trying to remove any and all traces of tears. "God, Mari, I'm sorry. You didn't need this on top of everything else."

"I get it." She gripped his hand hard in her un-casted one. She wanted to squeeze with both, to try and fill him with some of the strength that she had then. "Believe me, I get it."

"I'm sorry for what I said." He didn't look at her, didn't look at anything other than the floor. "God, I always feel like I'm saying something really awful to you."

"I can take it." She shrugged, but wouldn't admit the way his words had sliced her so many times.

"I don't know what to tell the team."

Mari knew this was the tricky spot. This was the moment that he was the most worried about. And God, she wanted to make it easier for him. To relieve him of this anxiety. But she couldn't do that. "You could try the truth."

"Oh sure." He scoffed a little. "'Sorry I've lied to you guys for the last four years, but I had cancer, and now I've got some sort of heart condition'?"

"It's an opportunity to." She bit her lip hard. "Then you wouldn't have to pretend like we haven't known each other for years."

"Right. And let them all know that I'm not only a liar but a jackass too."

She bit back the retort that burned the back of her throat. She wanted to be just a little mean. But she knew he wasn't trying to come off as a snob, as a guy who took his precious reputation so seriously that he couldn't be truthful with his so-called friends. But he sounded like a total snob.

"Tell me more about middle school," she said instead. "Tell me about why you made something so big a secret."

"It's not big to me." He looked at her then. "I don't remember it. How can something I don't remember leave me like this? Leave me with some fucking side effect?"

There was anger in his words, but Mari saw the pain. The confusion. The way all of this seemed to be hurting him in this minute.

"Because cancer doesn't care how old you are." She wanted

to hug him, but knew he wanted nothing to do with that right now.

"God, how am I going to do this at school?"

"I think you need to be honest," she said again.

"I can't do that."

"No, you *won't* do that," she clarified, starting to find her emotions running everywhere. "You can tell them. They're your friends."

"God, Mari, can't you be a little understanding, just once?"

"Me?" Hurt pushed into her heart, a quick punch and then an ache that radiated through her limbs. "I think I have been more than understanding, Jason. From the moment I walked into your AP Chem class and you pretended not to fucking know me."

"I apologized for that!" He sat up, words hot and fast at her. "How many times do I have to say I'm sorry?"

"I was understanding when you didn't want anyone to know that you knew me from camp or that you'd had leukemia. I was understanding when you let Lindsay and Madalyn discuss my vagina." She raised her chin, staring at him with hurt and anger. "I have been more than understanding, Jason."

"Maybe you need to stop relying on your *disability*, Mari. Maybe if you weren't always putting your life story out there for the entire world, people wouldn't make those comments."

"Fuck off, Jase." She backed away, the hurt growing like a tumor in her chest cavity, pulsating and tingling with each half-breath she took. "You get to be mad, but don't direct it at me. I didn't do this."

"No, but you made it so everyone in our school talks about cancer and how awful it must be. How terrible it must be for you since you're handicapped and poor." His words were harsh and full of spite.

"That was low." Her lips were so tight that the words could barely be said, holding her tears in check.

"Whatever." Jase stood, grabbing his stuff. "I don't have time for this."

"Jase . . ." Mari drew out his name, reaching for his hand, wanting to stop him.

"Sorry, do I know you?" He spat the words, holding his hands up like he was pushing her away, like he was afraid she might touch him.

Mari, feeling her heart wither from the words, the sting and stab of them, watched as Jase backed away from her.

"And good luck with AP Chem."

Jason Ellison knew just how to hurt her.

# Chapter Forty-Four

Jase's heart thudded in his chest. He sat in his car just outside the parking lot of the Daily Grind, his head pressed to the steering wheel as he waited for the triple and quadruple beats to subside. The part of him that wasn't angry remembered to press the button on the little device to mark an "event" like the nurse had said. Then he took out the provided cellphone and held the receiver to the pack, sending over the information.

And he fumed.

He could practically see the heat rising off his face and neck.

Without any other thoughts or really looking where he was going, he backed out of the cramped space near the zoo and hauled ass out. As he drove down Cherokee Avenue, the zoo on one side, the Grind on the other, he saw Mari come out in her wheelchair, but he didn't look at her, didn't try to see what she might be feeling, because he knew her well enough to know that it was a cross between anger and hurt. And at that moment, he didn't really care that it was his fault.

Whipping his SUV through lanes, around cars, he raced down the connector to his house. He didn't think of Mari. Or at least he tried not to. Because if he did, he might have to admit that he'd taken his pissy attitude out on her . . . again.

But he didn't think about her or his pissy attitude. Instead, he flew down the interstate toward the 75/85 split to 400. Not letting thoughts of Mari or his crapped-out heart in his head.

Sort of.

He parked his car in the three-car garage, his breath fast and tears filling his eyes, and he wanted to be anywhere else, be anyone else. Why had this happened? Just when things were going so well.

"Jason?" John Ellison had pulled up next to the car, then opened Jase's door to see tears leaking down his face. "Jason." His dad, not one Jase thought of as emotional, pulled him close, hugging him, letting him cry, even while Jase still sat in his car.

"Dad, this is all wrong." He pulled away, climbing out of his car. "I just want to be done with this."

John wrapped one arm around Jase, holding him up as they walked to the garage entrance and into the house. The bright kitchen opened up to them, bottles of sports drinks and waters with electrolytes stacked in the cabinets, and avocados, apples, bananas, and other "health" foods now filling the various bowls on the counters.

"Your mom went a little overboard." John helped Jase sit at the counter, handing him one of the bottles of water. "And yes, it feels wrong . . ."

"I'm benched." He couldn't stop the ache in his throat or the way his words sounded pinched, even to his own ears. "I'm not going to be able to swim for Georgia."

"One season won't keep you out if you want to swim," John assured him. "And if you don't want to swim, then you don't."

"Are you not pressuring me because my heart is worse than they've said?" Jase tried to laugh, but a really big part of him thought that might be the case.

"No, but it did make me think about some things." John slid in next to Jase. "I've always been the one to tell your mother that we needed to move on, to discourage you from going to camp and things like that, because we're done with cancer."

"We are," Jase agreed.

"And I remembered what middle school was like for you, when everyone knew about your past and I watched as your confidence shattered. I thought that maybe if we just didn't talk about it, didn't mention the whole thing, then you'd eventually just forget about it. That it wouldn't be a part of our lives anymore."

"Why did you let me go to camp, then?" Jase studied the way his fingers lifted one at a time over the countertop.

"Your mother." John sighed over a smile. "She's tenacious and talked to several experts. They agreed that camp would be a good thing for you. That because your cancer was now considered a chronic health condition, a place like camp would let you be with others with similar issues." John got up, crossing to the fridge for one of the sparkling waters that he seemed to like. "I argued that you wouldn't remember any of it, that it would just be depressing and most likely cause problems. It wouldn't allow you to move on." He sat back down. "I didn't want the reminder," he confessed. "I didn't want to remember the fear or worry over you when you were so sick. When all I could do was work to make sure we had money for your therapies, your meds, and whatever else was needed."

"Dad, I think this is the most you've ever said about any of this."

"Because I was wrong." The crack of the bottle opening was loud, breaking the silence after his words. "Because we can both see that we can't forget or ignore the fact that you had cancer. It might not be something we think about every day or, hell, every month, but it's always going to be part of your past." John Ellison looked at Jase then, serious eyes that were weary around the edges, smudged with what might be pride. "Leukemia, cardiomyopathy—those things are not Jason Ellison. They are small components that *shape* you, not *you*."

# Chapter Forty-Five

Mari stared at the lab assignment in front of her. The lab that Jase was supposed to help her with, the one that only seemed to remind her of the fight they'd had. Because they had never worked on it like they were supposed to.

Her head started to hurt.

Or maybe it was her heart.

Whatever was going on with him, it meant he wasn't talking to her. Not at all. At lunch, she hadn't seen him. He didn't come to sit with her. Instead, he was ignoring her, and she had even seen him talking with Lindsay in the hall. Smiling at her like he had in all of those Instagram photos before Mari came to AWP.

And that had hurt her heart.

"Five minutes until the bell." Mrs. Yother announced the first part to the class and then spoke a little lower to just her. "Mari? Don't you need to pack up?"

"Uh, I'm not finished." She knew she was the only one still working on the lab.

"Well, I guess keep going." Mrs. Yother turned to the rest of the class. "Silence, out of respect for your classmates who are still working."

*Ha, that pluralization was all for me.* Mari laughed internally, staring at the problems, trying to remember exactly what she was supposed to do and how, but there was a headache building at the base of her skull, one that said she was screwed.

The bell rang, and Mari tried not to watch as the class emptied.

As Jase all but ran out the door.

When no one else was left, Mrs. Yother tucked her long peasant skirt around her legs and sat on one of the lab stools. "How's it going?"

"Oh, you know, just another day in paradise." She was still thinking about how Jase had gone out of his way to ignore her all day.

"Mari, you were doing better before your car accident, but your grade has slipped again." Mrs. Yother obviously wasn't interested in easing into the conversation. She looked over Mari's lab report, the one that hadn't even been turned in yet.

Mari watched as she pulled a pencil out of her curly hair and began to mark it up.

"I know." She smiled tightly. "I'm working really hard on the makeup work, coming to the tutoring sessions as long as I can."

"I'm aware, but I can't cut you anymore slack. Right now, I won't be able to pass you."

The punch to her gut wasn't just an in-and-out motion. Instead, the hand that had slammed into her stomach reached in, grabbed her stomach and intestines, and snaked into her heart, where it squeezed and rotated, twisting everything around and rearranging her internal organs.

"Oh." Mari fought the tears that flashed into her eyes so fast she couldn't see straight. *This isn't over some stupid grade,*

Mari argued internally. This was exhaustion, recovery, and worry over Jase—no, Jason. "Is there anything I can do?"

"You need to get at least a ninety on the final exam and make sure all work is completed on time and turned in."

"Right." Like that would be easy. "Thanks for letting me know."

"If you can't pass the course this semester, you won't be allowed to take the second half. You'll need to think of taking College Prep Chemistry."

"Sure." She bit her lip so hard that the taste of blood didn't surprise her. "I'll talk to my counselor."

"Mari, you're very bright, and maybe if you hadn't transferred or had to miss school, this wouldn't be happening."

Mrs. Yother was trying to be kind, but it was coated in the praise that was so often offered to Mari for just living.

"You are an inspiration to your classmates and have been a benefit to our student population."

"Thanks." Mari smiled but hated everything the woman was saying.

"Just keep trying, and we'll work together."

The teacher had the audacity to reach out and squeeze Mari's hand like they were in this together somehow.

"We'll make it work."

"Uh-huh," Mari agreed but wanted to scream. She wanted to cry.

She wanted to find Jase and tell him how terrible everything was.

Because he hadn't been just her boyfriend.

# Chapter Forty-Six

Jase ran from the class as soon as he could. He was in his car and squealing out of the parking lot like something out of a movie. He could hear Mari talking to Mrs. Yother, struggling over the very thing that he was supposed to have studied for with her. The way that Mari had looked at him periodically throughout the day, the way he had ignored her at every turn.

Their first Monday back after break.

Jase's first Monday at school with his monitor. One he might not be wearing exactly as the nurse had told him to, pulling down the little electrode just far enough that his shirt covered it. The little device shoved into his pocket with a lot of prayers that it didn't make any sounds or anything.

"Where you off to in such a hurry, Jason?" Lindsay had pulled up next to him at an intersection and rolled down her window, her smile and cattiness oozing out of her luxury car and into his. "Where's your girl?"

"At school." He didn't refute that Mari was his girl, because Lindsay didn't need that kind of ammunition.

Lindsay smiled, seeming to find weakness in a situation like a stud finder against a wall.

"Right." She seemed to know that he had fought with Mari. Some innate sensor that Lindsay was attuned to. "Too bad. Want some company?" The light had changed, giving

Lindsay the left arrow, but she didn't seem to care that she was stopping traffic.

"No, but maybe later."

A horn blared, and Lindsay leisurely pressed the gas, waving to him from her open window as she moved out.

Why had he said that? Why had he given her an inch?

He went straight through the intersection before pulling a U-turn just after it, going straight back to AWP. He didn't know what arrangements Mari had made to get home, but he couldn't keep being an asshole to her. It made his skin itchy, like a sweater he'd outgrown.

~

Jase found her. She sat in her wheelchair under the overhang outside the school. Mari rarely looked pitiful, but right then, she looked worn and ragged.

But when he got out of the car and trotted over toward her, the wornness seemed to melt off of her, being replaced with relief.

"I thought you had to be somewhere after school."

He could hear all of the unasked questions in her voice.

"And you've been avoiding me all day. Why?"

"I haven't been avoiding you."

"Don't lie. It's unbecoming." She used her most affected tone, one that could be heard at the Country Club and garden parties.

"I've been avoiding you." He shoved his hands in his pockets to keep himself from counting them. There were always four fingers and one thumb on each hand, no matter how often he felt compelled to count them.

"What's up?" She stood, hopping around to the back of her wheelchair where she got her laptop and a book from the bag that hung on the back.

"I'm on pretty strict restrictions." He stared at his feet, both of them shoved in his school-issued loafers, but he couldn't look at her.

"Dr. H said you should get rid of all those time-consuming things, like girlfriends?" Her brow arched perfectly. He knew he shouldn't have looked up.

"It was suggested you find another ride." He shrugged. "Mom said something about Uber."

"Ride-sharing companies don't have to be accessible. Many won't carry passengers with disabilities." She recited it like a rule he should know but didn't. "But that's okay, I'll just wait for Leo."

"Did you get the Honda fixed?"

"It was practically totaled before the accident." Sarcasm dripped from her voice. "No, he's driving Dad's truck, so my chair will be strapped into the back and we'll look like the hillbillies that so many here already see us as."

"That's a bit harsh."

"When my boyfriend has been ignoring me all day and I feel like I failed the Chemistry lab he was supposed to help me with, well, let's just say I'm feeling a bit harsh."

"Okay, then." Her ire had changed, directed at him in a way he hadn't felt in a while.

"Whatever, Jase." She held her books to her chest, her eyes drilling into his. "I'm sorry. *Jason.*" She started to hop back around the chair with them.

"Mari, I—" He was cut off as the toe of her shoe caught on

the tiniest of lip in the sidewalk, and without preamble, her arms went out, notebook and laptop going to the ground with a thud. He didn't think, just reacted, reaching for her around the waist, pulling her close to keep her from falling. He held her close, like he had so often recently. His grip tight around her, his heart still pumping, now with added adrenaline. "You okay?"

"Fine." She pushed away with her non-casted hand and righted herself with little effort. "I can't handle this whiplash, this back and forth with you." Her hand flexed against his chest, and without words, she acknowledged what he'd been hiding all day.

The look on her face wasn't one he could instantly pull into his mind, but it was there. A little hurt. A little fear. And some anger.

"I'm sorry, I—"

"Nope. *I'm* sorry." She reached down and scraped at the ground, gathering her stuff that was splayed around her foot. "I'm sorry I ever let myself think that you were able to see past your own needs."

"Let me help—"

"Just go, Jason."

She again used his full name, and it stung each time.

"Let me be."

"Mari, if I could just talk to you."

"You've had ample opportunity. I was the one you left at the Grind the other night."

She angrily swiped at tears that he knew were definitely his fault. She still hadn't finished picking up her spilled items, so he bent down to do just that, but Mari jerked them away from him like he was made of poison.

"I don't need or want your help. There was a moment that I thought I might want something from you, that I could learn something about how to be like you. But you know what? I don't need anything you have to offer. I'm better with just me."

"Mari, we had a fight. It's nothing." He touched her arm, and she jerked away from him like she'd been electrocuted.

"I noticed you're hiding some things." She tapped her own chest where the electrodes would sit. "Don't want everyone to know? Don't want people to think your life is terrible like mine?"

"Come on." His gut twisted as he tried to think of what to say. "I'm just different than you."

"Well, there is a really big part of me that wishes I could be like you, Jason. That I could just blend and mesh with everyone around me. Hell, I would still be at South where people liked me, instead of here where I'm only seen as a diversity check-off. But if it would mean being a prick, I'm pretty happy with my life."

"Come on, I know how much you hate the look."

"Yeah, but I can live with the look for a few minutes over a lifetime of lying to myself." She looked past him, taking her things and shoving them into her bag. "Leo's here."

"Mari, we need to talk."

"About what?" She looked through him. "I'm done trying to be something I'm not. I had cancer, and now I don't. I have a disability. Not even a fancy prosthesis is going to change that." She sighed as Leo pulled into the overhang at the school in the old, white Ford pickup truck. "You hurt me. And it didn't start the other day. I blame myself for a lot of those feelings."

"Jase." Leo smiled, climbing out of the truck. "Mari said you couldn't drive her." He seemed confused to see Jase.

"I did." Mari wheeled past him, not looking back. "Jason can't give me rides anymore, but I'll talk to Giselle about maybe getting rides with her sometimes, and I can start taking the paratransit."

"Mari, we need to talk." Jase tried to stop her, taking the handle of her chair.

"No, we don't." She pushed hard with her chair, ripping the handle from under his hand. "We're done. Tell your mom I'll still speak at the gala, but this—whatever it was—is done."

"Mari." He stepped back, the look from Leo enough to get him to back away. "Come on. I've had a few bad days." He wanted to scream, to make her listen to him. "You get it more than anyone else."

"You've had a bad *year*." She nearly laughed. "I don't want your help. I don't want your friendship. Because all it does is make me feel less-than." Her voice was strained and even Jase knew it was from unshed tears. "And I am not less-than."

"You use your cancer and amputation as a crutch." He spoke harshly. "I know you don't want to hear that, but I wouldn't be a friend if I didn't tell you what everyone else thought."

"Everyone else, Jason? Or just you? Because here's the thing: I might talk about it, and to some it might seem like that's all I talk about, but it's because it was part of my life. One I can't ignore." She bit her lip, tears slipping down her cheeks in sad rivulets.

Jase was silent, his hands once again shoved in his pockets

as she stood and lifted herself into the cab of the truck, Leo taking her chair and tying it down in the truck bed. Neither boy said anything to the other. But if looks could kill, Jase would have been slivered into small bite-size pieces by Leo.

And all of Mari's words rolled and rocked into Jase's brain. There was a lot to what she had said, what she had demanded he understand, but he didn't want to hear it. Because it might mean he was wrong, and that coated his mouth in bitterness.

# Chapter Forty-Seven

Mari was in a foul mood. And her heart hurt. Because Jase—no, Jason—had decided that being an asshole was the best recourse whenever he was scared. Just like he'd done when she'd first come to AWP. Just like he'd promised to never do again. But here they were. And she was willing all of the anger and hurt to disappear into some other part of her body. Maybe the part they'd amputated. Then it would be gone and away, and none of it would hurt anymore.

"Wanna talk?" Leo asked the back of her head.

She stared out the window, watching the sun set and the mica in the asphalt reflect up at her. Traffic was stopped, which was not at all shocking, since it was a Monday and five o'clock traffic had started.

"Not particularly." She said the words, but she knew they were a lie. "I think I broke up with Jase."

"Dude."

"I know." She sighed over the word. "Like, seriously, one day we were fine, and the next it was like when I first started at AWP all over again."

"You mean Jase ignored you when you started at AWP? I got the feeling something else was going on then," Leo said. "Why didn't you tell me?"

"It was just all so weird. The whole transfer to AWP from

South and the scholarship that landed in my lap. Mom and Dad were thrilled. It was like when Nick and Kris got into Tech."

"But you never told us any of the bad stuff."

"I didn't want to upset you or admit that maybe I couldn't handle it." She chewed her bottom lip, anxiousness eating at her from the inside out. "And things had gotten better. Jase had been so nice, and we were dating, and he called me his girlfriend. And for, like, two whole weeks things were sort of wonderful."

"What happened?"

"Cancer." And she left it at that. She knew that what it all came down to was that Jason Ellison didn't want to have had cancer, but they didn't get a choice. Mari swiped at stupid tears. They only got a choice in how they handled it. What they did with it.

~

"Mari?"

Her mama came into her room, sitting on the foot of her bed and rubbing a hand down her one leg.

"Is everything okay?"

"Oh, fine." Mari was already in her bed, tucked under the two-tone bedspread, a deep maroon red on one side and a hunter green on the other. Her room being redone had been her Make-A-Wish several years ago, and it was lovely and made her feel at home.

"Leo said something happened today." Mama would know, because Karen Manos always knew. She knew her children intimately, each of them. It was like Karen could feel each of her children breathe, and she breathed with them.

"I broke up with Jase, or he broke up with me." She sniffled the words. Her face was red, she knew, from the crying jag that she'd allowed herself when she'd finally gotten home. All of the worries and anger that she'd been holding inside since the last Friday finally spilling out onto the soft pillowcase.

"Oh, Mari." Her mom pulled her close to her chest, holding Mari as she cried harder. "I'm so sorry."

"It's just all so stupid," Mari said softly. "Like, we like each other. We were friends before our hormones got in the way, but it's like we're from opposite planets."

"What happened?"

"I don't know, to be completely honest." Mari laughed a little, more tears slipping down her face. "We were arguing about stuff, and then we got mean."

"I know your temper." Karen brushed a hand over Mari's curls, like she had for as long as Mari could remember. "You said some things, huh?"

"Yeah." She remembered the look of hurt on his face. "But he did too. And we were both probably saying things that bothered us."

"What did Jase say, Mari?" Karen asked in her soft Mama voice. Not the teacher voice or the "We're going to be late for church, so get your rear in gear" voice.

"He said I use my cancer and amputation as a crutch." Her throat closed, and more tears flooded her eyes as she thought about the way he'd looked at her. The way he'd snarled the words. "And it's like he knows that I'm afraid I do."

"Of course he does," Karen said. "He knows you, Mari. What you said was probably just as hurtful because you know him."

Mari mulled over those words, letting them roll in her head, tinker around. She sighed. She had known exactly where to punch to get maximum effect.

"He went to the clinic over break." Fresh tears filled her eyes, and she wanted to hate them, but these weren't tears of anger, but of real fear. "Dr. H thinks he might have cardiomyopathy."

Karen was quiet as she held Mari.

Tears now seeped down Mari's face and onto her mom's arm. She sniffled and scrubbed at her face. "I really hate cancer."

"Oh, honey." Karen hugged her tight. "I know."

"Like, there's this tug of war in me." Mari pushed her hand into the center of her chest. "Because I know I would be different and my life would be different if I hadn't had cancer. Maybe I'd be interested in sports or cheerleading or something. Maybe I'd be on dance team."

"Be realistic, sweets." Her mom laughed. "I've always said that for God to choose you to have one leg, he picked the clumsiest person out there."

"So maybe I wasn't destined to be a great athlete, but I wouldn't have these worries in the back of my head. Do you ever think about what my life would be like if I hadn't gotten the infection?" Her voice was soft as she spoke, almost like she hated even asking the question.

"Oh, my sweet girl." Karen pulled her closer then, kissing her head. "Every time I watch you figure out how to do something. Every time you take an extra moment to make the accommodation for yourself, like when you ask for a cup with a lid so you can carry it or when you ask the person at Little Azio's to put your pizza in a box so you can carry it to your table without asking for help. Every time you do something like that, every time I see the way that your amputation has permeated your life, I think about the infection."

"Mama, do you think this prosthesis is going to work? Do you think it's going to be better or make me whole?"

"Mari Elizabeth Manos."

Her mother's cool hands cupped either side of Mari's face, making her look into her mother's eyes.

"You are whole. You are not broken or incomplete. You are beautifully and wonderfully made. A prosthesis won't change *you*. It's a tool, just like crutches or a wheelchair. It's not magic or made of flesh. For nearly five years now, I've watched you adjust and readjust to life with your amputation, and while there have been hiccups, you have done it with a grace and courage that I know many adults don't have."

"Lack of choice does that," Mari said, sarcasm dripping from her voice.

"You have always had choices, Mari. You could have given up. You could have said yes to the demands that South Side put on you. You could hide away from the world. But, Mari, you move and shake the world. You demand to be seen."

"But maybe if I didn't . . . maybe . . ." Mari didn't know what was supposed to come next. She just knew if maybe she was quieter, smaller, *less* somehow, then maybe people wouldn't notice her.

"Don't change who you are to fit in the world, Mari. Make the world change for you."

"Mama, I don't think I want this new prosthesis." The words were said before she'd even realized she'd been thinking that.

"Okay." Her mom didn't pressure her or tell her that she could be normal with a prosthesis, but she studied Mari. "Why?"

That was a harder answer. And one Mari wasn't completely sure she had a real answer for yet, but she knew that she was lighter now that she'd said the words. "It's like you said: it's not flesh; it's not magic." Her brows squeezed together as she thought. "And when I was at the office . . . I don't know. I felt like it wasn't about me. Like it was just about how the team could do something new."

"You've only done a couple of fittings. Don't you want to give it time?"

"Not really," she admitted to herself for the first time. "I remember Dr. Lee telling us that I probably wouldn't use a prosthesis, and I know that I always planned to do the opposite of whatever it was she said."

"Because you are contrary by nature." Her mom laughed a little.

"I don't know . . . She's right. I'm fast, and I know how to do this with one leg."

"Mari." Mama looked at her, knowing there was more.

"Mama, they're stupid expensive." She finally said the one thing she'd wanted to keep from her mom. "And I know that you and Daddy would cut off your own legs if it helped us somehow, but I'm not gonna use it, and we both know it. It's a waste right now."

"Mari, if you even *think* you might use it, let's do it. Let's do the PT and the shiny new prosthesis and try." Mama had that look in her eyes that she got when Mari was forced to act older than she was. "Because you're right: we would do anything for you."

"I don't want to, Mama." She sighed, a deep, deep breath that she'd been holding since that first meeting at South in September. "It's like you said: I should change the world for me. And I want to do that."

"I know it's easy for me to say. I'm ancient and don't know what I'm talking about, but if anyone can do it, it's the girl who told her ortho to fuck off."

"Oh, Mama." Mari laughed and then cried a little more. So grateful for her mom, her family. A family that saw her for who she was, not for what she was missing.

# Chapter Forty-Eight

"So, um, hey." Jase stood in the locker room before swim practice, feeling completely out of place since he was still dressed. Hell, he didn't even have his bag with him today. "I've been benched for a while."

"What?" Lucas spoke first, then several of his other teammates piped in. "Why?" Lucas's height and red hair always made him easy to spot, even among the whole of the team.

"I've got a heart thing." He didn't want to get into all of it. He'd spent most of the night before thinking about what he'd said to Mari and what he was going to tell people. "It's probably no big deal, but I'm benched for the next month."

"That keeps you out for most of the season." Lucas's brow furrowed as he stepped around the others. "You won't be able to compete at state."

"Yeah." He breathed the word. Oddly enough, there was a relief. It just sort of flowed off of him. "I'm pretty much done."

"But you've got records." One of the other guys spoke up. "You are the leg on the relays."

"I know." He shrugged. "I can't do anything about it."

"Dude. That sucks." Lucas sat down hard on the bench in the locker room. "How's this going to affect you swimming for UGA?"

"Hopefully, it won't." He didn't mention that it wouldn't

bother him if it did. That he had never been sure he'd wanted to swim with them to begin with. "But I can still swim with the club this summer." *Hopefully.*

"Ellison, I need to see you." Coach Bartlett came into the locker room then. "The rest of you hit the decks and warm up."

There was a flurry of movement as guys finished getting ready to swim, grabbing goggles and swim caps, then exiting the room, leaving Jase with his coach.

"I guess we know why your times have been slipping," Coach began.

"I guess." Jase shoved his hands in his pockets, feeling his right hand pulse against his thigh as he counted. It was like the stickers on his chest tightened as his coach looked at him. "It's nothing."

"Right," Coach agreed. "But, Jason, in the future I'm going to need you to be more open with your coaches. What if you'd had a cardiac event, and no one knew your health history?"

"Mom talked to you." His head dropped, and blood pounded in his ears.

"She did." Now his coach shoved his hands in his own pockets. "She was a lot more forthcoming than you were just now with your teammates."

"I told them the truth."

"Part of it." Coach leveled him with a gaze. "Now, I don't want to see you in this locker room for a month, and then you'd better have a note from your doctor."

"Yes, sir." And with that, Jase left the room, walking past his coach who now knew everything about him. Probably even things Jase didn't know.

He walked back outside toward the main building of the

school. His coat was warm, but his hands were cold, even in his pockets. Mari still had his gloves.

Mari.

Her name made his heart hurt in a way that had nothing to do with his potential cardiac issues. He walked past the main building, making up his mind as he walked. Most of the students weren't at school yet. Most everyone was still at home, classes not starting for another hour. Jase didn't go to his homeroom or even the lounge. Instead, he went back to his car, and without so much as a second thought, he drove home.

# Chapter Forty-Nine

"Are you sure you're feeling okay?" Olivia pressed her hand to his head.

"I'm fine." He smiled at her worry, the irritation from just the other day had melted, and now only nerves and the unknown remained. "Mental health day."

"Want to talk about it?" She sat down.

"I think I probably do need to talk." He stared down at the worn T-shirt he'd gotten from his dad one Christmas years ago. "You said you had journals from when I was on treatment."

"I do." Olivia nodded. "What I remember, and this is not something I'm proud of, was thinking that your illness was going to really mess up my doubles game." She laughed at the memory. "It was more of a shock factor, and that was just my most initial thought."

"Had I been sick for long?"

"God, it was like months of you dealing with cold after cold after cold. You would cry at night because your legs hurt." Olivia spoke softly. "I was so exhausted from being up with you at night that each time I took you to the doctor and they just said it was a cold, I wanted to hit someone."

"How was I finally diagnosed?"

"God, we were so lucky."

Olivia's eyes took on that faraway look that she got

sometimes when talking about him. It was like she was revisiting another town, another world he had been to, but just couldn't remember. Like a dream you know you had, but you can't find the plot points to tell about it.

"A resident was doing something at your ped's office that day. She saw the bruises on you, your little legs just covered, which we'd all dismissed as just being a preschooler. She suggested a CBC just to be safe, and that was that. The next thing I knew, we were being loaded into an ambulance and taken to Children's."

"Where was Dad?"

"Germany." Olivia scoffed. "He caught the first flight home, but between layovers and things, it took him a whole day."

"But I remember Gramma and Pops came." His mom's parents didn't live in Atlanta, having had to drive down from Raleigh. "They were here."

"You remember that?"

"I remember Gram taking me to the gift shop and basically buying me whatever I wanted." Jase laughed. "It was a free fall of candy, and Gramma never gave me candy."

"She did that while I was having a conference call with the doctors and your dad in some airport in Europe. I was having to sign all of these forms for procedures and trying to learn this new language that the doctors and nurses were speaking."

"Were you scared? I don't ever remember you being scared."

Olivia teared up, grabbing his hand and holding it tightly in hers.

"I was petrified." She didn't laugh over the words or try to make them any easier to swallow. "My baby was sick. Your counts were so high they had a hard time doing your initial bone marrow aspiration."

"What does that mean?" He didn't speak this language. He knew what these things were from his friends, from camp, but it wasn't completely fluent for him.

"Your white cells were spreading so rapidly, killing off all of your other cells, making no room for anything else in your body. It made extracting the bone marrow difficult," Olivia told him. "You were sedated, thankfully. But then the doctors were explaining your port and asking if we were adverse to blood transfusions from unknown donors, if we had a priest or pastor, just all of these things, and I was trying to answer everything while taking care of you."

Jase listened. He'd never heard this side of the story. Had never wanted to. He had spent most of his life running as far away from this story as he could. At camp, when others had shared their stories or discussed what it was like, he'd listened. He'd understood on some level, but not this one. Not the one where it was him and his life that were in jeopardy.

"I could have died," he finally said. And for the first time ever, he allowed that thought in his brain. His family had thought he might die. That it had been a real possibility.

"You could have." She nodded, seeming to understand that this was just now falling into his heart, his brain. "That was my fear every day for three years. Because even once you went into remission, I was terrified of what the chemo was doing to you. What the side effects were. What if you got an infection? When you were first diagnosed, I went to the parents' support group, and I heard a mom say that it felt like the *disease* wasn't killing the kids, but *infections*, the *treatments*. And as much as I tried to see your chemo as lifesaving, it was hard to see it that way. I held my breath for three years."

"I didn't know."

"Well, I couldn't tell my three-year-old that I was terrified he might die from the medicine I made him take." His mom laughed a little. "But I had the parents' support group. I had the other parents from Camp Chemo."

"I didn't know that you ever talked to any of the parents from camp." He whispered it, thinking back to his first summers at camp, trying to find a memory of his mom seeing a friend or someone he didn't know.

"Hold on." His mom got up, walked back to her office, and came back out with some notebooks and a photo album. "These are my journals and a photo album that I put together." She flipped through the pages before stopping on one of their entire family in front of the lake at Camp Chemo.

It was a spot he knew in his heart, his soul, but he had no recollection of either of his parents being there. His parents looked like they did now. His mom's hair had been longer in the picture, and his dad had less gray and probably a little more on top, but other than that, they looked the same. He didn't really recognize himself, though. The little boy in the picture was bald, just dark shadows and wisps of hair on his head. His eyes seemed huge on his face without the help of eyebrows, eyelashes, or hair to break it all up.

"When was this?"

"Just a few months into your treatment. Dr. V met us as we pulled into the parking lot to tell us that you were officially in remission." His mom's eyes clouded with tears at the memory. "And I hugged him."

"This was a family camp weekend?"

"Yeah, we stayed in one of the cabins and did camp stuff. It was the first time I'd seen you laugh in months." Now his mom reached forward and pushed hair off of his face. "It was the first time I thought we might make it through all of this intact." She ran a hand over the journals, fingering some of the pages before handing them to him. "It can't hurt you to look through some of this. It's your history." Olivia got up, leaving him with a kiss on the head and moving into her office.

"Okay." He said the word to himself as if preparing for what he might see.

With a little trepidation, he opened the first journal and started to read.

*Jason was officially diagnosed with acute lymphocytic leukemia today at 3:20 p.m. His oncologist is Dr. Vega and the team at Children's. We're currently inpatient on One West in room 1124, and our primary nurse is Lesa. Jason will have a small surgery tomorrow to implant his port and will immediately begin his first round of chemotherapy.*

The journal entry went on. It was almost clinical as his mother's neat script detailed his drugs, the dosages, and what the side effects he experienced were. Turned out Jase was allergic to Vancomycin, a heavy-duty antibiotic. It was probably something he should know in case he ever filled out forms for himself.

He read through the accounts of his first few rounds of chemo. A lock of his curls was taped to the pages from before his hair had started to fall out. Some of the passages were short, just saying that his mom hadn't had to hold him down that day for them to access his central line, that he'd lay there quietly and whispered to himself over and over that this was not an owie. Jase could read all of this, and it was like the story of some other child, not him. But then there were other passages that would trigger a memory so keen in his mind's eye that it was as if he was there all over again.

*"Okay, Jason, let me look in your ears." Dr. V held up the otoscope and looked through his ear. "Just a bunch of squirrels." The doctor tickled his tummy, and they both laughed.*

*Jason liked Dr. V. He was always honest with him, always told him when something would hurt and for how long. He let Jason play with his stethoscope and sometimes would let Jason look in his ears. Dr. V was funny and took care of him—his mama said so. And Mama didn't tell lies.*

Jase could practically feel the way Dr. V would press on his neck, feeling for any swollen glands. He could smell the antiseptic handwash everyone used, and it was visceral. He could practically taste it as the memories sat in his brain.

The entries became further apart. They still detailed each visit, what his counts had been, what Dr. V had told them, when he had officially been moved over to the cancer survivor program. When Dr. V had told them that he was retiring before Jase would return. His mom had cried while simultaneously thanking the doctor.

It hadn't bothered him the way it had obviously bothered his mother. He had never thought going to camp was a waste of time, like it seemed his dad had as Jase got older. He laughed at the entry from when he got home from camp and his mom had been so worried about everyone calling him Jase instead of Jason. He'd almost forgotten that it was at camp that he had gotten that nickname. That it was at camp that he came into his own that year. That he'd felt like his own person for the first time.

# Chapter Fifty

Sitting in the lobby of Dr. Lee's office was exactly how Mari wanted to spend the first day of winter break.

Especially because it meant she was getting her cast off. The lobby of her ortho's office was a weird mixture of adults and children. Dr. Lee also had adult patients, performing surgeries for hip replacements, as well as more experimental surgeries. Mari sat there, looking a little more pitiful than normal with her hand in the cast and missing a leg. But she busied herself with her phone, refusing to look at the pity the adults were sending her.

Mari: I want a shirt that reads "My leg tried to kill me."
Davis: You must be getting your cast off.
Mari: Are you around?

Mari wasn't sure where Davis was spending his winter break: the hospital or the Grind.

Davis: I'm around, but I've got another patient I'm with.

Mari thought that over. Davis was really good about not talking too much about the patients he saw at the clinic, privacy laws and things, but she also knew that it must be Jase. She didn't know how she knew this exactly. Only that Christmas break had started, which meant it had been about a month since his initial appointment.

Had it really been almost a month since she'd spoken with him?

She saw him at school, but . . . but it all sort of still hurt when she saw him. The ache was real and fast and still made her want to throw up a little.

**Mari: Will you tell him I'm sending good thoughts?**

**Davis: You bet.**

"Mari?" Dr. Lee's nurse called from one of the doors. "Let's get an X-ray."

Mari pulled herself with her one foot, then let the nurse take over, pushing her to the X-ray room. By this point, Mari knew the routine. They moved her as close to the large table as they could, and she placed her hand, palm down, on top. She heard the snap of the picture and then rotated her wrist for the next view while the X-ray tech changed out the films. Another snap, and then the nurse was back and wheeling Mari to an exam room.

"Can you tell my brother and his girlfriend to come in?" Mari asked. "I don't like the sound the saw makes."

"Of course." The nurse smiled before heading out. A few minutes later, Kris and Caroline bounded in, followed immediately by Dr. Lee.

"Any words for me today, Mari?" Dr. Lee asked, eyeing her with a small smile and a challenge in her eyes.

"Only if you tell me I have to keep this cast on." Mari smiled. "I'm ready to ditch this incredibly awesome chair."

"Sorry to be a downer, but I don't want you walking for at least a week, so around Christmas."

"Bitch." Mari said it, but didn't really mean it. And Dr. Lee knew that.

"But let's get this off. Want me to preserve it so you can take it home?"

"And what? Put it with my collection of leg casts? No, thanks," Mari said. She hadn't had anyone sign it or anything. She didn't understand the appeal of keeping casts. They were smelly.

"Wonderful." Dr. Lee smiled, pulling out the saw.

Mari immediately reached for Kris's hand with her left hand and turned toward him. "I really hate this part."

"I've never nicked anyone," Dr. Lee said proudly.

"And there's always a first," Mari mumbled, squeezing Kris's hand as the saw started up and the doctor put the saw to the cast. There was pressure and a vibration, and it was loud. Maybe it was the noise that really bothered Mari, but she squeezed her eyes shut anyway. The heat from the spinning blade made Mari itch to move, to get away, but she squeezed her brother's hand tighter. And when it got so hot she didn't think she could stand it anymore, there was a release, and relief was instant.

"Well. Look at that. My record remains intact," Dr. Lee teased, pulling the cast apart, the gauze and padding pulling apart.

Inside was Mari's shriveled arm, a pale white with crusty skin around where the edge of the cast had once been.

"And you didn't take off another appendage," Mari joked. "Nice work."

"Okay, lift your arm out." Dr. Lee took Mari's grief with a grain of salt.

Slowly, Mari lifted her arm, the air cooler on the newly exposed skin than any other part of her body.

"How's it feel?"

"Attached. Cold." She hadn't tried to flex it yet, waiting on the instructions. "Want me to bend it?"

"Give me a slow rotation," Dr. Lee encouraged. "Just until you feel any pain."

Mari did as she was asked, surprised by her own range of motion, but knew the order to wait on walking was a good one. There were more instructions before she was allowed to go, along with a prescription for PT, and that meant grueling sessions with Kelsey.

But she was out of the cast.

# Chapter Fifty-One

Jase was a little disappointed it wasn't Santa Austin doing his echocardiogram today. He thought it would have been fitting, since it was the first day of winter break. Instead, it was Steve who held the wand pressed to Jase's chest, moving the slime around, getting images of his heart. Steve had been kind enough to leave *SpongeBob* playing on the TV, and Jase tried to concentrate on it, what exactly was happening in Bikini Bottom that day.

But all Jase could think about was what Steve might be seeing on the screen. He talked to Jase some. Asking what he thought UGA's chances were in the playoffs. Jase hadn't even realized that they were playing in the playoffs, which said a lot about where his head had been these past three weeks since his last echocardiogram.

"Steve, can you tell me what my ejection fraction is?" Jase asked tentatively. "Or just if it's bad or good?" Because Jase didn't know what his numbers had been before, but he had spent the last three weeks googling what was good and what was not so good. What could be done if his continued to come back as not so good.

"Sorry." Steve looked at him sympathetically. "Against hospital policy. The radiologist has to read it first to get the official result."

"But Dr. H will be able to tell me something." His heartbeat felt like it was pumping out of his chest. He'd spent three weeks counting down to this appointment and whether or not he would be living with a heart condition for the rest of his life.

"Oh sure." Steve's smile was friendly. "Can you roll on your back?"

Jase did as he was asked and once again went back to watching *SpongeBob*, but his brain was anywhere other than Bikini Bottom.

~

Anxiety whirled around in his body. For the first time in recent memory, sitting in the lobby at the clinic made Jase feel sick. He briefly thought about asking the nurse for one of those blue emesis bags, but instead took deep breaths. He turned to his mom and his dad. Neither of them looked much better.

Jase could honestly never remember his dad coming with them to any of his appointments, which made this one feel all the more real, all the more serious. Because John Ellison was sitting there next to Jase's mother, holding her hand and not checking his email. Jase sighed, trying to clear out all of the bad air and feelings.

"Hey." Davis slid into the seat next to him.

"I didn't know you'd be here today." Jase was both relieved and filled with dread.

"I might have asked Heather when your follow-up appointment was." Davis smiled at him. "You don't have to do all of this alone."

"I know, but I forget."

"We all do," Davis said. "But I guess that's one of the great things about camp: like, we all get it." He paused for a second. "Video game?"

"Yes." It was said with relief. "Mom, we're gonna go play the video games in the exam area."

"Okay. I'll have them find you when they're ready." She smiled tightly, gripping his dad's hand even tighter.

Davis led him back, away from the noise and anxiety that often filled the clinic lobby. But what else could there be in a clinic for hematology and oncology patients? Jase didn't see the little kids who were trading Pokémon cards or the parents who weren't just discussing what they were there for, but also trading recipes, as well as the best way to get the numbing cream to work.

"How're you feeling?" Davis asked as they sat at the tabletop *Ms. Pac-Man*.

"Better, I think," Jase said. "I'm not sleeping on four pillows or waking up feeling like I'm breathing through a straw."

"That's got to be a good sign."

"I hope so," Jase agreed. "But I don't want to get my hopes up. I don't want to be let down when I can't swim the rest of the season or my heart is in fact in the toilet and I need a transplant or something."

"Is that a possibility?" Davis had concern all over his face, but not a lot of fear.

"I guess, but I don't think it's that bad," Jase admitted. "Did you know that I washed toys for Heather back after Mari's car accident and she said I sucked worse than you did?"

"Did you lick the toys? Because I didn't think anyone could ever be worse than me." Davis laughed, but it trailed off. "Want to tell me about Mari?"

"Not really." Jase's voice was soft.

"She hasn't said much to me." Davis shrugged. "But I think she's protecting you."

"Which I totally don't deserve." Jase chased the ghosts around the screen, not looking at his friend, but still thinking about Mari and all of that. "When she first got to AWP, I pretended I didn't know her."

"Wait, what?" Davis stopped playing then, and Jase could feel his stare. "You pretended not to know Mari?"

"Yeah. I was really freaked out. No one at AWP knows that I had leukemia, and her being there . . ." Jase trailed off because he knew he sounded completely ridiculous.

"But now everyone does, right? Like when y'all started dating or whatever."

"No," Jase admitted, gesturing to the clinic walls around them. "So, I mean, she has a really great reason for not talking to me."

"And then?" Davis said, obviously trying to piece it all together.

"We fought some more." Jase looked at his friend, feeling like a total jerk. "I screwed up, and that's just that."

"Jason?" His dad called from around the corner. "They're ready for us in room 10."

"Okay." He shrugged to Davis. "I guess it's time to find out my fate."

"Whatever it is, it'll be okay," Davis said.

# Chapter Fifty-Two

Late-afternoon light filled the boutique near Midtown Atlanta. Absently, Mari flexed her now un-casted wrist, the scar a bright pink down the inside of her wrist. Her mama had been right: she hadn't been allowed to walk out of Dr. Lee's office a few days ago, but Mari being Mari had been walking on her crutches the next day. And there was no looking back. Giselle and Mama were rifling through racks of dresses and formal wear while Mari went to find the saleslady.

"Hi, there." Mari smiled at the lady in the dressing room nook of the Atlanta Junior League's secondhand shop. "I'd like to try on these." She held up a couple of floor-length dresses that her mom and Giselle had found for her. This time of year, the department stores had them for the parties, but even at the less-expensive stores, they were out of Mari's price range. She already hated that she was spending money she'd marked for Christmas presents for this stupid dress. But she was not going to ask her parents for money for it.

"Oh sure!" The older woman—clearly this was her after-retirement job—jumped to it. "These are just lovely!" She took the dresses from where Mari had been holding them under her arm, pressed against her side, but they'd still dragged over the carpeted floor. "Let's see. Right in here."

She pushed back a curtain, opening a small nook. There

was a long floor-length mirror, and that was about it. No bench or stool, just some old hooks and the mirror on the walls.

Mari smiled pleasantly. "I hate to be a bother, but do you have an accessible changing room?" She gestured awkwardly to her very-hot-pink forearm crutches. Just in case the lady had completely missed the fact that Mari was disabled.

"Oh, of course. How thoughtless of me." The lady backed out of the nook and moved to the end of the changing area, where there was a larger curtained-off area. "We usually use this for storage overflow. I forget about it sometimes."

"Right." Mari smiled through the explanation because she'd heard it at least three times before. She stood out of the way, pressed against a wall as the lady moved a clothing rack with dresses and other clothes out of the room before going back in and hanging up the dresses Mari had on the hooks.

"Here you are!" The saleslady motioned to the room like it was the Showcase Showdown on *The Price Is Right*.

"Great." Mari walked in, looked, and then put on her biggest smile again. "I am so sorry to ask, but do you have a stool? Or a chair I could use?" Because she was going to have to sit down to try on these dresses. She wasn't sure how, other than this being a larger nook with a three-sided mirror, that the owners thought this might be accessible. But she bit her lip and smiled.

"Oh." This seemed to startle the woman. Like Mari had asked for her to find an antique fainting couch instead of a folding chair. "Let me see what we've got."

So now Mari stood in the dressing room and waited.

"Here we go!" A tan metal folding chair with paint that

was chipping was provided like it was indeed that antique fainting couch.

Mari smiled, but was internally grimacing because that stupid thing was going to be cold on her butt when she sat down. But at least she had something.

Moments later, she stood in a dressing room in her bra and underwear and briefly wondered why they didn't use better lighting in these places. Mari wasn't thin. She was round, with hips and breasts, and needed to really think about buying a new bra. But bras were not cheap, and she didn't understand spending that kind of money on something no one was going to see. Her stomach wasn't flat; it had two rolls separated by her belly button.

She slipped a column of silk over her head, dark midnight blue that had a corset that laced up the back. It was her pick, the one she wanted to look amazing on her at the gala in just a few weeks.

But as she looked in the mirror, it was anything but.

The top was just a little too tight, pushing at her breasts, making her look smushed and out of proportion. But the bottom was what made it look incredibly weird. Instead of flowing out like a bud vase around her leg, it clung to her residual tissue, scooping under where her leg should be and then flowing down, highlighting the fact that she was missing a leg.

She stood staring at herself in the three-way mirror. Nothing about this dress worked. Not the top and definitely not the bottom.

"Can I come in?" Mama and Giselle were right outside.

"Sure." She knew Mama would see the same things. The cupping around her missing leg, the unflattering top. "I guess it was just too much to wish for." Mari sighed, running her hand down her right hip where her leg should be.

"Yeah, it's just not a good cut," Karen agreed. "Try the other one." It was red and more of an A-line cut, which they both knew would flatter her more.

"Sure."

"I'm going to go back out and keep looking," Giselle said, but Mari could see the sadness in her eyes. The want for the dress to just magically fit better and be better. "I'm sure there's something here."

"Thanks!" Mari said, sitting on the chair and undoing the hidden side zipper before pulling the dress off. It was such a pretty dress, and she'd already thought of the shoes she might wear or the earrings she could maybe borrow from Ellie. Maybe the red would be better.

Slipping it over her head, she knew instantly that it fit better. She didn't feel squished, and it flared out nicely from her waist. But the dress itself was nothing special. There were no pretty embellishments or sparkles to catch in the light. It was just a red dress, with simple cap sleeves and a belt.

"I think this was a bridesmaid's dress!" Mari called through the curtain. "I mean, it's fine, just plain."

"It fits nice." Karen came into the room and straightened the sash around the back. "But you're right: it does have that polyester feel of a bridesmaid's dress." She turned to Giselle. "Something to keep in mind if Nick ever gets his act together."

Giselle laughed. "Oh, he knows. But honestly, I think I'm just going to propose and get it over with. He can wear the ring, and it'll be great."

"I love that idea." Karen smiled. "After basketball season."

Nick didn't plan on trying to go pro. Instead, he was looking at master's programs.

"There's a really mean part of me that likes the idea of doing it, like, at his last game or something, but he'd hate that kind of attention."

"True. When we threw a surprise party for him when he was seventeen to make up for the fact that he didn't have a big sixteenth party, I thought he was going to disown us." Karen laughed.

Mari remembered it all because it had been just a year after her amputation. That had been why they'd missed Nick's sixteenth birthday.

"Let me change. Unless you found anything else?" Mari changed the subject.

"I did find one thing, but it's not your typical style." Mama held up a black dress. It was a fitted strapless top with a high-low black skirt and sheer black panels breaking up black silk. "Giselle assures me that it's appropriate for the gala."

"And if it works, we could find you a black shrug or something to go over your shoulders if you're worried about it."

"Can't hurt to try." It wasn't Mari's style. Nothing about this dress said prom. It was classic and refined with a name brand that even Mari knew. The price tag wasn't attached, which made Mari just a little suspicious, but she tried it anyway.

The top flattered her chest for once, instead of making her look weird. It had the tiniest bit of a sweetheart neckline, accenting her collarbones and making her neck look longer. She imagined if she wore her hair up, she might look like a ballerina or something. The skirt draped out over her hips, the front reaching just below her knee and the back just brushing the ground. With the right flats—because she was not going to wear any sort of heels on a night when she would definitely be standing all night—it wouldn't even need to be hemmed.

"Mama? Giselle?" She called once she had the dress zipped.

They both stepped in, and Mama's voice hitched a little. "Well, that's lovely."

"And it doesn't look like a bridesmaid's dress." Giselle eyed her a little more shrewdly. "A little pendent necklace, nothing too big or flashy. Some studs for earrings. Or simple hoops. Your hair down. We could blow it out."

"And I have a velvet cape," Karen said, just remembering. "It'll be perfect."

"Did you find everything?" The saleslady was back with a beaming smile.

"Yeah." Mari smiled. "We did."

The saleslady explained that the dress had been sitting on the rack for a while—which Mari didn't believe for a minute—and gave Mari a big discount on it. Mari knew better. Mari knew that this lady was taking pity on her and all but giving her the dress. But given that so much of her meager salary from the bookstore was going to this stupid event, she didn't much care.

Just then, a vibration in her pocket from her phone surprised her, but not nearly as much as who the text was from.

**Jase: Can we talk?**

# Chapter Fifty-Three

Jase debated going to the Daily Grind. It was the spot they met at the most, but instead he sat outside of Mari's house, waiting for her to get home. He didn't know what to do, how to feel, what anything really meant at the moment. But as he'd left the hospital with his parents, still unable to really process anything, he knew that Mari's would be a safe place.

He sat on the porch swing, not wanting to face Leo or one of her other brothers, not sure what he'd say to them anyway. Her mom and Ms. Austin went in through the side kitchen door, giving him and Mari privacy that he probably didn't deserve.

"Hi." He didn't shove his hands in his pockets like he wanted to. Instead, his fingers typed on his pants like he was writing a dissertation.

"Hey."

She stood in front of him on her crutches, and he realized that her cast was gone. And he hadn't even known she'd had a doctor's appointment coming up. God, he was the biggest tool.

"I needed to talk to you." He finally worked the words out.

"Okay." She still didn't sit. Her very being was imposing at the moment. "Talk."

"I didn't handle things right the other day."

"Which day in particular?" She arched that brow that could either make him laugh or, like right now, make him sweat.

"Pick one. All of them." He breathed out the words. "I had been feeling crappy for months, almost since the start of school, but I could ignore it." He chewed on his lips, nerves overriding almost everything.

"But then you couldn't," she filled in, sitting down on the swing with him, but not close.

Not like before when she would all but crawl into his lap, grip his hand, touch his face. This was Mari from school, not even the Mari from camp who had been his friend.

"Yeah." His gaze dropped, and he stared at his shoes, but they never offered any answers.

"Do you feel okay?" She started to reach out to touch him but jerked her hand back.

"Tired," he admitted. "I get short of breath sometimes and a little dizzy."

"Oh, Jase," she whispered his name. "Why didn't you say anything?"

"I didn't know that I had anything to talk about," he admitted slowly. But he held it in his heart that she had called him Jase.

"I'm sorry." She said the words so easily, like they didn't take anything from her. "How was your appointment? And before you get mad, Davis didn't tell me, but why else would you want to see me?"

"I missed you," he said to her question. "And I did go back to Dr. H today." He pulled his coat tighter around him. Not sure if he was cold from the December air or the news.

She didn't come closer, but he could see the concern in her

face, her brown eyes filled with kindness. The day was done, and he was exhausted from . . . everything.

"Want to tell me?" She didn't press, didn't come closer and beg him to tell her all of it.

"So, after most of my life barely knowing that I had leukemia, it did leave me something to remember it by."

"Oh, Jase." She sighed his name with understanding and sadness.

"According to Dr. H and my new cardiologist, my ejection fraction isn't terrible by cardiomyopathy standards, but it's enough to warrant daily medication and monitoring."

"Swimming?"

"Fine." He shrugged. That had been the least of his concerns. "I can even rejoin the team, but I'm not sure if I'm going to."

"But you're supposed to swim for UGA in the fall."

"I was never sure I really wanted to, and this month off has been . . . an experiment of sorts, to see what my life would be like without swimming. And while I miss the ability to work out my frustrations and irritations in the water whenever I want, I don't want to compete anymore."

"What exactly does the cardiomyopathy mean? Like, I know about it on a basic level because it's been part of my survivorship plan forever, but I'm not sure what it is."

"My heart doesn't pump out blood as efficiently as it should. There's a number scale they use, and anything over fifty is fine. Below that, and you get the classification of cardiomyopathy."

"What's your number, Jase?"

"Forty. It's not terrible, and my cardiologist seems to think that if I take my meds and behave, it could potentially get better."

"What's 'behave' mean?" She eyed him suspiciously. "I've known you for a while. Behaving isn't your strong suit."

"Oh, take my meds, rest when I need to, weigh myself every day and see if I'm retaining fluid. Be healthy generally. Work out, but not to exhaustion. That type of thing."

"No huge, drastic lifestyle changes like . . . I don't know . . ."

"Not like the loss of a limb or anything." He tried to joke, but from the look she gave him, it wasn't that funny.

"I'm sorry, Jase." She did the unexpected then, reaching out and taking his hand. Holding it, offering comfort in the most basic physical way.

And his raw, slightly dysfunctional heart needed just that.

"I'll be fine, really. It just means that even though I might have been through with cancer, it wasn't through with me."

"Cancer: the gift that keeps on giving."

# Chapter Fifty-Four

Since the day after Christmas, Jase had been carting in various ficus trees laden with twinkly white lights.

"Not that corner," his mother directed like the drill sergeant she was.

"Mom, remember I have a heart condition."

"And your doctor said that exercise was important." She didn't give him an ounce of pity. "You might not be swimming right now, but you will not become a couch potato."

The new argument in his house was if he would swim summer team with the Atlanta Country Club or not. It was far enough away that Jase was content to let it simmer for a while. Plus, it might be fun. He wasn't sure just yet. He still had some symptoms from what he now knew could be considered early stages of heart failure. But he no longer felt like he was breathing through a straw or exhausted at all times.

He'd made some headway with his parents over the past few weeks. Then, on Christmas Day, when everyone was still full of revelry and enjoying time with extended family, Jase had sat with his mom, updating his new phone.

"Mom?" Jase was still in pj's and knew that his hair needed to be combed or something. Sleep was gone, newly discovered half-caf coffee in a mug and a cinnamon roll right next to him.

"Merry Christmas, Jason." She smiled, and it was that smile

that was all happiness and still a little sleepy. "Christmas is much more enjoyable now that we don't have to stay up until three in the morning putting together impossible toys."

"Merry Christmas, Mom." He smiled. "Mom, I know that Mari is the speaker at the gala, but I'd really like to say something this year."

Olivia Ellison studied him, taking in his entire appearance before speaking, her voice thick with emotion. "You would?"

"Yeah." This idea had been in his head for a long time, one that meant more than just saying a few words about the importance of charity or something like that. "I think it's time."

Now the day of the gala was here. Jase spent most of the morning moving trees, helping iron tablecloths, and polishing more silver than he knew existed in the city of Atlanta. This busywork kept his mind from thinking too much about anything other than the task at hand. But he knew that in a very short time, he would be standing in front of this room. And that the room would be filled not only with adults but a handful of his friends.

"Do you do this every year?" Lucas polished a giant bowl inscribed with someone's name for being the volunteer of the year.

"I usually get roped into doing something," he admitted. "But I've been here more this year."

"Trying to make amends?"

"Maybe a little."

Lucas nodded in return. He still didn't know the whole story, but didn't push it either.

"I've got some friends coming tonight I want to introduce you to."

"Other swimmers?"

"Uh, no." Jase didn't elaborate on how he knew Davis, Noah, Paige, and MF, but was excited that they would be coming that evening. "Just make sure you find me."

"Sure."

Jase polished more, his brain moving from one thought to another without ever settling on anything in particular, but when Mari walked in, whatever he had been thinking slid out of his brain.

He walked over to where she was talking with his mom and Margaret. Margaret would be there tonight, along with some other people from camp. If Jase hadn't been nervous before, all of these people, each of them important to him in different ways, being there would have set his stomach on fire.

When Margaret and his mother walked away, leaving Mari by herself, he made his move.

"Hey." He smiled at Mari, drinking her in. He hadn't seen her since that day a week and a half ago, the day he'd gotten his official diagnosis of cardiomyopathy. But here she was, standing in the nearly decorated ballroom of the Atlanta Country Club, smiling at him.

"Hey." Mari's eyes darted around the room, seeming to take all of it in. "You still coming tonight?"

"Oh yeah," he promised. "I wouldn't miss you talking about camp for anything."

"I think I might be less nervous if you weren't here."

"You're going to be fine," he assured, taking a step toward her, smiling because she was there and not moving away.

"I hope you're right." Mari looked around more. "This looks swankier than I imagined."

"Olivia Ellison doesn't do anything unless it's swanky."

"That does not help my nerves."

"Any reason Mom wanted you here before the event? Surely she's not going to make you polish silver."

"No, no." She laughed. "I asked if I could come and check the stairs to the stage and podium with my shoe." Mari gestured down to her dress shoe, no fancy heel or red bottom to indicate that it was a shoe that meant something to the girls at his school.

"Smart." He would have never thought of that. "Have you done it?"

"No. Wanna show me the way?"

Jase reached out and held on to Mari's arm just above the cuff of her crutch. And she didn't pull away. She smiled. It was soft, a little kind, and maybe a little shy. Baby steps, Jase decided. Baby steps.

"So, this is the stage and the stairs." It was one of those mobile things that a lot of schools and offices used for temporary staging. Three little gray steps led the way to the stage. He watched as she walked up the steps, taking them like she'd been going up and down steps like this her entire life.

"Okay, I'm good." She grinned, and for a brief moment, Jase's heart and stomach eased. "I can't wait to see you tonight."

And with that simple statement, he knew he was ready.

# Chapter Fifty-Five

Well, hell, if those millions of little lights that Jase had had to check over the week didn't make the ballroom look like it was right out of some winter fantasyland. His tuxedo didn't itch the way it had the year before, probably because he wanted to be there this year. He wanted to be a part of this night.

Even if he was still so nervous that the possibility of throwing up gave him pause. Breathing out through his nose, grateful that his new meds worked and he could in fact take a deep breath now, he scanned the room. Mari should be here any moment.

And then she was there.

He nearly choked.

Mari stood with her family, the men all the more intimidating in their formal wear. And he vaguely noticed that her mother, Ms. Austin, and a woman who he guessed was Kris's girlfriend were there too. But he couldn't take his eyes off of Mari.

Her straight hair was the first thing he noticed. He couldn't remember ever having seen Mari with straight hair. Her hair was straight, down, and longer than usual. She looked elegant and, well, much older than the sixteen he knew she was. Her makeup was soft, but more than what she normally wore. She didn't fidget or pull her foot up with nervousness like she did at school sometimes. No, she looked confident and lovely. Simple earrings and a small necklace that sparkled just a little in the candlelight around the room.

"You gonna just stare at her?" Davis came over, pushing Jase on the shoulder. "It seems we clean up well."

"Well, at least she does." Jase couldn't pull his eyes away. "You the only one here?"

"Paige and MF are ogling Heather's husband and looking at the silent auction stuff."

"Right."

"Go talk to her." Davis pushed, rolling his eyes at Jase's obvious befuddlement.

"Yep. As soon as those linebackers who are her brothers and dad go away."

"I don't think that's happening." Davis laughed. "Don't let some giants who could play professional sports stop you from talking to Mari."

"You're not helping." But his feet finally unstuck, and he managed to move past a few couples already dancing and to where Mari was with her family. "Thanks so much for coming." He tried finding his adult voice, the one that said he was part of the event this evening.

"Jase." Mari smiled, and the relief in her face was evident.

"Do you mind if I take Mari and show her around?" He asked her parents. "Davis and some others from camp are here, scoping out the silent auction and stuff."

"Sure."

Ms. Manos smiled at both of them, and Jase was pretty certain it was honest and not the look she would give a boy she wanted to filet because he had been cruel to her daughter.

"You were made to wear a tux," Mari commented softly, her eyes shining up at him. "You should really just wear one all the time."

"You look amazing." The dress was strapless, a large expanse of her shoulders and back bare for his touch. "Just gorgeous."

"Thanks." She blushed prettily. "Where are our friends? I'm dying."

"Camp friends or school friends?"

"Lindsay is not my friend."

"Addison and Zeke are here too." Jase smiled at her immediate refusal of Lindsay.

"I guess we need to keep them separate." Mari's brows drew together. "Uh, show me camp people. They'll settle my nerves."

"Mari." He stopped her, placing a finger on the little wrinkle between her eyes, smoothing it. "I promise that tonight will be good."

"It's okay. I just want to protect you." She shrugged. "It's the least I can do."

# Chapter Fifty-Six

Mari did feel the most centered with her camp friends. Paige and MF grilled her incessantly about her breakup with Jase and what was going on now.

"I'll forgive you for not telling me." Paige hugged her. "But next time I need to know all of it."

"There is no next time." Mari shook her head, her straightened hair around her shoulders still an unusual feeling. "But thanks for being cool about it."

"We're generally cool." MF laughed. "You ready for this?"

"Sure." Mari breathed the word. "It'll be fine. This crowd will be eating out of my hand."

"Who doesn't? That's the real question," Paige teased.

"Mari, dear, you ready?" Olivia Ellison sparkled in a silver gown that just brushed the floor.

Mari was sure she hadn't bought hers at the secondhand shop.

"Oh, uh, sure." Now butterflies moved into her stomach as she thought about her speech. Her notecards already on the podium, her thoughts mostly centered.

"Great, Jason will introduce you, and then you'll go."

"Okay, great." She stopped then, the words Mrs. Ellison said fully penetrating. "Jase is introducing me."

"Here we go." Olivia just smiled, a spotlight appearing on the podium, and Jase walked on.

Seriously, he should always wear formal attire.

"Good evening." Jase smiled at the crowd as they quieted down and turned to where he was on the stage. "Thank you so much for joining us this evening at the Atlanta Country Club's annual New Year's Eve Gala. We are here tonight to give back to our community, and this year, we are lucky to have a charity that means a lot to me as a beneficiary."

Mari's breath stuck as she stood just off the side of the stage, listening to Jase speak.

"Camp Chemo was started in 1983 by a group of industrious nurses at the children's hospital here. The nurses noticed that children with cancer needed a place to go and just be kids. Not be *sick* kids. But there wasn't a summer camp that could handle many of these kids' serious medical needs.

"Camp Chemo now has year-round programs that include family camps, sibling camp, retreats for teenagers and young adults, and many other programs."

Mari watched as Jase took a deep breath and then looked to where she stood on the stage.

"And I have been lucky enough to attend Camp Chemo since I was seven years old."

There wasn't an audible gasp or anything. This hadn't been a secret from a lot of people in the room. But Mari couldn't help but wonder what the reaction from those who went to AWP was. Were they shocked?

"When I was three, I was diagnosed with acute lymphocytic leukemia. I received chemotherapy, and once I was old enough, my parents decided that a week at Camp Chemo would be beneficial to me. And it has been. It allowed me to be friends with others who had experienced cancer just like I had. And it was while I was at camp that I met our speaker for tonight. Mari Manos has a way of making everyone around her comfortable. She is someone who has taught me about the balance that cancer survivors walk every day. How our survivorship might not impact everything we do, but it is our story. Mari lives her life with that story and never shies from it.

"Mari is a junior at Atlanta West Preparatory. She is the epitome of Camp Chemo and has even helped coin one of the camp's sayings: 'Camp Chemo, where hair and limbs are optional.' Please give a warm welcome to Mari Manos."

Mari heard him say her name but was still so shocked it was like her foot was stuck to the ground. It had surely been hours (mere nanoseconds) before she finally moved over to the podium where Jase stood. He smiled warmly at her, stopping her once she was close enough. Jase put his hands on her bare shoulders, warmth and sparks seeping into her skin, then he reached around her, hugging her, his warm lips right next to her ear.

"Thank you for teaching me about balance."

"Jase . . ." She drew out his name, not at all sure what to say. "How am I supposed to talk to these people now?"

"We'll talk later." He let her go and walked down off of the stage, leaving Mari standing in the spotlight, all eyes on her as she began to talk.

"Like Jase said, Camp Chemo is the only place I know of where hair and limbs are optional."

# Chapter Fifty-Seven

It felt like hours before Jase was able to get close to Mari again. After she spoke, they were both overwhelmed with people wanting to talk to them.

"Jason." His dad came close, smiling warmly. "You did wonderfully."

"Thanks, Dad."

"I know you've struggled with this. I'm proud of you."

"Thanks, Dad." He didn't have other words, still overwhelmed by it all. He looked past his dad, who was being taken away by another partner at his firm, and saw Lindsay, Lucas, and others he went to school with. They all stared at him, a little unnerved. For the first time since middle school, Jase got the look. Slowly he walked over to them, not sure what to expect from them now. Would it be middle school all over again?

"You had cancer." Madalyn stated it, with her knack for the obvious and all.

"I did." He didn't shove his hands in his pockets even though he wanted to.

"You knew Mari before she came to school." Lindsay eyed him. "Like, y'all were a thing or something?"

"Or something," he agreed.

"Is your heart thing from something to do with your cancer?" Lucas asked, studying him.

"It is, actually."

"Whoa." And there was a long stretch of silence as his friends seemed to have a hard time deciding who he was now. Like he was a new person and not the guy who had gone to school with them since ninth grade.

"Jason, I don't know what to think about this," Lindsay said after a minute. "Like, you're Jason still, but there's a whole part of you we didn't know."

"It's fine, Lindsay. I know you don't think too much about anyone other than yourself." Her mouth fell open, but for once Lindsay didn't speak. Jase didn't want to be nice to her, to let her off for all of the horrible things she'd said to and about Mari this year.

"But you were a total ass to Mari when she first came." Addison sized him up with her eyes. "That was bullshit."

"It was." He admitted it. "And I would have been fine never saying anything to any of you guys about it, but it wasn't fair to you or myself."

"How long have you been going to camp?" Zeke asked. He looked the least surprised out of all of them. "And I knew. My mom is on the board."

"Oh." Jase wasn't sure how that made him feel. "Then you knew I was an asshole all along."

"You hiding that you had cancer never had anything to do with why I thought you were an asshole." But it was said with a smile.

"Come on, let me introduce you to some of my other

friends from camp," Jase said to his friends, his heart no longer pulsing in his throat. Ease, happiness—it all washed over him.

"Hey." Addison stopped him, separating him from the rest of the group. "You know Mari still has, like a, thing or something for you."

"I didn't do this to get back into her good graces." He said it, but even as the words left his lips, he knew it wasn't completely true. "Okay, maybe at first it was to get Mari back, but the more I thought about it, the more it was about me."

"Be nice to her," Addison warned. "I don't know everything going on with you two, but she's had a shitty year."

"I'll be nice," Jase assured him.

"And you did good."

"Thanks for your approval," he teased, but there was a chunk of him that meant it. "Thanks for being her friend when I wasn't."

Mari was still trapped by the many well-wishers. "Hi, folks." Jase came over to her. "Can I have Mari for a few? We have quite a few friends here." Like the parting of the Red Sea, Jase slipped his arm around her shoulders and ushered her out of the group of people.

"Thanks." She breathed the word. "I was getting claustrophobic."

"Want a breath of air first?"

"Before what?"

"Oh, I've introduced all of our friends."

"Jase." She stopped him right before they went out into the night. "I don't know what to say."

"I promised it would be a fun night." He noticed that he didn't have that urge to count his fingers. Instead, a weight of anxiety had melted off of him. He led Mari out onto one of the empty verandas that overlooked the pool and golf course. From his spot, he could also see the light from downtown and Midtown. The city seemed to glow around them.

"But you didn't just start telling people you had leukemia. You, like, announced it."

"You said something one time: that you were in control of your story. It stuck. This way, I'm in control of mine."

"I never meant to make you share that part of yourself. I understand the desire to keep things like this to yourself."

"And for some people, it's the right choice, but not for me, not anymore."

"That's pretty brave of you, Jason Ellison."

"Please don't call me Jason anymore." He took off his coat, noticing her shivers from the cold night air. "Here. Just don't think you'll be able to keep this like you did my gloves."

"Those gloves are really warm."

She smiled, and it was so big that Jase saw her two bottom teeth, and even without his coat, he felt warm.

"I'll get them to you, though."

"Looks like it's almost midnight." Jase watched as servers passed out party hats, sparkling cider, and champagne. "After the countdown, they'll all come outside. We used to be able to see the peach drop, but now the club has its own fireworks."

"Of course it does." Mari laughed teasingly. "Before they built the new Braves stadium, we could hear the fireworks on Saturday night home games."

"Want to go inside?" He stepped closer to her. "I bet I could convince the servers to give us the champagne, instead of sparkling cider."

"No." She looked up at him, her hair long and straight, her face confident, and her brown eyes almost black in the night. "I think this is exactly where I want to start the new year."

"Me too." He touched her hair, just the rubbing the ends between his fingers. They could hear the shouts and excitement building inside, but they didn't move, listening as the party started the countdown from ten.

"It's going to be a great year." Jase stepped in closer, reading her body language, seeing if she wanted him to step away, to stop.

"I think so." Mari smiled.

"Resolutions?" His hand moved from her hair to behind her neck, tilting her face up at him.

"Goals." She whispered it. "And it's to kick your ass at Capture the Flag this year."

Fireworks began, lighting the world around them, the booms and pows drowning out the noise as guests cheered from the other side of the veranda.

"Oh, Mari. With Davis back, you guys don't stand a chance."

"I guess we'll wait and see."

There was nothing separating them. Mari looked up at him. Her eyes glittered. Then, carefully, with crutches still around her arms, she touched his waist, curling into the back of his dress shirt.

"It's after midnight and, I think, incredibly appropriate for you to kiss me." She smiled as she said it.

With the fireworks sounding off around them, Jase dipped his head down, kissing Mari's soft mouth.

New year, new promises, new things surrounding them.

# Epilogue

Mari watched as Cason, the newest camper in her cabin and Davis's girlfriend, smiled sweetly up at Davis, her acting skills better than Mari had thought they would be.

"This was not her idea." Jase pulled Mari into him, his arm around her waist, her crutches almost a non-factor.

"Oh, it totally was." Mari smiled up at her boyfriend, happy to be in this place with him. Cason had come up with the most diabolical plan to help their team *finally* win Capture the Flag. "She came up with it all on her own. I was too busy pouting because I knew that you and Davis would be unstoppable."

"Well, not this year." He circled her waist then, their foreheads pressed together.

"It's about damn time." She smiled. Happiness filled her heart. The last seven months, while not full of only good things, had been so much better than she'd ever thought they could be.

"Well, it looks like your New Year's goal happened." He smiled before pressing a sweet kiss to her temple. "What's next?"

"Figure out how to keep you from flirting with sorority girls in the fall." She said it but didn't mean it. "I mean, I got a four on the AP Chemistry exam. Everything is great."

"You're welcome for that." He smiled.

It was such a lovely smile. One that she knew he only used with her.

"Oh, come on. You know it was all Caroline." She mentioned Kris's girlfriend who had spent all of Christmas break making sure Mari was able to do the work. "Someone was busy licking his wounds."

"You two better start moving!" Noah called as he jogged past them, heading back toward the ball field. "You don't want Grant to find you in an indecent position."

"They are way too busy being worried about Cason and Davis to even think about us," Jase assured him. "I'm not sure they even know that we're dating."

"So true." Mari grinned. She was grimy from playing in the woods. Sweat was making her hair stick to her head, her curls having seen much better days, but God, she was happy. Camp, Jase, Cason, Davis—her favorite people in her favorite place. "Nothing could make this better." She sighed happily.

"I don't know," Jase teased, leaning in, starting to brush his lips over hers.

"Evening." Margaret, in her infinite camp director wisdom, appeared behind Jase. "I do believe that the rest of camp is headed out to the ball field for snack."

"Of course." Jase nodded, a grin that was a mixture of embarrassment and happiness on his face. "We were just headed that way."

Mari smiled at the director as Jase moved away from her, still holding on to the top part of her arm—holding on to her when he couldn't hold her hand. Margaret followed them toward the front of camp, her smile saying that she knew exactly what she'd interrupted . . . again.

"Nice evening, huh, Margaret?" Mari smiled. She should have been paying attention, a rookie mistake, for sure. But as she tripped and started to fall over a stupid tree root, Jase swooped in, his arms keeping her from falling.

"It's all about balance, Mari." He did his best imitation of her arched brow.

And it was.

# Acknowledgments

"Yet those who wait for the LORD Will gain new strength; They will mount up with wings like eagles, They will run and not get tired, They will walk and not become weary." Isaiah 40:31

This verse sat on my heart as I wrote this book. Because there were times that I felt weary and tired, but the story of Jase and Mari was so personal, something I felt needed to be told.

I was in middle school when I found out a friend from my chemo days hadn't told anyone in her school that she had cancer when she was younger. And middle school Kati was baffled that someone could make the choice not to tell others. I wanted to play with those themes, that idea.

Mari Kesselring and the entire team at Flux, thank you. Thank you for seeing the need in this story—that cancer survivors are so rarely talked about and so rarely get any attention. You knew that this story needed to be told. Thank you for guiding me and answering unending emails.

Eric Smith and the gang over at PS Literary. Thank you for recognizing my unique stories, my desire to tell these specific stories, and giving me the outlet for them.

Sarah Taplin, this cover is everything I've ever envisioned. Thank you for being a brilliant artist and making sure that I finally saw a girl that looked like me on the cover of a book.

Jessica Minton, thank you for reading this and making sure I captured what it's like to be an amputee. I know that's odd, since I am one, but thanks for assuring me we all feel some of these things.

Avery Schroeder, thank you so much for helping me navigate what most independent schools are like. You're the best.

Dr. Jordyn Griffin, Dr. Geoff Jackman, Dr. Whit Boone, Dr. Howard Katzenstein, Lesa Boone, Sarah Woznicki, and Dr. Brooke Cherven, thanks to each of you for answering my medical questions and helping me make sure this book was as authentic as it could be. Jordyn, sorry it kept you up until 2:00 a.m. while we were at camp, but thanks anyway.

First Baptist Raleigh, thank you for giving me a room to write in when I needed a place to camp out.

Jen Foster, Jennifer Davis, Amy Freed, Elise VanderMeer, Anne Mitchell, Heather Neal, and Stacy Criscione, you ladies are some of the best friends a girl could ask for. Thanks for letting me go weeks without responding to a text, for reminding me to eat, and for making sure I stay off of social media and actually write.

Elizabeth Keenan, Samirah Ahmed, and Sangu Mandanna, thank you for being the loveliest and most brilliant people out there. Thank you for listening to me whine and assuring me that my words are not all terrible. Thanks for making me laugh when I mostly wanted to cry.

Julie Dao, Mara Fitzgerald, Kevin Van Whye, Jessica Rubinkowski, Heather Krazsinksi, Austin Gilkinson, Rebecca Caprara, and Jordan Villegas, oh thank the heavens for each of you. For talking me down, reminding me that writing is what we do. We tell stories and hope that someone maybe gets a little something from them.

Megan Bannen, you are a beautiful friend who understands the importance of a good donut and appropriate GIFs.

Lily Lopez, Tia Bearden, Mary Dunbar, and Rachel Merridee, thanks for being the best CPs and friends a girl could have.

Sunshine Forever!

Once again, Camp Sunshine and my fellow counselors. Thank you. Thank you for always believing in me and what I can accomplish. Thank you for a place where hair and limbs are optional.

Campers, past, present, and future, still no kissing at camp. Your counselor knows all and sees all. Each year, you teach me so much about what survivorship looks like, and I am so proud of each camper that I have been blessed to know.

And last but always first in my heart, my sweet and understanding family. Jason Gardner, you are the only reason I can do this. You give me countless praise and love. You were the only reason I ever thought to try and have my stories published. I'm at a loss for words as I think of your goodness, your love, your sheer brilliance. You are phenomenal.

Kennedy and Eleanor, you are the light of my life, and being your mom is my greatest joy. Continue to find the balance in your own lives, be brave in your choices, and live out loud. —Mama

# About the Author

Kati Gardner is a recovering actor, wife, and mom. She is a childhood cancer survivor and amputee who writes books about disability and kissing. Originally from Atlanta, she now lives and writes in Raleigh, North Carolina. *Brave Enough* was her first novel. You can find her on Twitter at @AuthorKati, on Instagram at AuthorKatiGardner, and at katigardner.com.